THREE SISTERS

O. J. MULLEN

Boldw**oo**d

First published in Great Britain in 2023 by Boldwood Books Ltd.

Copyright © O. J. Mullen, 2023

Cover Photography: Shutterstock and iStock

A CIP catalogue record for this book is available from the British Library.

Paperback ISBN 978-1-83751-501-1

Large Print ISBN 978-1-83751-500-4

Hardback ISBN 978-1-83751-499-1

Ebook ISBN 978-1-83751-502-8

Kindle ISBN 978-1-83751-503-5

Audio CD ISBN 978-1-83751-494-6

MP3 CD ISBN 978-1-83751-495-3

Digital audio download ISBN 978-1-83751-497-7

Boldwood Books Ltd
23 Bowerdean Street
London SW6 3TN
www.boldwoodbooks.com

Catherine Campbell
Love you, sis

PROLOGUE
GREAT WESTERN ROAD, GLASGOW

19 December

Lewis Stone was angrier than he'd been in his life.

It was after midnight. The party would carry on into the wee hours for those with the stamina to go the distance. Tonight, he wasn't that man. As he was leaving, the muted strains of Abba's 'Dancing Queen' followed him to his car. He drew his coat tightly round him against the freezing air, carefully testing each step on the road glistening like glass in the sub-zero temperatures. Parties, especially Christmas staff parties with an open bar, were better avoided. This one was

supposed to be a 'thank you' to the workforce for another successful year. It should've been fun. Instead,
because of the antics of his business partner, Damian
Morton, it had descended into a fiasco that might well
have serious consequences further down the line.

Some inquisitive bright spark had discovered
Damian and a female colleague behind a room divider
and imagined it was a great idea to take the screen
away so the crowd could watch them going at it on top
of a table. Their clothes were on the floor, abandoned
in the moment – blind drunk, the couple hadn't realised they could be seen and had carried on frantically doing what they were doing: the woman had her
legs wrapped round her lover; her head was back and
her eyes were closed. His teeth were gritted with lust,
the veins in his neck bulging under the skin. Their
climax was met with laughter and thunderous ap-
plause from the audience and, with the aplomb of the
truly pissed, Damian had taken a bow before they'd
run from the room to catcalls and lewd comments.

People had enjoyed the show; they'd thought it was
funny. Lewis hadn't been one of them, although he
knew it was no more than alcohol-driven high jinks, the
kind of scene played all over the country at these events,
regretted in the cold light of day. In the twenty-first cen-

tury, having sex with a junior member of staff was problematic and exposed an employer to accusations of sexual harassment and exploitation, industrial tribunals and the negative publicity that went with them.

But it wasn't just that. Damian had lost the plot tonight, not once but twice.

In recent months they'd been in talks with the giant American retailer Lassiter-Accardi about a potential deal that would be a game changer if it came off. Overnight, Stone Free's iconic lines would be on rails and shelves in hundreds of outlets worldwide from Campbeltown to Cape Town. Lewis and Damian's 'baby' would become a brand name and the dream they'd had as hungry young fashion designers in Glasgow would be a reality.

But nothing was signed. Until it was, confidentiality was vital; a leak might well sink the whole thing. When the ink was dry on the contracts a joint press release would break the news to the media. That was the plan, or it had been before an inebriated Damian staggered onto the small stage, wrestled the microphone from the DJ and, in a few slurred sentences, trashed everything they'd agreed.

Under the lights, his face was sweaty and twisted by booze. Beside him, Tina, his accomplice, grinned

stupidly, the public exhibition of their passion apparently forgotten.

Damian put a finger to his lips. 'Shhh! Fucking
shhh, will you? Got a Christmas secret for you.'

Another voice yelled, 'No, you don't. We've seen
her!'

'Got your hands full there, mate!'

At the back of the room, alone at the bar, Lewis
wondered just how much more degrading it could get
and wished he weren't there to see it. When he realised where Damian's little speech was going, it was
already too late.

Damian boomed into the mic. 'Stone Free's
heading for the big time. Lassiter-Accardi wants us.
Yeah! They know quality when they see it and want to
take us on. So, get those summer holidays booked.'

Most of the people were drunk or getting there and
didn't understand what he was talking about; it didn't
stop them cheering. Beside him, Tina stifled a giggle.
Lewis saw it and fought an urge to haul his mate off
the stage and beat some sense into him. The state of
play with Lassiter-Accardi was confidential, yet his
'girlfriend' was in on it; the irresponsible idiot had obviously told her.

Damian swayed and waved a limp arm at the
room. 'This year's been great. The next twelve months

are going to be even better. Trust me. Can't say more. I can't. Lewis will kill me.'

Lewis felt eyes watching him and knew that this wasn't the moment to show emotion. The DJ took over. Loud music ended the wayward lovers' moment in the sun; they stepped off the stage and disappeared into a sea of bobbing heads. Lewis balled his fist impotently at his side. Tomorrow his partner wouldn't remember much about his little speech, but on Monday morning they'd be having a frank conversation; some hard talking would be done, home truths that shouldn't have to be said would be.

Lewis wasn't interested in excuses – there were no fucking excuses. If it had been somebody else, anybody else, behaving the way he'd behaved tonight, they'd be looking for a new job.

Lewis was heading for the door when a female voice stopped him. 'You don't look like a guy who's enjoying himself.'

Blue eyes in a pretty heart-shaped face studied him. Long red hair fell to luminescent bone-white skin revealed by the swell of her breasts beneath an off-the-shoulder leopard-print blouse, a perfect match for the black leather skirt hugging her slender thighs.

On another night he'd have been more than happy to find out more about this lady with the cheeky attitude, but Damian's tacky indiscretions had soured his mood. Lewis said, 'Really? I thought I was making a pretty good job of disguising it. How did you guess?'

She edged closer until they were almost touching. 'Maybe I'm psychic.' She held out her hand. 'Mari, pleased to meet you, Mr Stone. Can I buy you a drink?'

'No need, it's free.'

'Even better.'

'I'm leaving, so no, thank you.'

'Are you sure?'

It was impossible to misunderstand the meaning behind her question and, in spite of his anger at Damian, he felt himself respond. 'Have we met? I ask because I don't recognise you but you know who I am.'

She smiled and let her arm brush gently against him. 'I'd be surprised if there was anybody here who didn't.'

'There's a difference. They work for Stone Free, you—'

'That's right. I shouldn't really be here.'

'Then, why are you?'

'A friend brought me. I hope you don't mind.'

Lewis didn't mind. If he hadn't been in such a foul temper he would've shown her how much. He said, 'Of course not, you're welcome to stay as long as you like.'

She reminded him. 'Mari.'

'Mari, yes. But, as I said, I'm leaving.'

She tilted her head and looked up at him. 'Are you telling a girl willing to gate-crash your party you haven't time to dance with her? Surely not, Mr Stone?'

'Don't take it personally.'

She ran her fingers suggestively along his lapel. 'If you won't dance... there must be something we can do. Give me a minute to get my coat and I'll come with you. We can think about what it might be on the way to your place.'

She kissed him on the lips; he caught notes of mandarin and fig in her scent mixed with something cool and green, and almost gave in. Almost.

* * *

He pointed the red Golf GTI towards the West End and gunned the 2.0L four-cylinder turbocharged engine, already regretting turning the woman down; he could've been taking her to his bedroom instead of going home alone. The conversation had been brief but enough to discover three things: her name was Mari, she didn't work for Stone Free, and she wanted him. All he'd needed to do was forget about his partner, Lassiter-Accardi, and bloody Stone Free for a few hours and match her lust with his own.

The traffic lights at the junction of Byres Road and Queen Margaret Drive forced him to wait. Lewis drummed his fingers impatiently on the steering column, still thinking about Mari's blatant sensuality. Damian had made an idiot of himself and endangered the deal with the Americans with behaviour that had been tawdry and indefensible. But at least he knew how to let go. How to enjoy himself. Stone Free was a voracious beast that had demanded everything they'd had, taking and taking until there was nothing left.

It was time Lewis learned to live a little.

Christmas was six days away. Glasgow was in party mood – he might as well join in. He opened the window, slipped a Bon Jovi *Greatest Hits* CD into the player, and turned the volume all the way up. 'You Give Love a Bad Name' blasted from the speakers. What would her reaction be if he suddenly reappeared – would some other horny bastard have made a move, already be chatting her up, chancing his luck? Probably. Guys would be queuing up to speak to her.

Bugger it! He'd go with his luck and book a room. They'd stay in bed the whole weekend, drink bottle after bottle of champagne, and catch up on the fun he'd missed out on.

When the lights changed, he took a right into a crowded Byres Road, searching for an opportunity to turn round and go back. He stamped the accelerator to the floor and the car lurched forward. Suddenly, a face flashed at the corner of his eye, white and terrified in the headlights: a female; there and gone. Lewis slammed on the brakes but not in time to avoid her. He felt a double bump under the wheels as the car skidded and came to a halt. For a second, the world stopped, then people were running towards him, others covering their mouths with their hands, rooted where they stood.

Lewis saw their shocked expressions and wanted to be sick.

PART I

1

Imagine you had a secret so terrible you couldn't tell anybody. Ever. Because if you actually said the words out loud the world would see who you really were.

I didn't realise it, not then – none of us did – but that chilly winter's night in the West End of Glasgow would change all of our lives irrevocably; it would be the last time the three Kennedy sisters were together; the beginning of the end of our family.

And if I had known where the road would take me, what would I have done differently? I can answer that. Everything. But I couldn't see into the future and the choices I made were mine. All mine. Now I have to live with them.

* * *

We came out of Òran Mór into Byres Road, giggling hysterically, holding on to each other down the stone steps of the former Kelvinside Parish church into the street. Not drunk but getting there, oblivious to the freezing air stinging our cheeks. Even by Glasgow-in-winter standards it was bloody cold. On the icy pavement Molly pointed an accusing finger at Sam.

'You blew it, girl. That guy fancied you. You could've been away there. We wouldn't have told Colin, would we, Alex?'

Sam wiped laughter tears from her eyes. 'As if my self-worth wasn't low enough.'

Molly said, 'What was wrong with him?' which set us off again.

'You can't be serious?'

'Of course I'm serious. You've always liked them a bit rough. Don't deny it.'

'There's nothing to deny. It isn't true. Colin isn't rough.'

'Colin's the exception. The rest were dogs. Absolute bow-wows. Alex will back me up.'

I wisely avoided going there. 'You're forgetting, Molly, Sam's happily married. As for her admirer, actually, I thought he was quite nice.'

'Quite nice? He was so out of it he could hardly stand.'

'Okay, but apart from that he was nice.'

That cracked them up. When she stopped laughing, Molly shook her head at her twin. 'Trust you to take the moral high ground. You've always had impossibly high standards. How does your poor husband keep up with them? It must be hell for him.'

She'd wandered onto dangerous ground so I shepherded her away from it. 'Careful, Molly. You're getting personal.'

Her reply was unrepentant. 'It had to be said and it's been said.'

'No, it didn't. You're out of order. Watch it.'

Sam took it better than I had but wasn't going to let the comment pass unchallenged. 'Make your bloody mind up, Molly. A minute ago I liked them rough. And seriously, do you think bombing out somebody who's blind drunk is a high standard?'

'Definitely. What do you know about him?' Molly answered her own question. 'Nothing. You should've been asking yourself why he was blind drunk. What had driven him to it? Did he lose his job this afternoon? Could be he'd had to have his dog put down, or his father's bald and he'd just noticed he's going the same way. There are a hundred reasons, but whatever it is he's obviously in a bad place. Maybe you were sent to save him.' She looked up with mock awe at the snow falling from a dark sky. 'Sam: the Miracle of Christmas.'

I sensed Sam's growing irritation and cut the banter short. 'You're full of it, Molly, you do know that, don't you? And, since you feel so strongly, you save him.'

We joined arms and strolled towards Hillhead subway station, ignoring the stares of passers-by. For us, attracting attention wasn't a new experience. It had been like that all our lives. Meeting up in the week before Christmas, spending time in each other's company, even getting a little drunk, had started while we were at university and only seeing each other in term breaks. The tradition had assumed a greater significance when our parents died, cementing us as friends first and sisters second.

At thirty, I was a widow. I'd lost my husband, Freddy, to cancer eighteen months after the wedding. His death had been devastating. Somehow, I'd survived – just – but apart from going to work and seeing my sisters whenever their hectic schedules allowed, I'd retreated into a small, lonely world of my own.

Samantha and Molly were twins, two years younger

than me and as different from each other as it was possible to be: Sam, dark-haired, serious and intense, married to Colin, a successful property developer in the
city, who lived in a five-bedroom house in Newton
Mearns; Molly, irreverent and unattached; a natural-
born rebel, vulgar and very funny, who drank Guinness, watched football and rugby, and had a collection
of wigs – I'd lost count of how many. She even had a
blue-and-white one for when Scotland were playing.
Mad! But that was her. Tonight's little number was a sil-
ver-and-purple bob cut that screamed for attention and
perfectly framed her face. My sisters shared the high
cheekbones of our mother. I'd inherited flatter features
and an aquiline nose nobody had taken responsibility
for. Molly used to tease me I'd been adopted.

We walked in a line, me on the inside, Sam in the
middle, Molly nearest the kerb. I asked Sam what was
intended to be an innocent question. 'Will Colin be
waiting up for you?'

'No, he'll have gone to bed.'

'Wake him up.'

A snowflake landed on her eyelash; she blinked it
away. 'Believe me, I intend to.'

I frowned. 'Too much information, thank you very
much.'

Molly leaned in. 'Too much information about what?'

Sam and I replied with one voice. 'None of your business!'

'Well, if that's how it is I'd rather not know. It's bloody cold, isn't it?'

Sam snapped at her, 'Serves you right for dressing like a teenager. Those days are over, accept it and let them go. Move on, for fuck's sake.'

Molly fired back. 'What, and look like you? An old married woman. Is that what you mean?'

'No, I mean instead of somebody who wears skirts up to her arse, Molly. As for your latest wig – Christ, what's that supposed to be about?'

'I didn't expect you'd understand; it's a statement.'

'Oh, yeah, it's that, all right. What does it say: I need help?'

I stepped in to referee, the role I'd played all my life. 'Seconds out, sisters. Neutral corners. Molly, don't be so touchy. And, Sam, keep your opinions to yourself.'

We went on, not speaking. Suddenly my feet went from under me on the icy surface and I went down. My fingers clawed the air for something to hold on to and found Sam. She pulled me up. When I was safely back on my feet, shaken but unhurt, I said, 'Christ, these pavements are treacherous. Watch your step. I could've broken my ankle. And it would've been my own fault for putting on these shoes. Bloody idiot.'

Sam reassured me. 'No chance. You're indestructible and besides, I had you.'

At the corner of Cresswell Street we stopped to let a taxi pass. The for-hire sign was on. Molly said, 'If I'd flagged him down I'd be at the flat in twenty minutes.'

'Why didn't you?'

'Because – cold or no cold – I prefer being here with you two.'

Sam squeezed her sister's hand. 'What a sweet thing to say. I told Colin the same thing when he came home late. Again.'

'That you'd rather be with us?'

'Something like that.'

Just then, Molly's mobile rang and she lagged behind to take the call, giving me the opportunity I needed to speak to Sam. 'Were you having a row?'

The harsh street lighting drained the blood from Sam's face, reminding me of Freddy in the last months, when I'd watched the force within dwindle a little more each day until there was nothing of him left. He'd been courageous, more concerned for me than for himself. The end hadn't been quick. And courage hadn't been enough.

Sam answered, carefully choosing her words. 'We don't do rows. That needs people to be in the same room. My husband's too busy chasing money, among other things. I can't pin him down long enough to have a proper argument – he makes sure of it.'

'What, then?'

'The latest instalment in the war of attrition we call a relationship.'

'But you just said you were going to wake him up. I assumed you meant for sex.'

Sam studied me. 'You've always been an enigma, you do know that, don't you?'

'What the hell does that mean?'

'Wise and, at the same time, bloody naïve. I was joking – a bit of festive irony. If you must know there hasn't been any of that in months. Even then, it only lasted about two minutes.' She sighed. 'Seven months, one week, and four days to be exact. But who's counting?'

I ignored her assessment of me, not certain it wasn't the truth. 'I'm sure it'll work out.'

'Are you? Why?'

'Because it's you and Colin. You love each other. Always have. Of course it'll work out.'

Sam's bottom lip trembled. 'It won't. It's gone too far.'

'Don't be silly. Most couples go through rocky spells. Par for the course, isn't it?'

'Is it? I bet you and Freddy didn't.'

It was the wrong thing to say and Sam realised it immediately. 'Oh, Alex. How stupid of me. I didn't—'

I shrugged the clumsiness away. 'Don't worry about it. We weren't married long enough for it to go bad. Sometimes in the morning when I wake up it feels like a horrible dream, then the awful reality comes crashing in and it's all I can do to drag myself out of bed.'

It was my turn to bubble; the festive season could be difficult. People remembered things it would've been less painful to forget. The happy mood had taken a turn for the worse. Sam tried to rescue it. 'What happened to Freddy was terrible. I've no idea how you came back from that, yet you have.'

I smiled a sad half-smile. Now who was being naïve? 'Only in public. I don't believe you do. Not really. The best you can hope for is to find a reason to go on. It's either that or sink under the dreadful weight of it. When people die we put them on a pedestal, which makes it even more difficult to let them go. Somehow, telling myself that helps. Does that make sense?'

'Perfect sense.'

'I loved Freddy but he wasn't a saint. Nobody is.'

Molly stopped fidgeting with her phone and leaned across. 'In case you haven't noticed, I am.'

I laughed. 'Yeah, in your dreams, girl.'

Snow piled in drifts at the kerb and salt had been spread by gritters – a task that wasn't finished and wouldn't be any time soon according to the forecast. It wouldn't be enough. The temperature that had hovered in single figures all day was plummeting and a hard frost on Byres Road glittered like a zillion stars in a black sky.

Near the entrance to The Curlers Rest, the oldest watering hole in this part of Glasgow, I stopped to drop notes into a beggar's plastic cup. A straggly beard and a wispy moustache covering his face made it impossible to say if he was young or old. He was sitting in the lotus position – I'd never managed to feel comfortable in it at my yoga class – on a piece of torn cardboard with his back pressed against the pub's whitewashed wall, wearing a camouflage jacket and several jumpers that peeked out at the wrists. His cheeks were chalk, hollow under a navy woollen hat pulled down over his ears. On the ground in front of him, scratched in pencil and barely legible, a card read 'Hungry and Homeless'. But he wasn't alone; he had a companion, a tan-and-white mongrel better cared for than he was himself. The dog recognised a friend, tilted its head and I was smitten. I hunkered down and drew my fingers through his coat feeling the heat from his body. He wagged his tail. I spoke to his owner and didn't get a response. The man stared impassively ahead through empty, red-rimmed eyes, without acknowledging the money or me, and I guessed he was on something. Of course he was. How else could he survive the freezing cold and the abject misery of his situation?

I'll remember the scream for the rest of my life.

The screech of brakes trying and failing to gain traction on the icy road made me look up from my one-way conversation with the beggar to see Molly fall under the wheels of a red car. When I'd slipped on the pavement my sister had caught me. This time Sam's outstretched hand hadn't been enough and I started to run.

2

Lewis had seen the woman too late to avoid her. One second she wasn't there, the next she was in front of him. His reaction was instant. He slammed his foot on the brake and felt the car skid and slew. After a delay that in his brain went on forever, he'd heard a dull thud as it crashed into her body, followed by two bumps in quick succession that told him the sickening truth: he'd run over her.

Not once, but twice.

He sat with his hands on the steering wheel, too numb to move, aware only of a rushing sound in his ears like being underwater. The car was new – barely six months old – yet the air bag hadn't deployed, a fact that wouldn't register until much later. The door flew open, a hand stretched across him to turn the music off, and a deep male voice asked, 'Are you okay, mate? Are you all right?'

It took a moment to realise he was talking to him.

The good Samaritan helped him out of the vehicle. Lewis saw a shoe with a broken heel in the road and short blonde hair matted with blood. Mercifully, the face was turned away, sparing him the full horror. Two people bent over the victim, while the crowd watched him in silence, their expressions a mixture of curiosity and contempt.

Minutes ago he'd been a businessman on his way home from the office Christmas party – usually four hours of listening to employees with half a bottle of Prosecco down their necks telling him what he was doing wrong – an event he got through by restricting his alcohol intake to a glass of red wine nursed most of the night and left unfinished, and grinning until his jaw ached.

Not this year. Damian had seen to that.

On the pavement at Byres Road, Lewis tried to speak and found he wasn't able to. Finally, he managed to whisper, 'I didn't see her. I didn't see...'

'Hold on. The police are on their way.'

'The police?'

'Yes, they'll be here shortly. If you're wise you won't

say anything to anybody. Do you understand? Not to anybody.'

'Yes... yes, I understand. What happened... did you see?'

The man at his side was forty-something, with kind eyes and a shaggy salt-and-pepper beard. He came closer. 'Listen, when I tell you not to speak to anybody, that includes me. You're obviously in shock. Wait till you've got a grip on yourself.'

It was good advice. Lewis ignored it. 'Did you see it?'

'No.'

'Did anybody?'

'No idea, mate. Probably. I was on the other side of the street. As soon as I heard the brakes squeal I knew it was bad and started running.' He took Lewis's arm, led him across the road and sat him down on the freezing kerb.

'The police will take over. Until then, close your eyes and breathe deeply. You'll feel better.'

Lewis pressed his balled fists to his temples, talking to himself, desperately trying to hold on to a reality that had slipped away from him. He said, 'She stepped out in front of me. There was nothing I could do. There was nothing...'

The man put a comforting hand on his shoulder.

'It's best if you stay calm, it really is. For your own sake.'

Lewis lifted his head, tears in his eyes. 'Is she dead? She's dead, isn't she?'

'I don't know, mate.'

3

I bent over my sister, whimpering her name over and over. We'd been laughing on the church steps about the drunk guy in the bar fancying Sam, the Kennedy girls on a Christmas night out together. Now, Molly was unconscious and broken in the road, her arms and legs at crazy angles and there was blood everywhere. The purple-and-silver wig had come off and was yards away in a pool of ice water. The reality was too much. I couldn't take it in. Two passers-by were helping, one on his phone calling for an ambulance, the other giving Molly CPR. The guy had obviously been trained: after the double-handed compressions he tilted her head and pinched her nose, sealed her mouth with his and breathed into her. When she didn't respond he began again, refusing to be panicked, methodically going through the procedure. Kneeling beside him, I fought an urge to grab hold of her and shake her awake. Instead, I begged my sister to open her eyes. 'Molly. Molly. Don't do this to us. Please, don't do this.'

Breaking away to talk to the beggar had been a mistake I'd regret for the rest of my life. I was the eldest, the big sister, a responsibility I'd always taken seriously. Guilt kicked in, insidiously whispering its poison, telling me I was to blame, this was my fault; if I'd stayed with them instead of stopping to give money to a stranger it wouldn't have happened.

I wouldn't have let it.

Sam was surrounded by the crowd on the pavement. Her and Molly were closer than even they sometimes realised. Born nine minutes apart, from the moment they could talk the twins bickered over everything. When they were small it had been sweets and toys. Growing up, they'd adored the same popstars and raided each other's wardrobes without bothering to ask permission; more than once they'd stolen each other's boyfriends because they could. But underneath the rivalry was a bond, a genetic connection that was impossible to break, and with her sister bleeding in the street Sam stared unblinking like someone in a trance.

I wasn't aware of the flashing blue light until a policeman gently tried to lead me away. Leaving Molly felt like an act of betrayal and I wouldn't go. A female constable nodded to him to let her handle it and I collapsed against her, sobbing uncontrollably.

'She's my sister. I have to stay. I have to. She needs me.'

A second police car arrived from the direction of Partick Cross and parked at an angle in the middle of the street, followed by an ambulance that rolled to a halt behind the red car. Two paramedics leapt out, threw the back doors open, and immediately started working. Molly didn't move. Seeing them lift her onto a stretcher was heart-breaking and surreal; I couldn't look and turned away. My senses seemed heightened and dulled at the same time. Colours were so bright I had to shield my eyes, silence roared in my ears and, unbelievably in the circumstances, I registered it had stopped snowing.

Sam had forced her way to the front of the crowd but wouldn't come closer, standing ashen-faced, arms hanging helplessly at her sides, as lost as anyone I'd ever seen.

On the other side of the road, a man sat on the kerb with his head in his hands. Instinctively, I knew he was the reckless bastard who'd run Molly down. Before the officer could stop me, I broke away and threw myself at him, punching and kicking. He held up his hands but didn't defend himself even when blood spurted from his nose.

Two policemen pulled me off and spoke to him. 'Is the red Golf yours?'

He wiped the blood on his sleeve and nodded.

'Have you been drinking this evening, sir?'

'Yes... no... not really.'

I screamed at him. 'Not really! Not really! You're pissed!'

I was hysterical but that didn't mean I was wrong. The policeman signalled to the other PC to get me out of the way, produced a breathalyser, and spoke to the driver. 'I'm going to have to ask you to blow into this for me.'

'I'm not drunk.'

'I'm not accusing you of anything, sir. I'm asking you to take a legal breath test.'

'And I'm telling you it isn't necessary.'

The officer glared at his colleague struggling to hold me back. 'Are you refusing to take the test?'

'Of course not. I had a half a glass of wine three hours ago.'

The policeman handed him the breathalyser. 'Then, you've nothing to worry about, have you?'

4

QUEEN ELIZABETH UNIVERSITY HOSPITAL, GOVAN, GLASGOW

Four weeks later

Sam tapped the arm of her chair to a rhythm only she could hear. I watched the rise and fall of her finger, irritation welling up inside me, wanting to snap at her to shut up. Since the accident I'd become irrationally angry over the smallest annoyances to the point where I struggled to stop myself from screaming like a mad woman and running away. Now, I lashed out at the surgeon who'd operated on Molly four weeks ago in the early hours of a Saturday morning.

'Where is this guy? How much longer does he expect us to wait?'

The criticism was unjustified and unfair. We'd been treated with extraordinary consideration and kindness, having even the smallest decisions explained to ensure we were fully informed. I knew I should've been on my knees thanking God for the NHS, except I wasn't talking to Him and doubted I ever would again. All day every day depression followed me and I understood why it was called 'the black dog'. I'd been here before but this time was different. This time *I* was different. Ranting at every fiddling annoyance was my default response, a coping mechanism to stop me from smashing things or ripping the skin off somebody's face.

The silence was broken by the ticking of the clock on the wall and my voice sounded belligerent even to my ears. 'You know what he's going to say, don't you? You know what he's going to tell us?'

Sam looked at the floor and didn't answer.

I drew my shoulders back defiantly. 'Well, he can fuck right off.'

'Alex...'

'Her head moved, Sam, I saw it. Not much. Just a bit. He didn't believe me. None of them believed me, but it happened.'

'Alex... Alex, listen.'

I turned reluctantly. Behind Sam, Colin stood, his expression dull and drawn, hands clasped in front of him, lips pressed in a tight line, as though he had no part to play and wanted none. If Sam needed help to deal with the loss of her sister it wasn't coming from him. She said, 'They've tried their best. The doctors. The nurses. Everybody. There's no more they can do. It's down to us.'

I drew back sharply, as though I'd been slapped. '"Down to us." What are you talking about? What do you mean?'

'To do the right thing. Down to us to do the right thing by Molly.'

She could've added 'and ourselves' and not been wrong.

The death of a loved one is a hurt like no other. Nobody had to tell me; after the crushing diagnosis that had meant the end of everything I'd known, my husband, Freddy, had taken months to pass, long enough to get used to the idea of him not being there without ever getting close to accepting it.

Whatever this was, it wasn't that. What had happened to him had been heart-breaking. But it hadn't been anyone's fault. Molly's future had been stolen from her by a reckless fool who'd walked away from the accident unscathed and whose life had gone on unaltered. I'd replayed the horror of that night a hundred times in my mind, searching for the tear in the cosmic continuum that would have allowed me to step into a parallel universe and change the outcome. I hadn't found it because it didn't exist, and doubt over what might have been joined the black dog relentlessly stalking me.

If Sam hadn't caught me when I'd slipped.

If I'd broken my ankle.

If I hadn't stopped to speak to the beggar and stayed with my sisters.

If! If! Bloody if!

All I could think about was Molly on the pub steps, her usual incorrigible self, winding Sam up about her drunken admirer and how, minutes later, she was gone from us forever.

The certificates of professional excellence in matching gilt-edged frames on the wall above the desk were meant to reassure us; they didn't. Not even the one in the middle from Johns Hopkins Department of Neurosurgery. My own certificate was admittedly more modest, but it hung proudly behind the dispensary counter in the little chemists I owned. God alone knew when I'd be ready to return to that. But no, it wasn't possible to be reassured, because in the end, fancy cer-

tificates were just words, while, in a private room surrounded by screens, a machine was keeping our sister
alive. This wasn't the first time we'd been in this office,
though it might be the last. That was what Sam was
trying to tell me.

'We have to let her go, Alex. We have to.'

'Let her go and do what, Sam? Carry on as though
she never existed? I can't.'

Sam moved closer, so close I could see the red fleck
of a tiny broken vein in the white of her left eye. Mine
felt as if somebody had rubbed sand in them; bursting
into tears umpteen times a day and hardly sleeping
hadn't helped.

Sam took my hands in hers and spoke softly, trying
to reach me. 'Neither can I. Molly's our sister and always will be. Just because someone isn't here doesn't
mean we leave them behind. We're here. You and me.
And, even now, she's depending on us to take care of
her.'

I pulled away. 'Ending someone's life isn't my idea
of taking care of them. It's only been four weeks.'

'Mr Gupta thinks—'

The dam inside me broke and I was on my feet,
shouting, 'I couldn't give a flying fuck what anybody
thinks! People recover, they just do. Medical science
admits it only knows how approximately 10 per cent of

the brain works – 86 billion neurons. An estimated 100 trillion connections. And they understand a measly 10 per cent. So please don't tell me what some bloody doctor with fancy certificates on his office wall thinks. Forgive me for not being impressed but, honestly, I don't bloody care.'

Sam stayed calm, speaking slowly, as she would to someone too young to understand the adult world. 'I've read all that, too, and I want to believe it every bit as much as you do. But this is his job, Alex. This is what he does. We have to trust him.'

My outburst had come at a price; I was trembling and near to tears. Denying the evidence of my own eyes, clinging to wishful alternatives because the truth was too painful to accept, had exhausted me. My reply was flat, like an obdurate child in a room full of grown-ups, defeated though not ready to give in. 'I don't. I don't have to trust anybody. It isn't his sister lying in that bed. If it was, I bet he'd have a different view.'

Sam tilted her head, doing her damnedest to disguise the pity behind her next words. 'He wouldn't, Alex, he really wouldn't. The facts would still be the facts.'

Since we arrived, Sam had done the talking; her husband hadn't said anything. She was a strong character and I guessed that when the front door closed on their house in Newton Mearns, the dynamics would be the same. Sam addressed him directly, willing him to support her. 'Colin. Please. Tell her letting Molly go is the hardest thing we've ever done. But it's the right thing. The only thing. And we won't stop loving her, will we?' She watched his face and answered her own question. 'No, no, of course we won't. How could we?' Her fingers gripped the edge of the chair, the other hand pulling on his lapel. 'Alex needs to hear it from you. We both do.'

Colin shifted awkwardly, glanced at the clock and played for time. 'What I think doesn't count. The doctor will be here in a minute.'

Sam lost patience with him. 'For God's sake – he told us his prognosis weeks ago. What's changed? What's different? We're still in this bloody hospital and Molly's still in a coma, breathing thanks to a ventilator. Her heart is beating, her skin is warm, but her eyes stay closed and she doesn't react to pain or light.' She lowered her voice, as near to pleading as I'd ever heard her. 'We need your help, Colin. *I* need your help. Alex and me... we're too close. Is Molly alive or dead?'

Alive or dead?

it had to be said and it's been said

For almost a month we'd substituted every synonym we could think of rather than put those three words together. This was the first time they'd been spoken out loud. The impersonal white walls melted away and, like some bizarre out-of-body experience, I saw myself hunkered down on the icy pavement talking to the beggar on Byres Road, turning to see Sam reach out as my sister's scream and the whine of brakes melded in the freezing air and split the December night. I'd been luckier than I'd realised; when I slipped Sam had caught me. The second time she'd tried to catch her sister, she'd been too late and now Molly was on a ventilator and we were in a doctor's office about to debate her future.

Sam's fingers dug deeper into the chair and she repeated her question to her husband. 'In your opinion, is Molly alive or dead?'

The edge of Colin's mouth twitched, yet he refused to commit himself, wary of voicing a view that, either way, was doomed to be wrong. His reply was cautious, lacking conviction. 'If it was me, I'd hear what Gupta has to say before I decided anything.'

Sam lost it. She beat her fists against his chest. 'I'm asking you! Why don't you just answer me?'

'Okay, I will. How can anybody be absolutely certain there's no hope Molly will come back?'

It wasn't what Sam had wanted to hear. 'It's nice to know you're there when I need you, Colin.'

She turned her attention to me. We'd always been different, never more than now with so much at stake. If we'd had it in us to find a united front and share the terrible responsibility it would've made a difficult thing, perhaps not easier – that was too much to ask – but more bearable. It was becoming obvious that wouldn't happen because, while one of us needed this to go on, even if ultimately it was futile, the other longed for it to be over.

The door opened, momentarily easing the tension. Mr Gupta was wearing a white coat and carrying a folder. He nodded to each of us in turn and sat down behind the desk. I'd researched him on Google: Sandeep Gupta was forty-two years old, married with four beautiful children whose pictures were regularly posted on their mother's Facebook page. He'd been born in the southern Indian state of Kerala and educated at the All India Institute of Medical Sciences in New Delhi and Johns Hopkins in the United States. Why he was working the graveyard shift on a weekend in Glasgow was a mystery I hadn't had the energy to explore.

He'd spoken to us after he'd operated on Molly. My memory of the conversation wasn't vivid enough to be called a memory, more a series of fragmented images unconnected by time; the longest night of my life had passed in a dream until a grey dawn became a grey day.

The operation had lasted almost eight hours and, understandably, the surgeon had looked tired. We'd shaken hands with him, a formality that didn't bode well, then gone to a private room down the corridor where he'd explained in a quiet voice I'd had to strain to hear. The list of Molly's injuries and complications had gone on and on, though the one that stuck out had come in the first sentence. 'Your sister has suffered what's known as a coup-contrecoup, which means—'

Sam had interrupted. 'Both sides of the brain have been traumatised.'

'That's right.'

Given I'd witnessed Molly lying in the road like a discarded toy, my question had been pathetically naïve. 'How is she? I mean... how is she? Did the operation go well?'

The weariness on his face had morphed into something deeper; he'd hesitated before delivering the bad news. 'Molly is unresponsive.'

'Will she recover?'

He'd spread his arms in a gesture of powerlessness. 'Modern medicine is considered by many to have existed less than one hundred years. Tremendous strides have been made since Alexander Fleming stumbled across a mould he identified as "penicillium". Nevertheless, in some respects we are only just emerging from the Dark Ages. It's those limitations, those gaps in our knowledge, that give us reason to believe in miracles.'

The surgeon had skilfully avoided answering the question. I'd needed clarity. 'What exactly are you saying?'

Mr Gupta had studied us, judging if we were strong enough to hear what he had to tell us. 'Your sister is on life support. With the trauma Molly has sustained, recovery to any degree is unlikely.'

I'd pushed him to drop the doctor-speak and be specific. 'How unlikely?'

A shadow of what might've been resentment had passed behind the neurosurgeon's eyes. 'In my assessment it would be *very* unlikely. I'm sorry I haven't something better to report.'

Denial had washed over me. 'How can you be sure?'

'It's my job to be sure.'

Sam had said, 'Can we see her?'

'It would be better to go home and come back tonight or tomorrow.'

I'd spat the words at him. 'Better? Better for who?'

He'd forgiven me and answered with kindness.

'Better for you. Molly's in good hands. The best hands, trust me. We'll look after her. But there are difficult days ahead for you. You must look after yourselves.'

Four weeks further on we were here because he'd asked us to come. Mr Gupta pulled a pair of wire-rimmed reading glasses from the breast pocket of his white coat, opened the file and started to read, flicking through page after page, while the clock on the wall ticked the seconds away. When he reached the end, he removed the glasses and rested his elbows on the table. I felt a tightness in my chest and the acid burn of fear in the pit of my stomach. Sam's fingers found mine and squeezed. This had been coming from the second the car crashed into Molly; it was inevitable. Knowing that didn't make it better. Whatever the moral or medical arguments, none of the options were worth a damn – on that, at least, Sam and I were agreed. Now, we were settling our differences for our sister's sake as well as our own.

Mr Gupta put his palms together as though he were about to pray. Sam shot a look at me; she'd had the same thought. God was persona non grata as far as we were concerned.

He'd had his chance and blown it.

Gupta said, 'Your family is going through a period of unimaginable sorrow and stress. The last thing I want is, in any way, to add to it. Let me begin with a word of reassurance. Please believe Molly isn't in pain or discomfort of any kind, and, whatever you decide, that won't alter. I asked to meet so we can, hopefully, move closer to agreeing the way forward.'

Immediately, I saw exactly where this was headed and rose angrily out of my chair.

'You want to turn the machine off. That's what this is about, isn't it?'

Mr Gupta didn't react. He'd been in this situation many times; none of this was new to him. He spoke with the same calm I remembered from the first meeting, when exhaustion had hung on him like a cloak. Breaking the terrible news to our family was his last act before going home and falling into bed. 'No, it's about doing what's right for Molly. This is an incredibly difficult thing for everyone involved to deal with. I think it will be useful to lay out what the law has to say on these situations.'

I reacted to the phraseology. 'Our sister isn't a "situation".'

Sam put her hand on my arm. 'That's not what he meant, Alex.'

'Isn't it? That's what it sounded like to me.'

Gupta waited a moment and went on. 'The decision to end life support lies with the family and the medical team. Molly didn't make a Living Will detailing her wishes, which leaves the final say with the people in this room. Are you in agreement about what you want to do?'

Sam replied for both of us. 'No, no, we aren't.'

The surgeon nodded; it was what he'd expected. 'Tell me your thinking.'

I seized the opportunity. 'You admitted medicine is still in the Dark Ages. Four weeks isn't long. I can't let Molly go, it's too soon.'

Gupta smiled a sympathetic half-smile. 'That isn't quite what I said. Our understanding of how the brain works is a long way short of complete but we still know a lot.' He swung his attention to Sam. 'And you?'

My reasoning had been driven by emotion, hers wasn't. 'You told us the chances of Molly recovering were extremely unlikely. Has that changed?'

'I'm sorry to say there has been no improvement since your sister was admitted, so, reluctantly, my answer has to be no.'

'Then I say we let her go. Let Molly go.'

The surgeon's expression gave nothing away. He drew on his experience, gently prompting us towards a decision. I resented every word and didn't want to hear it.

He said, 'It may be helpful to consider what you

would want if the positions were reversed. Molly has suffered a series of injuries any one of which could've been fatal. Without the combination of machines and medication to support organs that are failing or have failed, this conversation would be unnecessary.' He looked at me and destroyed my objection in a sentence. 'Four weeks or four years, time isn't a factor. Nothing will change because nothing can change. Please accept my apology for being so blunt but a person who has no brain function will not regain consciousness or be able to breathe by themselves. In reality, we've already lost them.'

5

The conservatory was illuminated by a grey light that matched the mood of the men inside. Damian Morton's expression told the story: he wasn't happy. What was meant to be a discussion, an exchange of ideas, had become a monologue delivered by him. Lewis's contribution had been close to nothing. Damian finished on a low note. 'It's a trade-off, isn't it always? Exposure at the cost of the margins. And, as usual, the manufacturer – who does all the real graft – is at the short end of the stick. Except, with the contracted quotas and their high-street presence, it's guaranteed to be a very thick stick.'

Lewis didn't respond and Damian realised he'd been talking to himself the whole time. Lewis was a friend but he couldn't take much more of this. The relationship was falling apart, a tragedy given all they'd achieved, going from employing one woman and her teenage daughter working part time on second-hand PFAFF industrial sewing machines in a roller-door lock-up down a side street in Shettleston, to one of the fastest-growing clothing businesses in the country.

Success had come relatively quickly. They'd reached a point in their development years ahead of even their most optimistic forecasts, due in part to Lewis sinking money he'd inherited into the project. The brand had had a solid reputation for marrying an edgy style with ethically sourced materials and for striking fair trading deals that benefitted the locals, but it had remained small. Until a rock icon wearing a Stone Free jacket on the Pyramid stage at the Glastonbury Festival name-checked the label to 200,000 people live and a television audience of millions, sending demand through the ceiling. Since then, the phone hadn't stopped ringing with investors who hadn't given them the time of day before.

Stone Free was hot.

The question they had faced was which direction to go in. Until Lassiter-Accardi had entered the picture. Now, crunch time had arrived and they wanted to put the deal to bed. But for the best part of a month,

Lewis hadn't engaged with the proposal, spending his time at the house in Sherbrooke Avenue in Pollokshields, languidly doodling designs on scraps of paper, balling the results, and throwing them away.

Damian knew Lewis was a big-picture thinker, a creative guy with vision, flair, and the energy to make things happen. By comparison he was a plodder. But his partner's characteristic energy was missing, the roles had reversed, and Damian was the one forcing the pace while Lewis had largely become a passenger. He'd aged. There were lines on his face, tension in the set of his mouth, and he was clearly finding concentrating difficult. His friend understood why. Since the accident, getting him to focus on anything had been impossible, as though he no longer cared – about Stone Free or himself. He'd rejected the offer of a few beers in the once-familiar surroundings of the Horseshoe to talk about what was going on with him and hadn't come near the office, fielding calls from his home when he bothered to answer at all.

This meeting, like the previous three he'd cancelled, was supposed to have been about their response to the numbers the Americans had put forward. That needed the senior partner to be present in the room and clearly he wasn't.

The weather during the first month of the new

year had been horrendous. Today, the pattern contin-
ued, with rain falling from a moody sky in a steady
stream, drumming a quiet, relentless beat on the conservatory's glass roof. Lewis seemed to have forgotten
Damian was there, gazing down the length of the lawn
to the Victorian brick wall at the bottom separating
the property from its neighbours.

Damian broke into his thoughts. 'Lewis. Lewis.'

'Oh, sorry, man. I was miles away.'

'Yeah, you were.'

'What were you saying?'

This was the cards-on-the-table moment Damian
had been avoiding. He said, 'It doesn't matter. We can
come back to it. There's something more important we
need to talk about.'

'More important than the roll-out proposal?
What?'

'You.'

'What about me?'

'If you really don't know, you leave me no option
but to tell you. This can't go on. It just can't.'

Lewis was taken aback. 'What can't go on? We're
doing great, aren't we?'

'"Great" isn't how I'd describe it.'

'What's wrong?'

Damian waved an arm at the room. 'Take a look at

where you live – a long way from the one-bedroom flat in Hamiltonhill you were in when we met. Remember the ASBOs upstairs and the toilet that didn't flush half the time?'

Lewis hoped there was a point to this unsolicited stroll down memory lane. 'Where are you going with this?'

'It was fun. In many ways more satisfying than having power players throwing silly money at us validating our belief in what we were doing.'

'I'm hearing a "but", Damian.'

Damian ignored him and carried on making his point. 'You and me flying by the seat of our pants, not sure if we could pay the electricity bill at the end of the month, was fantastically exhilarating. Real white-knuckle stuff. Great memories and I'm glad I have them. But those days are gone and neither of us is keen to revisit them. Stone Free is a success and it's going to be a monster. The downside is that people are counting on us when they weren't in the past. Their jobs, their mortgages, the well-being of their families, depend on an idea we came up with one night when we were pissed. Stone Free's a great concept and a great brand name. "Saving the world one T-shirt at a time."' He laughed. 'Our first business plan was literally written on the back of a fag packet. If we screw up it has to be because punters stop buying our clothes, not because we lose the plot and run out of steam.'

'Who's running out of steam?'

'You.'

The truth dropped like a brick between them. Lewis took a deep breath and let it out slowly. 'You're telling me I'm not pulling my weight and I know you're right.'

'Just when the doors to the big time are finally starting to open, you're AWOL.'

Lewis nodded. 'You deserve better from me. All I can do is apologise.'

'Not necessary. We've known each other too long and too well. It's the accident, isn't it?'

Lewis drew the palm of his hand over his tired face, distorting his features. 'I can't stop thinking about that woman. Every time I close my eyes I see her and hear the thud of the car smashing into her. The bumps beneath the wheels. The squeal of the brakes. Christ!' He shuddered. 'I go to bed exhausted and wake up the same way. Honestly, I couldn't tell you when I last had a decent night's sleep.'

'You were breathalysed and let go. If there had been the slightest suggestion you were to blame – any-thing at all – they would've taken you to the nearest police station and charged you. Instead, all you were asked for was a witness statement. It wasn't your fault.'

Lewis gave a disgusted grunt. 'Tell that to a family with a sister unconscious in a hospital bed. I doubt it'll be a great comfort to them. It isn't to me.'

'Nevertheless, for the sake of your health you have to get past it. The business needs you back. *I* need you back. These people have given us an opportunity and are expecting an answer. They won't wait much longer.'

The phone vibrated on the table like an angry bee. Lewis's mobile wasn't slim and small and covered in soft Morocco leather; it didn't play Tetris, Clue or chess or have built-in GPS. All it did was allow him to make and receive calls. He lifted it and forced a lightness he didn't feel into his greeting. 'Oliver, what can I do for you?'

Oliver Shawcross was a partner in Campbell, Mckinnon and Shawcross, a legal firm in Spiers Wharf, Port Dundas, in what had originally been the offices of the Forth & Clyde Navigation Co and the City of Glasgow Grain Mills and Stores. Lewis's late father had been his client. He'd met the son after his parents were fatally injured in a train crash in India, when an express ploughed into the bus they were on at a level crossing in Rajasthan. Paul Stone's estate had included a modest amount of cash and two houses – one in Sherbrooke Avenue in Glasgow and a second property at Loch Morar, where Lewis had been when the tragedy occurred; Oliver had driven up to break the sad news in person rather than over the phone and they'd become friends. Years later, outsourcing the fledgling Stone Free's legal work to his firm had been a no-brainer.

Small talk wasn't necessary and the lawyer got to the point. 'It's not good, I'm afraid, Lewis. Molly Kennedy, the woman involved in the accident—'

'I know who she is, Oliver.'

Shawcross made a mental note to choose his words more carefully. He'd spoken with Lewis twice since the new year and both times found him irritable and quick to react – a far cry from his usual laid-back self. 'Of course you do.'

'What about her?'

'They turned off her life support.'

Lewis groaned and covered his eyes with his arm. 'Oh, Christ. Then she's dead.'

'Yes.'

'When was this?'

'The family met with the doctor a few days ago and came to a decision last night. I've only just heard. In case you're worrying, this doesn't change anything for you. It was an accident then and it's still an accident, albeit a fatal one.'

'I'm all right. It's her family I'm thinking about. They must be devastated. Find out when the funeral is. I'd like to send a wreath and a card.'

Oliver held the phone nearer his mouth. 'Lewis, forget I'm your lawyer. I'm telling you this as a friend.'

Lewis guessed what was coming and shook his head. 'Fire away, I'm listening.'

'By all means send flowers but I'd hold off on a card if I were you.'

'Why?'

'Sympathy, especially coming from you, may not be appreciated. Even if you keep it brief, landing on the right words and the right tone won't be easy.'

It was good advice; Lewis was inclined to ignore it. He said, 'I'll make it "deepest condolences", something like that. It was my car that hit her. It seems wrong not to recognise that.'

Lewis's attitude unnerved Shawcross. He said, 'To you. To you it seems wrong. But you aren't them, are you? In their position a show of kindness from the driver who ran down their sister six days before Christmas could be the last thing they want. Promise me you aren't considering actually going to the service.

Because, as your lawyer never mind your friend, I have to advise you that would be extremely unwise.'

'Don't lecture me, Oliver, I don't appreciate it.'

'I'm not.'

'Really? That isn't how it sounds.'

'Well, it does to me.'

Lewis had heard as much as he wanted. 'Come back to me with the funeral arrangements and for fuck's sake, credit me with having some bloody sense.'

Damian let a minute pass before he spoke. 'Look, mate, my advice is to forget about everything – the business, the accident, the whole bloody lot of it. I've already suggested we go and get rat-arsed like we did in the old days. C'mon, let's do just that. God knows we deserve it. The problem is you've bottled things up and it's crippling you. Grab your jacket and we'll fix it right now.'

Lewis stared at him; he hadn't heard a word.

6

Sam studied her reflection in the bedroom mirror: the black dress with its matching coat and hat had hung forgotten in the back of the wardrobe, the shoes with their appropriately small heels bought specially for her mother's funeral, worn only once on the day and never again since, still in the box. Death hadn't been unexpected given their mother's failing health, but it had still been a terrible time for all of them. Without her sisters, Sam wouldn't have got through it. A hollow-cheeked priest had read the familiar committal 'Ashes to ashes, dust to dust' prayer at the graveside in a barely-audible voice, the words ripped from his mouth by a bitter November wind, adding them to the gold and bronze leaves blowing across the cemetery between the standing stones. And as the coffin was lowered into the hard ground, she'd seen Alex silently mouth reminders that they were the daughters of the lady in the casket, raised to be strong, independent women able to deal with life on life's terms and suffer the pain of parting with dignity. At the end, they'd each lifted a handful of earth and allowed it to trickle from their fingers into the hole.

Today was not that day.

Where there had been three, now only two remained. Molly should've had decades ahead of her – the best years of her life; the joys of children and grandchildren, basking in their triumphs, commiserating in the inevitable failures. Always there.

Colin shouted anxiously from the bottom of the stairs, 'I'll bring the car round the front! Are you ready? We can't be late.'

Sam took a final look in the mirror; the dress suited her. What a pity somebody had to die before she got to wear it. She sat the pillbox hat on her head and straightened it into position, wiped the tears threatening to have her mascara running, and drew down the veil. Sam sighed. 'As ready as I'll ever be.'

* * *

Lewis hugged the inside lane of the M74 in the hire car he'd had the presence of mind to arrange, leaving plenty of space between him and a Vauxhall Astra with a yellow 'Kids on Board' sign in the rear window. Three small shiny faces smiled baby-teeth smiles at him. One of the children waved. He didn't wave back. His hands gripped the steering wheel tight, eyes darting nervously to the side mirror and back to the road. A hundred yards from the Rutherglen/Cambuslang exit, the driver signalled his intention to turn off. Lewis let out an exaggerated sigh of relief, as though some terrible threat had been removed.

The change from a guy going purposefully about his life to what he'd become dismayed him. He could count on one hand the number of times he'd driven since the accident. His confidence was shot. To rediscover it he needed to face his demons. Oliver was a shrewd observer of human nature who knew Lewis better than he knew himself and hadn't been wrong about what was in his mind. When he'd called with the funeral arrangements, the lawyer had repeated his warning about the wisdom of attending the service. 'A wreath as a show of sympathy, fine. I don't have a problem with that. Doubt many people would be offended. But, as I've already said, anything else is madness, though if you really are thinking of going it might be worth asking yourself why. The deceased won't be affected. The family won't want it. Who does that leave?'

Silence from the other end of the line told him he wasn't getting through. Once Lewis Stone got hold of a thing he didn't let go. Before he ended the call, Shawcross had added a jaundiced aside to the mini monologue falling on deaf ears. 'Then again, why listen to me? You know your own business best. Or, you used to.'

* * *

It was cold but the rain had stopped. Lewis edged along the leafy approach road with the hum of the nearby motorway fading in his ears. He rolled down the window, savouring the rain-washed air and the quiet, so silent he might have been in the depths of a forest instead of the grounds of a crematorium on the outskirts of Glasgow.

The trees parted. Daldowie's squat grey facade loomed into sight. His immediate reaction was disappointment. Those who came to this place were in pain. There was no comfort to be found in the concrete lines of the aesthetically barren building. The architect had deftly distilled the desolation of grief in a joyless, depressing memorial and probably imagined he'd made a fair stab at a difficult brief.

According to Google, Daldowie had three chapels: East, West, and South. The Kennedy funeral was at eleven o'clock in the East. Mourners dressed in black milled around the entrance in groups, chatting to each other, putting off the inevitable until the last minute. The hire car's arrival got their attention. Some stopped talking to check if it was anyone they recognised and returned to their conversation when they saw it wasn't.

Lewis pulled into a parking space, cut the engine, and surveyed the scene through fresh eyes. The mourners were strangers to him. He was a stranger to them. What Oliver had been banging on about suddenly made sense. This wasn't right.

He didn't know these people.

There was no place for him here.

What the hell was he doing?

The family would be sitting in the front row doing their best to support each other. Emotionally fragile, still coming to terms with their loss, scarred by the aftermath in the hospital and the decision no one wanted to ever have to make.

For a long time, he rested his head on the steering wheel, his cheeks flushed with shame at what he'd almost done. The psychological trauma they were suffering was beyond anything he could measure, let alone understand. Recovering from it – if that was even possible – would take time. For the man who'd killed their loved one to be standing with those who'd come to pay their last respects could send them over the edge. Thanks to Oliver, he'd avoided causing more hurt; they'd already had more than enough.

The accident replayed in his head. He saw the woman's face – the abject terror on it the second before he crashed into her. Remembering made him feel ill. Lewis got out, grateful for the chill air against his skin, leaned against the car and vomited on the ground. Hot bile burned his throat and splashed his shoes; he gagged and vomited again, wiped his mouth with his hand and looked across to the East chapel. People were still arriving, some crying quietly. Lewis got in, turned the key in the ignition, and pulled away.

* * *

Colin slipped into the pew behind the sisters. There had been so much tension between him and Sam, the last thing anyone needed was for it to erupt, today of all days. This way all of them got the space they needed to grieve. The tragedy could've been a wake-up call; so far it was just another issue to divide them.

They couldn't discuss anything without ending up shouting at each other. Alex, the usually pragmatic eldest of the Kennedy girls, had been in trouble before the decision to turn off Molly's life support. Since, she'd become a different person, someone Colin didn't recognise. Sam was doing better, at least on the surface, but she was deep; it was difficult to be sure.

In the centre of the chapel towards the front, the mahogany coffin rested on a table decorated with a simple white cover. Not long ago the cold dead body inside had been a vibrant woman, a smart, funny ball of impish energy. Colin had been in the neurosurgeon's office and heard his bleak assessments. When they'd switched the ventilator off, he'd covered his eyes with his hand. It hadn't seemed real.

Alex and Sam had made the arrangements. All three siblings had abandoned their parents' faith the moment they no longer lived under their roof. This was intended to be a non-religious dignified farewell and celebration of a life. Given the circumstances, there wouldn't be much celebrating.

To the left-hand side of the mahogany coffin a TV screen repeated images of Molly and her sisters in better days as the familiar piano intro of Adele's 'Someone Like You' filled the chapel. Molly had been a huge fan, the song one of her favourites.

It was all too much for Alex. The brave show at their mother's funeral wouldn't be repeated today. She bowed her head, her shoulders shook and she broke down. Sam put an arm round her and whispered something Colin couldn't hear. Whatever she'd said helped. Alex nodded slowly and dried her tears with a tissue hidden in her sleeve. Colin lifted a memorial card and ran a finger gently over the face smiling back at him lit by the freshness of youth and the possibilities that lay ahead. In the photograph, Molly's hair was shoulder length, dark brown like Sam's. Nobody had asked his opinion about which picture to use. This one was new to him. He hadn't seen it before and guessed his sister-in-law would've been seventeen or eighteen when the camera caught her essence.

A woman radiating a quiet calm introduced herself as Amy, a humanist celebrant. 'Molly was a free spirit. A bright star. She wouldn't want any of you to be sad at her passing. Death reminds us of our own mortality and of others we have lost. But because a person has died doesn't mean we stop loving them. They live on in our hearts and minds and memories. I'm going to start by reading "When I am dead, my dearest" by Christina Rossetti.'

She took a moment to compose herself and began.

'When I am dead, my dearest,
Sing no sad songs for me;
Plant thou no roses at my head,
Nor shady cypress tree.
Be the green grass above me
With showers and dewdrops wet;
And if thou wilt, remember,
And if thou wilt, forget.'

Colin closed his eyes and blocked it out.

7

I'd learned that people react differently to death, grieve in their own particular way. Sam's was to talk nonsense about things that weren't important, as though the very ordinariness of it would keep the pain she was feeling at arm's length.

She unpinned her hat and fired it across the room. It hit the wall, dropped to the floor and lay like a dead bird. 'Sometimes I worry I'm losing my mind. This morning, I was looking in the mirror asking myself why I'd forgotten this outfit. Now I know – it's depressing. And as for that monstrosity of a hat... it's the ugliest bloody thing I've ever seen. What possessed me to buy it? Answers on a postcard.' She turned to me.

'Isn't this the bit where you jump in and disagree with me? I'm not hearing it.'

I took a bottle of The Famous Grouse from the drinks cabinet and poured a whisky for each of us. One wouldn't be enough but it was a start. The humanist had melded the memories and anecdotes we'd shared with her into a story that accurately told who Molly had been. Not perfect but rather a flesh and blood woman we recognised.

Sam accepted the drink and raised her glass. 'To Molly.'

I answered, 'Molly,' and sat down in an armchair by the flame fire.

We didn't speak again until Sam shrugged. 'So that's that. All over bar the shouting.'

I shot a sharp look at her. 'For you, maybe.'

'What do you mean?'

'I mean it isn't over for me. Think about it a minute. The man who ran our sister down is walking around scot-free. He killed her. Whatever way you look at it he killed her, Sam. And he's getting away with it. At least, he thinks he is.'

Sam pulled her shoulders back, unable to hide her surprise. 'Yes, she died, Alex, but it was an accident. She fell in front of him. I know, I was right beside her.

Hasn't it occurred to you I might have had a few sleepless nights myself? Been on a guilt trip of my own?'

'No. Why would you feel guilty?'

'Maybe because I stopped one of my sisters from falling but I didn't stop the other one. How do you imagine that makes me feel? I'll tell you – fucking awful! The only consolation I have is that it was an accident. A tragic freak event. So please don't turn it into something more. I can't cope with more.'

The last thing I wanted was to hurt her, but I couldn't help myself. 'A freak accident that might not have happened if the bastard hadn't been drinking – he admitted it to the police. They should've arrested him, there and then. What happened to zero tolerance? Isn't that the law in this country, or did somebody change it?'

Sam put her glass on the coffee table and leaned forward. 'Alex, listen to me. Don't do this to us. We were both there. We saw it. Molly slipped. You can't—'

'I can and I will because it's the truth. How much or how little alcohol was in his bloodstream isn't important, his reactions were impaired. You heard the bloody music he was playing. Nobody could concentrate on the road with that racket going on. Which makes him responsible. In my book that's manslaughter. So shove your "that's it", okay! I won't hear it.'

Sam breathed slowly through her mouth. 'I don't like the sound of this, Alex. This isn't you. You're scaring me. It's done. It's over. We need to get past it and start living our lives. Yes, it won't be easy. But we have to try or Molly won't be the only Kennedy sister who died that night.' She hesitated, no doubt gathering the courage to say what she was really thinking, not knowing the reaction it would receive. 'Alex, shouldn't you be getting back to work?'

She held up her palm to stop me interrupting. 'Yes, it's in good hands, but the fact is you have too much time on yours, and this... this is the result.'

I stared into the flames. 'I can't. I'm just not ready yet. And you can relax, Sam. I'm not asking you to do anything. Molly was your twin. I thought all that stuff they say about twins feeling each other's pain was—'

Sam jumped to her feet, towering over me, her face twisted in rage. 'Don't dare! Don't you dare try your emotional blackmail on me. It won't work.'

'I'm telling you what I thought, that's all. Nothing more.'

'Well, you thought wrong, didn't you? We went out. We drank a bit too much. The pavement was icy. You slipped and so did Molly. I caught you. That's the only difference. Scratching around for somebody to blame might help you in some perverse way; it doesn't help me. Molly will still be dead. So start accepting it and get a grip. You heard what the humanist said. When somebody we were close to isn't here any more it doesn't mean we stop loving them. Of course it doesn't. I'd do anything to rewrite the past and have her walk through that door. Anything, Alex. But it isn't going to happen. It can't happen because she's...'

The atmosphere in the room had changed, the roles reversed, and it was my turn to be the comforter. I held Sam tight, whispering, 'I'm sorry I upset you. I know it's hard. It is for me, too. And we will keep loving her – what else would we do? I just find it impossible to live with the fact that the man who mangled her body and put her on that life-support machine has got away with it. That can't be right. That can't possibly be right. Tell me you agree. Tell me I'm not alone in this. I've lost Molly. I can't lose you.'

Sam drew away from me. 'You're all I have in the world, Alex. That won't change. But we have to get a hold on ourselves and come to terms with what is. We aren't the first people who've had someone taken from them. They let the driver go, whoever he is. I'm not spending the rest of my life hating a guy I've never met for being part of something that wasn't his fault. Maybe you can't understand that.'

I said the next words slowly. 'Lewis Stone.'

Sam's hands flew to her mouth. 'You know his name? How?'

I could have added, 'Not just his name. Where he works and where he lives,' but something told me to hold back. 'I overheard him tell the police.'

Her reaction was everything I'd expected. She looked away, awkwardly, not wanting to say what she needed to say. In the end it was short and final. 'Alex, listen, this isn't easy though I have to get it out. You're deluding yourself, not facing up to what is. I can't go there. I don't want to go there. I didn't think I'd ever hear myself say this to my big sister, but you're on your own with this.'

* * *

I could have been angry and resented her poor opinion of me, but that wouldn't change her mind. Sam didn't get it. She hadn't lived the nightmare I'd been through – happier than I'd ever believed it was possible to be before a sombre consultant delivered the shattering news it was all about to end: Freddy – my lovely Freddy, my beautiful man – wasting away before my eyes; the endless tests and the tubes coming out of his body; the doctors with their clipboards and their white coats telling me to prepare myself. How could anybody who hadn't been there and seen his pain for themselves possibly understand? The cancer, insidious and relentless, had been too powerful to challenge; it was always going to win. Molly's death was different – there I had a focus, a flesh and blood killer to turn my fury against. And if I was alone in the fight, so be it.

8

It was only 4 p.m. and the sun was setting on another bleak day for Lewis.

He pinched the corners of his eyes and turned the PC off. Among the emails had been one from the Americans forwarded to him earlier by Damian with a line of question marks along the bottom. Lewis hadn't replied; sooner rather than later Damian's patience would run out. He had a point, there was no denying it: the proposal was the opportunity they'd dreamed of propped up on stools in the Horseshoe Bar off Renfield Street, eking out their pints because they couldn't afford another round. Now, when it was finally in their grasp, it seemed hollow and empty, more trouble than it was worth. Damian had told him he realised he'd need time after the accident and had given it to him. But unless Lewis freed himself from the downward spiral he'd been in since Christmas, a showdown was on the horizon. Then again, showdowns took energy and Lewis didn't have any.

He uncorked a bottle of Chateau Svanidze Mukuzani 2017 that, according to the marketing blurb, was 'a legendary Georgian full-bodied wine with intensive cherry, redberry and oak tones and a long finish'.

It was alcohol, and that was everything he needed to know.

Beyond the conservatory's ceiling-to-floor glass panels, the garden was a darkening void broken by a flurry of fresh snow drifting languidly to earth. Mother Nature was reflecting his own lethargy. Its warmth reminded him that at this moment in Glasgow, poor buggers were lying in shop doorways under strips of cardboard, not sure if they'd be alive in the morning. He nursed the glass of Chateau-what-the-fuck, then took a sip. Feeling sorry for himself needed to end. Damian had told him to his face it couldn't go on. Too many people believed in the project and were depending on its success; disappointing them wasn't an option.

He laid the glass down, pushed it away, and put his

head in his hands as he had on the kerb in Byres Road. Oliver hadn't called back. Lewis suspected he'd had as much of him as he could take and decided to back off. If that was true it would be a significant loss and he'd have only himself to blame. Oliver was a good man to have in the boat, a wise counsellor even though, more often than not, Lewis ignored his advice and went his own way. Of course, he'd been right. His assessment of how the dead woman's family would react to the man who'd killed her showing up at the funeral, perhaps pathetically, embarrassingly, breaking down or attempting to shake their hands, had been frighteningly accurate and come perilously near being realised. Lewis having witnessed their grief first-hand, albeit from the relative safety of the crematorium car park, it wasn't difficult to get where the lawyer had been coming from. If the positions were reversed, Lewis was in little doubt what his response would've been. He'd have decked the bastard before a sorry word came out of his mouth; hit him and kept on hitting him until somebody dragged him off.

Outside, the flurry had become a steady fall. Lewis considered going to bed but dismissed the idea. What was the point? It was still early. He wouldn't sleep, he had too much on his mind. Strangely, not the proposal. In fact, he'd forgotten about it until the email reminded him, a far cry from his reaction when he'd first been told an offer was in the wind. They'd discussed the deal at length in the second half of the old year – some days it had seemed it was all they discussed – excitedly exploring the potentials, identifying the long-term implications, in the end agreeing it was everything they'd wished for. A no-brainer.

It demanded nothing from him except a yes, a signature, and a few PR gigs. Why he hadn't just let accountants and lawyers wade through the fine print and thrash out the details was a mystery to both of them. Was it a power thing? A reluctance to hand over his baby to somebody else? Surely not? For all its ethical values, Stone Free was a business created to make money. Damian was excited, recognising it as an important step in their development. Global exposure for the brand – and only the beginning. Although he was the junior partner he was just as invested in the project and deserved better. So why not sign the papers and be done with the damned thing?

Lewis sat on the brown-leather sofa and opened a book given to him as a Christmas present. He'd started Donna Tartt's *The Secret History* on New Year's Eve, hoping the modern masterpiece would take him to a better place in his head. According to the bookmark, he'd read fifty pages. Lewis couldn't remember a single one of them – the characters, the setting: it was all a blank. He stared at the cover, willing the story to come to him. A fragment even, to prove he wasn't going insane.

He closed the novel and set it down, shaken by what his loss of memory revealed about his state of mind.

The partnership hadn't always been smooth. Damian had never been slow to press for what he believed was in the best interests of Stone Free. They were both strong characters who, inevitably, had had their share of shouting matches. More than once the loud differences of opinion had damn near come to blows. But when the dust had settled, they'd laughed about it and gone to the Horseshoe Bar. Passion was good, they'd told each other. More than good, essential to drive the project to greater heights. The global roll-out of Stone Free was mega, yet Damian was tiptoeing round him as though he were a highly strung child who required careful handling. As for Shawcross, he'd simply disappeared off the face of the earth since he'd said what he felt had to be said.

These men were his friends or pretended they were.

No, that was crazy – they *were*. They'd proved it time and again.

It was him. He'd walked away from the accident on the surface seemingly unharmed, except something inside had shaken loose. The signs were undeniable and they were everywhere; disengaging from the business at a crucial moment, turning up at a funeral where he wasn't wanted and hiding in alcohol weren't the actions of a man in command of himself. Not remembering a damned thing about the book was, by itself, of no importance, yet it told him what Damian and Oliver had already sussed: he was having a breakdown. But though their conclusion was right, they were wrong about the cause of his emotional collapse. Lewis knew something he wouldn't share with a living soul. Yes, she'd been under the wheels before he could react. And yes, he was sure the half-glass of wine he'd drunk earlier hadn't been a factor, otherwise the police wouldn't have let him go. The shameful truth he couldn't forgive or forget was that, as he'd gone down Byres Road that Friday night, his head had been full of the lady with tantalisingly long legs.

Driving hadn't been his priority. Fuck! In spite of the difficult conditions, he hadn't been paying attention and because of it, a family was broken and a young woman was dead. He picked the wine up and walked to the end of the conservatory, seeing his reflection in the glass. Somewhere in the night a dog barked, a baying lonely sound that touched a chord in him, stirring emotions better left alone. Another animal joined the first. The barking got louder as one became two, rising to a deafening crescendo in his head, until it was all he could hear.

Lewis downed his drink and tried to hold on to what was left of his sanity.

9

I moved quietly through the rooms, measuring my steps like an intruder. Molly was gone but this was still her flat and in my heart I knew I had no business being here. In the spare room I laughed out loud at the row of teddy bears lined up on the pillows acting as wig stands. Her favourite sat in the middle, a cuddly one-eyed little guy called Angus she'd had since she was a child, with a blue-and-white wig on his furry head. The tartan scarf Molly wore when she watched Scotland play was wrapped round him like a shawl and I remembered how she'd scream with delight and hug him when the team scored. I draped the scarf over my shoulders, hoping it might bring me closer to what I'd lost. It didn't, of course it didn't, because it was just a stupid lump of wool and I longed to be able to come to terms with her death. But until somebody took responsibility for it, I couldn't. That 'somebody' had to be the man behind the wheel on Byres Road that December night: Lewis Stone – he was the cancer that had brought my beautiful sister's time with us to a premature end.

And he was still out there, living his life as though nothing had happened.

* * *

It was dark. I released the rusty latch, praying it wouldn't creak, and pushed the old wooden gate open as the first snowflakes arrived like an advance guard scouting enemy territory. I saw them and cursed quietly. This was difficult enough without snow making it harder to see. I used the hedge as cover, hurrying, staying low. Remarkably in the circumstances, I wasn't afraid. Sam and Molly had often joked about my single-minded determination, a trait they'd mistakenly assumed they didn't share. I recognised it in myself; once I'd settled on something there was no going back. If I needed proof, I only had to look at where I was right now.

The sound of barking made me stop and look anxiously at the lights in an upstairs window. Any second it could open and some angry man demand to know what I was doing in his garden. If I told him I was spying on the house over the back wall he'd call the police, no question about it.

My actions were driven by emotion – I hadn't thought it through. There was nothing that could even vaguely be called a plan. My car was parked three streets away behind a line of vehicles, their windscreens opaque with frost. On a night like this, the owners would be stretched out in front of flat-screen TVs, pondering whether another glass of wine to round off the evening would feel like such a good idea when the alarm clock on the bedside table rang at seven o'clock in the morning.

Under the Barbour's fur-lined hood, my mouth was set in a grim smile. This was crazy. But crazy or not, it had to be done. The law had failed; our sister's killer hadn't been called to answer for his crime. Accepting it wasn't an option I could allow myself to consider.

On Byres Road, the police car's flashing light had bathed the scene in electric blue. I'd watched them lift Molly's body onto a stretcher and into the back of the ambulance, not knowing I'd never speak to my sister again, or that a month later I'd be a reluctant part of the decision to switch off the ventilator and end her life. Across the street, officers had been with the driver, breathalysing him. I'd expected the guy to be charged – it hadn't occurred to me he wouldn't be. When they'd let him go, I'd felt the first pinprick of betrayal that would grow to a raging storm and end with me creeping through a stranger's back garden in the snow.

The ground beneath my feet was hard. With each step my breath puffed in a gossamer cloud and vanished in the freezing air. If Sam could see me now, she'd go bat-shit crazy. I was the eldest, the sensible sister, the voice of reason.

This wasn't me.

Except, now it was.

Climbing over the brick wall was a challenge. Somehow, I managed it and dropped to my knees on the other side. The house at the far end was everything I expected from a property in one of the most expensive streets in Glasgow. Mr Lewis Stone had done all right for himself. Instead of spending years of his life behind bars, he was living it large on the South Side.

Not for much longer.

The conservatory was rectangular with a tiled roof, the space bigger than most people's living rooms; a nice spot to relax after a hard day at the office. In summer, the bastard would no doubt dress in Ralph Lauren polo shirts and Tommy Hilfiger jeans and entertain his smug friends and business associates over boozy Sunday lunches that would carry into the evening. As the afternoon drew on and the wine did its work, they'd talk of many things, these privileged wankers, but the death of a much-loved sister whose life had been snuffed out in her prime wouldn't be one of them.

Through the snow, even from a distance, I recognised him. He stood on the other side of the glass panels in the amber glow of an overhead light, one hand thrust into his trouser pocket, the other holding a drink, almost as though he'd been waiting for me.

Nonsense. Byres Road was weeks ago; he'd have forgotten about it, erased it from his memory as though it hadn't happened. His kind could do that.

With every hour he went unpunished, the pain of losing Molly grew to a physical hurt so sharp it kept me awake at night. I wasn't 'over it' – whatever that was supposed to mean – and didn't expect I ever would be. Seeing the man responsible for so much sorrow made me want to tear his face off, rip out the eyes that hadn't registered my sister slip into the road in time to turn the wheel and avoid hitting her. It had been an accident – everybody, even Sam, said so. As if that made it okay.

For me, it was far from okay.

Molly was still dead.

Coming here had clarified an important point for me: I wouldn't be satisfied until Lewis Stone had suffered like Molly. Anything less was an insult to her memory.

The snow was heavy now, heavy enough to all but obscure the building and the conservatory. I narrowed my eyes and peered through it. Stone was still there; he hadn't moved. There was something odd about him; what was he thinking? He emptied his drink and walked away.

Seconds later, the light went out and I was alone in a white world.

10

Sam leaned provocatively against the frame of the
kitchen door, waiting for Colin to notice she was there.
He was already dressed, sitting on a bar stool in the
nook by the French windows leading to the garden,
absorbed in something on his tablet. An empty coffee
cup on the gold and grey veins of the Calacatta marble
top they'd paid silly money for even at trade prices
told her he'd been up for a while. She saw his broad
shoulders stretch the material of the black Hugo Boss
T-shirt he was wearing and remembered the morning
he'd arrived home unexpectedly with a hunger in his
eyes she'd been happy to satisfy. They'd torn each other's clothes off and he'd had her on the couch, then
again, slowly, deliberately, upstairs in their room.

Once, in the middle of a dinner party, he'd ravished her against a wall, while yards away their unsuspecting guests discussed the failure of American foreign policy as though any of them had a clue what they were talking about.

They'd laughed about that escapade for months.

They had been exciting times. Great times. Sam hadn't seen that look in ages. She wanted those days back; the tension between them had to end. Either she forgave him for what he'd done, left the messy past behind and made a commitment to get back what had been lost, or...

Or what? Carry on like this? Many unhappily married couples preferred it to the alternative. Sam understood why. Splitting up would be complicated; the business and the house would need to be sold, the credit cards cleared, and whatever was left in their bank account divided between them. The prospect of starting again, years older with a lot less wherewithal, didn't appeal, and she thanked Christ they didn't have kids; that would put the tin lid on it.

When the new wore off, most relationships went through phases, peaks and troughs they succumbed to or survived depending on the strength of the bond between the people involved. She'd read somewhere that, in the UK, 42 per cent of couples divorced before their thirteenth anniversary. Sam had no interest in being a part of that depressing statistic. She didn't lie to herself though. There had been moments – not moments, months – in the last year when she'd hated Colin with every atom of her being. A part of her still did. But they'd built a life together and he was her husband.

When she'd woken up, it had taken a second to realise that, once again, she was alone in the bed. Reality had rushed to greet her, and with it a shaft of clarity – Molly was dead, the funeral was behind them, and her marriage was on the rocks. The only thing it was possible to change was the relationship.

Somebody had to make the first move. That somebody had to be her and the time to do it was now.

Sam despised herself for being weak but, God help her, she loved him.

Colin pretended he hadn't heard his wife come downstairs and braced himself for the barbed exchanges that had become the norm whenever they were in the same room together, until he grabbed his car keys and escaped with her accusing rants ringing in his ears.

He looked up, expecting yet another vitriolic monologue. It didn't come. Sam leaned against the frame of the door watching him with an intensity he recognised and he felt himself respond. Painted finger-nails released the ties of the midnight-blue three-quarter-length satin dressing gown; the smooth mate-rial opened revealing her nakedness underneath. Colin hadn't been prepared and gasped. Sam came to-wards him, eyes lowered. Halfway across the floor the dressing gown fell from her shoulders. She dropped to her knees and began unbuttoning his fly.

Colin grabbed her wrists so hard it hurt and pulled her hands away. 'No, no. I can't do this.'

Sam pleaded with him. 'Don't turn away from me, please, Colin. Leave me some self-respect, at least. After all this time, surely I deserve that?'

He heard the desperation in her voice and felt for her. 'It isn't right, Sam. I'm sorry.'

'You're rejecting me, I can't believe it. You're re-jecting your wife.'

Colin couldn't listen to any more; he ran from the kitchen and up the stairs. Minutes later, Sam heard the front door slam, then the growl of his car bursting into life, and realised it was hopeless. He'd humiliated her. Again. Or maybe she'd humiliated herself. It didn't matter. Well, the bastard would pay for what he'd put her through. If she couldn't have him, she'd have the house and every bloody penny he'd ever earned.

* * *

The vegetarian café and delicatessen wasn't somewhere Oliver Shawcross would normally consider going. He was headed there because Damian had suggested it. He hadn't said why. Oliver hadn't asked, though he guessed it would be to do with Lewis.

It was a typical Scottish winter's day – blue skies, weak sunshine, and a wind so cold it nipped his eyes and caught the back of his throat. The snow had gone; only random humps of discoloured ice remained. He paused on the Great Western Bridge straddling the River Kelvin to give a *Big Issue* seller a coin and gaze down at the brown water rushing below with its crown of foam floating on top created by agitation of the detergent in the sewer. It wasn't as bad as it looked apparently – nevertheless, he didn't fancy drinking it.

In some circles it was fashionable to loudly declare yourself a fan of Glasgow. Oliver wasn't and never had been. He'd come to the city a wide-eyed student from Pittenweem, a fishing village in the East Neuk of Fife, met a girl and never gone back again except to visit his parents. When his father passed, followed eighteen months later by his mother, the 'Kingdom' held nothing for him. He'd sold their property and bought a flat in Partick, his first step on the property ladder.

Not being Glasgow born and bred allowed him to take a detached view of the 'Dear Green Place'. The natives, in the main, were friendly. Like anywhere in his experience, the nice ones were nice. He liked the architecture and the history but cuts to public services had taken a toll; the amount of litter in the streets was a disgrace. Covid had done the rest, as it had in so many city centres all over the country, painting a picture of what somebody had accurately described as 'managed decline'. In the buzzing West End, it wasn't so noticeable and he was grateful for that.

Damian was already in a seat by the window and waved him over. They'd never quite gelled; the lawyer had always been Lewis's man. Neither offered to shake hands and Morton said, 'I've ordered coconut chickpea curry and a couple of garlic naans, is that okay? I can cancel and get us something else.'

Oliver scanned the blackboard in the centre of the tiled wall with today's specials written on it in chalk, the shelves on either side stacked with gluten-free pasta, cartons of vegan milk, and boxes of Fair-Trade chocolate from around the world.

It was lunchtime but he hadn't anticipated they'd actually be having lunch. He liked what he saw and said, 'No, it's fine. I'll go with whatever you're eating.'

Damian smiled. 'I could've picked any number of

things, really. Everything they serve is made in the kitchen downstairs and sells out. By this afternoon they'll have nothing except the odd croissant and a few chocolate brownies. The brownies are excellent, by the way, you should take some with you. The coffee's good, too. Their own blend roasted on the premises. I come here a lot and rate it the best in town.'

The lawyer wasn't interested in food and had no talent for small talk. His reply lacked enthusiasm. 'Pleased to hear it.'

Damian noticed the reticence and got to the point. Oliver Shawcross was a busy man; now he had him here he didn't want to lose him. 'You're probably wondering why I wanted to meet.'

Oliver raised an eyebrow. 'It had crossed my mind, yes.'

'It's simple, really. I need some legal advice. The problem is, at this stage it has to stay under the radar. If it got out it would be damaging to Stone Free. That can't happen.'

Oliver heard the same tentative introduction every other week. He hadn't expected it from Lewis's partner. 'If this is going where I think it's going, I'm not the best-placed person to talk to.'

Damian disagreed. 'No, you're without doubt the best-placed person. In fact, I wouldn't be talking like this with anybody else. I called you because I want your opinion, not some smart arse who doesn't have the foggiest about the situation.'

'You mean Lewis?'

'I mean Lewis.'

'All right, I'm listening, but you have to understand there's a line, and as soon as I reach it, I'll stop.'

'Your loyalty is admirable.'

'Client privilege trumps loyalty every time. I'll remember that even if you don't.'

A waitress with a stainless-steel lip-stud chose that moment to arrive with their food. She oozed youth and slid the plates in front of them with the mandatory, 'There you go.'

Damian thanked her and Oliver said, 'Why do they always say, "There you go"? Or that other gem, "No problem". Why should doing your job be a problem? I don't get it.'

'No idea. Put it down to hospitality in the twenty-first century.'

'Is that what it is? We live and learn. You were saying...'

'When did you last speak to Lewis?'

Oliver thought about his answer with his mouth full of curry. 'Not sure – a week ago, maybe – why?'

'Then you aren't aware he went to the funeral.'

Oliver frowned. 'I'm sorry he did that.'

'That makes two of us. Which is why I'm concerned about him. He isn't returning my calls, and with the best will in the world...'

Oliver was ahead of him. 'Stone Free could go into freefall.'

'Yes, it could. The danger of messing up the Lassiter-Accardi offer is that word of the company's fragile state will spread – fast. That will mean fewer orders and, more importantly, job losses, yet I haven't been able to get him to discuss it. At one point I suspected it was a matter of trust. Or maybe cold feet. I'm pretty sure it isn't either. We always had hopes of some day floating the company on the stock exchange.'

'Surely it would need to be a lot bigger?'

'You're right, it would. This deal would've multiplied our capitalisation many times over. On its own not enough, but it gets us closer.'

'Is it still live?'

Damian gave up on the chickpeas and pushed his plate away. Just talking about the implications made him lose his appetite. 'The mark of how much they want to do business is that – in spite of the fact we've messed them around – they've given us a few more days.'

'Then, try again with Lewis.'

'I intend to, but the problem is much bigger. As I said, Lewis *is* Stone Free. In any company, the first thing investors and partners look for is stability. When the man at the top gives the impression of being flaky...'

Damian didn't finish the thought; he didn't need to.

Oliver followed his example and edged his lunch to the side. 'So what're you asking and why are you asking me? You believe Lewis is suffering some kind of breakdown?'

'I absolutely do but it's beyond that, I'm afraid. He's lost it completely, no doubt about it. He's my friend, yours too, come to that, but in business there are no friends. I want your help to stop him before he does more damage.'

11

Hard light flashed off the Cessna's nose as the seaplane banked and began the slow decent to the calm grey water of Duck Bay. In the distance, on the eastern side of the loch, the craggy snow-capped summit of Ben Lomond dominated the horizon like an extinct volcano biding its time. A majestic scene; a mental picture worth savouring. Colin wasn't in a place where he could appreciate it – he could barely remember how he'd got here. His last fully formed recollection was at Anniesland Cross, impatiently waiting for the lights to turn green, still visualising the shame on Sam's face as he ran from the room. The drive out of the city was a blur, a disconnected montage of images until he pulled off the main road and pointed the car towards Luss. In his younger days he'd brought women to the village on the banks of arguably the most romantic stretch of water in the world. They'd walked along the edge of the loch, hand in hand, heads close together, his mind on fire with thoughts of seduction.

The irony didn't pass him by; he was here to escape a woman who'd tried to seduce *him*, except this one was his wife.

The tawdry scene in the kitchen shocked him. Sam's sad failed attempt at reconciliation had left them angry, diminished and even further apart. And as stunning as the beauty on every side was, it didn't make processing the disaster their life had become easier.

Humiliating her, humiliating both of them, had been unavoidable but sex wasn't the problem. Which meant it wasn't the solution. Running away from his wife and his home had probably not been the solution, either, though he'd do it again.

Sam's emotions swung from hating him to wanting him back, deluding herself into believing they could put the past behind them and make a fresh start. Perhaps, other couples could do it. Other couples weren't them. A year down the line, maybe even three or four, the cracks would reappear because once they'd formed they couldn't be unmade. By then, there might be children to complicate an already complicated situation and they'd be trapped. He'd been besotted with Sam Kennedy once. It hadn't lasted. Maybe it wasn't possible to sustain that intensity with another human being.

He walked to the end of Pier Road and stood on the wooden jetty with the cold wind pinching his eyes and ruffling his hair, as alone as he'd ever been. Out on the loch a pair of white-fronted geese skimmed low across the water in perfect symmetry. Colin envied them. It would've been easy to use Molly's tragic death as a turning point, cleave to each other and carry on. Easy, but wrong. Sam had coped admirably with losing her sister, or so it had seemed. This morning's debasing performance had shown the reality, that underneath was a fragile woman desperate to salvage, by any means and at any cost, what she could from the wreckage of a marriage that had gone off the rails. Colin didn't shy away from the part he'd played in it. He loved Sam Kennedy and always would, but he wasn't 'in love' with her.

Two words but all the difference in the world.

12

I slumped in the chair by the fire where I'd huddled for most of the night, depressed and exhausted, with no idea what time it was. Going to bed hadn't been a consideration; I wouldn't have slept, so what would've been the point? In the early hours of the morning – I wasn't sure when – I'd closed the door to Molly's place and driven back to my flat, shrugged off my clothes and put on the dressing gown kept in the back of the wardrobe and only worn when no one was around. The shapeless garment wasn't flattering; Freddy had hated seeing me in it. Now, I couldn't have cared less. Normal stuff – like making coco or reading a few chapters of the Agatha Christie novel on the bedside cabinet before my eyes closed – belonged to another me.

'Normal', whatever that meant, no longer existed.

Dark thoughts circling like a predatory beast on the edge of my consciousness had come painfully into focus and crystallised with the quiet 'click' as Molly's life support was turned off. I could still hear the sound and knew I always would. More even than the horror of the accident, that had been the defining moment. From then, I'd focused my energy on the man who'd killed – in my mind it had become 'murdered' – my sister.

My palms cupped the half-full whisky glass in my lap. It was the first but it wouldn't be the last, yet alcohol wasn't delivering the way I'd hoped. Every time I closed my eyes the hellish scene was waiting. The images and sounds haunted me: Molly's broken body behind the skewed car, while through the open window the radio blasted out a rock song in a mocking soundtrack. He'd had the bloody window open! Who drove like that in the middle of winter in Scotland? I pictured the driver on the pavement talking with the police, admitting he'd been drinking. Witnessed him blow into the breathalyser, waiting for him to be taken away and charged.

I'd read there were ways to beat the test. If I'd realised it would end in a hospital room with that damnable 'click', nothing would've stopped me from strangling the bastard with my bare hands.

Losing Molly had changed me. If it had been Sam and Molly creeping through somebody's garden at midnight I would've disapproved but not been surprised. The twins had been impetuous teenagers who'd grown up to be quick-to-react adults. That wasn't me. I was more measured, less of a 'mad arse', to use one of Molly's less ladylike expressions. Being protective of the younger girls was one thing, this had become something else.

What in God's name was I doing?

Lewis Stone lived in a fancy house. Finding him in the conservatory had been a stroke of luck. I hadn't had many of those lately. Peering into the darkness, he'd cut a strange figure. This guy had got away with murder, he should be happy. He hadn't looked happy, he'd looked... lonely.

I lifted the whisky to my lips and noticed the trembling in my fingers. The sip I'd intended to take became a gulp, starting a fire in my gut and coursing through my veins, forcing the question I'd avoided asking myself into the open: nothing would bring my sister back, so where was I going with this?

The answer came from somewhere deep inside. I

heard my voice, brittle and profane, whisper to the empty room, 'All the way. All the fucking way.'

13

Sam stood in front of the bedroom mirror assessing her naked reflection, her eyes running over her smooth pale skin, searching for blemishes and finding none. Colin's reaction had been a hammer blow, and her confidence – already eroded by his absence in their marriage – had plummeted. It wasn't that she hadn't taken care of herself; she had her nails done once a month, her hair cut and blow-dried regularly. Add a lapsed gym membership replaced by a personal trainer she worked out with twice a week and the end result, at twenty-eight, would've been enough for most husbands. Though, apparently, not hers. Realising he didn't desire her was a crushing knock to her ego.

Sam had made a point of examining her face every

day for the tell-tale signs of age, pleased to not find them. The body in the glass was lithe and svelte, the long legs still show-stoppers; she looked sensational. This morning Colin had run from the kitchen as if the prospect of making love to her was more than he could stand – the single most demeaning thing that had ever happened to her. Yet, it proved something she hadn't been ready to admit and it had sod all to do with her figure or her appearance. He had no interest in saving their marriage.

Time to accept it and move on.

Hot tears brimmed in Sam's eyes. Colin had shown what he was capable of the night of their wedding. She'd been a bloody fool to marry him and was paying the price for allowing him to treat her like a doormat. Offering herself to him had been an act born out of insecurity and desperation. And though his reaction had been the deepest cut of all, she didn't blame him.

How could she expect her husband to respect her when she didn't respect herself?

She showered and dressed, still stunned, desperately needing to talk to somebody. Traditionally, that somebody had always been Alex.

Sam's big sister had a gift for taking the emotion out of a situation, allowing the person to arrive at a decision not driven by anger, resentment or fear. When

Molly or Sam went to her, she'd let them speak without interrupting, then ask a question that invariably produced a solution: 'If the situation was reversed and I was where you are, what would you tell me?' Alex would pause to let them think about it before continuing. 'You see, our gut talks to us. It knows the answer. All we have to do is listen.'

Yeah, Alex was the wise old owl they'd leaned on since they were teenagers. Helping her and Molly navigate a path through the dodgy boyfriends who'd broken their young hearts had been a full-time job. In spite of her unhappiness, Sam recognised her mistake: she should never have allowed her disaster of a relationship to get this far. If she'd stepped in earlier instead of being afraid, Colin would've remembered it was her he loved.

It was all so obvious she could kick herself.

She called Alex on her mobile, frowning when there was no reply. A few minutes later she tried again with the same result. The sisters had keys to each other's flats – a throwback to their days as students. It was Saturday, Alex could be shopping or having lunch in town. Sam hoped she was enjoying it because she hadn't been the same since the final difficult visit to the hospital, when she'd buried her head in the bedclothes, weeping, and held Molly's hand as her life force faded. Nobody who'd been there would forget that day and how it had ended. Sam couldn't think of Molly without wanting to cry. She'd be driving or washing her hair and suddenly see some snapshot from the past in her mind's eye. Sam didn't dwell on them: nothing good lay down that road.

At some point Colin would come back and she didn't want to be there when he did. Alex lived in Shawlands in the flat she'd shared with her late husband. Maybe she'd let Sam have the spare room until she sorted herself out.

* * *

Sam parked her car and walked to the flat she'd been coming to since she was in her late teens, dropping in with Molly after school to bask in their big sister's happiness. Alex had just married Freddy, a quietly spoken guy who clearly adored her, following her with his eyes as she moved around the room, listening to every word she said. Freddy had been the love of Alex's life – there had been no one since and Sam didn't expect there would be. Her abiding memory of them together was Freddy playing piano in the next room while Alex made her famous pasta sauce in a huge cast-iron pot, shooing them out of the kitchen so she could add the secret ingredient she refused to reveal no matter how much the twins had begged.

Alex and Freddy had had it all. Loving life. Loving each other. Then, Freddy had got sick and Alex had looked after him. Without meaning to she'd become Sam's role model for what marriage should be. If Sam could've been anybody in the world she'd have been Alex – more than a sister, she was the best friend she and Molly would ever have.

The curtains were drawn, a sign all was not as it should be. Sam climbed the stairs with a quiver of unease in her stomach. No way Alex would've gone off without telling her; she had to be ill.

She rang the bell and rang it again, and when she got no answer, took the key from her bag and slid it into the lock, overwhelmed with anxiety about what was waiting for her on the other side of the door. The hall was cold and unlit; shoes lay where they'd been kicked off. She stepped inside, resisting the urge to run. At the door into the lounge, she hesitated. Sam had already lost one sister and was terrified of losing another.

What she saw shocked her; Alex was unconscious on the floor. She ran to her sister and fell to her knees, feeling for a pulse. Sam fought down panic and fumbled for her mobile, intending to call an ambulance, then stopped. A whisky bottle had rolled across the carpet and was resting against the skirting board. The glass tumbler wasn't far, hidden behind a cushion on the chair by the fire.

Alex wasn't ill; she was drunk.

Sam hadn't understood how profoundly Molly's death had affected her sister and was ashamed. She'd come for help, for sanctuary and advice, because her life was falling apart, expecting Alex, as usual, to be there, never guessing how much pain she was in.

Alex's skin was clammy, her breathing coming out in stentorious bursts that echoed in the room. Later, she'd have the mother and father of headaches. Somehow, Sam manhandled her onto the couch, brought a cover from the bedroom and draped it over her. At the very least she'd be dehydrated. A glass of water would help; a couple of paracetamol from the medicine drawer wouldn't be unwelcome, either.

Sam settled down to wait. It might be hours before she surfaced. Hours, days, what did it matter? The roles had been reversed: Alex needed her and she was there.

14

I opened my eyes and immediately regretted it. The room spun like a fairground Waltzer a mile in the air above me. I'd laughed at jokes about drunk people holding on to the floor. Now, I got it. And it was anything but funny. I lay still, hoping it would stop. It didn't. In fact, it got worse. Nausea crashed over me, the urge to vomit so strong my hand went to my mouth in a reflex. It passed and I fell back, trembling and weak, cold sweat filming my brow, my throat on fire and a vile taste in my mouth. I'd never been hungover. I could handle alcohol well enough when circumstances demanded it – the annual Christmas night out with my sisters was an example – but months could go by when not so much as a drop passed my lips.

Not for any particular reason. There were no family skeletons, nothing like that. I just wasn't a drinker.

End of story.

Freddy had been the same. After we'd moved in together, cans of lager left from New Year would sit forgotten in the back of the fridge before he thought about popping one. On our first wedding anniversary he'd taken me to an expensive hotel in Rome. The management had arranged a box of Swiss chocolates and a bottle of champagne to help us celebrate, a nice gesture much appreciated. We'd fought each other for the chocolates; they hadn't lasted ten minutes. The wine travelled home in our suitcase and was still there a year later for our second anniversary. A sad irony, because Freddy wasn't.

I scanned the room, trying to make sense of it, afraid to move, sensing I wasn't alone. A noise from the kitchen made my heart leap in my chest, bringing a fresh wave of nausea. I almost lost it and was lucky to recover. Then, a voice I recognised said, 'Okay, where's my sister? You know – that sensible woman who keeps the other brats in line.'

I was too ill to appreciate the humour. I said, 'Sam. What are you doing here?'

She was wearing jeans and a blue T-shirt with 'I've had my patience tested. It was negative' written on it in black capital letters.

'You recognise me. Good. We can rule out brain damage. And the question isn't what am I doing, it's what have you been doing? What the hell have you been doing, Alex?'

'I don't know. I don't remember.'

'Well, if you don't know, nobody knows. How do you feel?'

'Terrible, really terrible.'

'Too much booze will do that. Aren't you supposed to be the responsible Kennedy girl?'

'Not any more.'

'Obviously. We need to talk, though not until you've eaten something.'

'Oh, no, please, I couldn't. I couldn't keep it down.'

'If you'd had the same reaction to whisky we'd be having a different conversation. I've made scrambled eggs.' Sam lifted the water and the paracetamol she'd brought from the kitchen. 'These will help and, believe me, you'll need them. You've just woken up. This is the first stage.'

'You mean it gets worse?'

'I mean it gets worse, yeah. Sit up. I'll bring a tray and you can tell me about it.'

I held up a hand. 'No, no, honestly, I can't face it. Maybe later.'

'In case you haven't noticed, it's later already. Most of the day's gone. How about having a shower and giving it a try when you come out? Your blood sugar's low; you have to have food. Believe me, Alex, you'll feel better. My cooking isn't as bad as it used to be. Thanks to Delia and Jamie I've improved. And water, get plenty of water down you. You're dehydrated.'

I saw the determination in her eyes, dragged myself to the bathroom and stood under the shower, letting it run as hot as I could stand before turning the mixing valve to cold. When she reappeared, Sam said, 'How do you feel? Better?'

'A bit. I've never understood why hungover people don't get sympathy.'

She laughed. 'Because their pain is self-inflicted. The night before they were convinced physiology didn't apply to them and they kept partying.'

'So the poor buggers don't deserve any, is that it?'

'Absolutely. There's a price to pay for everything. In your case the price is feeling like death warmed up. It'll pass. And then the fun will really begin.'

'What do you mean?'

'I'm talking about the screaming heebie-jeebies.' Sam checked her watch. 'Give it an hour, two at the most, and strap in for Anxiety Central. I'll get the scrambled eggs, shall I?'

I put my head in my hands. 'Oh, God.'

Sam turned at the door. 'Do I hear a "never again" coming on?'

'You bitch, you're enjoying this.'

''Course I am. Other people's hangovers are the best. So long as it isn't you, what's not to enjoy?'

15

Lewis had stayed in bed watching the day fade to night before forcing himself to get up. The effort drained him. He mooched around in torn jeans and a washed-out T-shirt, going from one room to another, switching the TV on and switching it off again before a programme had the chance to start. Opening a bottle of wine was an option – and if it stopped at just one it wouldn't be an issue, but if it did, that would be a first.

His mobile registered four unanswered calls – one from Oliver, three from Damian. At the heart of their concern would be the deal. The extended deadline was almost up, the opportunity was slipping away. Damian's anxiety would be off the charts. Lewis realised he wasn't being fair to his partner. Since the beginning of the year the business had been in limbo. Of course, it could carry on – for a while anyway – without something serious going wrong, but a time would come when the lack of a firm hand on the tiller would start to show. Joe Public wasn't interested in what went on behind the scenes so long as they could get the chinos or the shirt they'd spotted in some glossy fashion mag at a price they could afford. But Stone Free's investors would take a different view.

He shook cornflakes into a bowl, splashed milk on them, and carried his 'breakfast' to the conservatory. Outside it was as dark as it had been the previous night – it matched his mood. His mobile rang. He saw it was Damian and for a second thought about not answering but changed his mind.

'Damian.'

Damian's anger travelled down the line. 'You selfish, poor-me bastard! It's gone, we've lost it!'

Lewis didn't understand what he was talking about. 'What do you mean? What's gone?'

Damian sounded close to tears. 'The deal, the fucking deal. They've withdrawn their offer. We messed them about so they've dropped us.'

It felt as though the oxygen had been sucked out of

the room. Lewis reacted like a man clutching for something – anything – to hold on to. Words tumbled out of him. He said, 'I'll speak to them. Get them back onside. They want us, that's why they chased so hard. They're bluffing.'

'No, you won't. And you're wrong, it's finished. Lassiter-Accardi *did* want us. Not any more. I tried getting in touch with the guys negotiating for them. Guess what? They've blocked me. The bastards aren't taking my calls. As far as they're concerned, you, me, Stone Free – we don't exist.' Damian marshalled his anger. 'From the beginning I've been happy to let you take all the credit even though we were in it together. Well, as of today, that's over. All you had to do was sign the bloody agreement, and you wouldn't do it because you were scared to relinquish control.'

'That isn't why and you know it.'

Damian ploughed on as though his partner hadn't spoken. 'You're pathetic. You've put the whole factory in jeopardy, and you've cost us millions, Lewis, do you get that? Fucking millions!'

'Damian, I'm sorry. There will be other deals, believe me. Better deals. Stone Free is too strong a brand for—'

'Stop! Just fucking stop talking! I'm bringing in the

lawyers. You aren't fit to be MD. Fight me on this and you'll lose, even if it takes years. By then, there may not be a business. But one way or another, you're fucking history. You're out, Lewis.'

16

The silence was the silence of siblings; there was nothing awkward or uncomfortable in it. Sam's keen eyes scrutinised me for signs of improvement as the water and eggs did their work. I got it. Finding her dependable elder sister like this was hard. I'd never been the rebellious one, that had been Molly, her motto 'Why just do it when you can overdo it?' If it had been her suffering after a wild night, it wouldn't have been a surprise.

Sam had her own experience with booze. Five months into her marriage she'd discovered her husband kissing another woman. He'd said it was a mad moment, nothing more, yet the betrayal had crushed her. It was the woman she couldn't forgive. The bitch had known what she was doing – a man with his new wife waiting for him at home; it hadn't deterred her. Sam should have ended it there and then, a mistake I knew she regretted. Instead, she'd put it behind her, lying to herself that some guys needed time to adjust and almost believing it. Almost. Her response had been to drink and keep on drinking, often unable to remember how she got to bed. One morning, depressed and defeated, she'd reached out to me. I had explained as gently as I could that if she wanted her marriage to survive, the drinking had to stop. What she was doing would never make her husband realise how much he needed her. How much he loved her. And, as quickly as she'd started, she'd quit.

When I finished eating, Sam said, 'Feel better?'

'Apart from the brass band rehearsing in my head, yes.'

'Give the paracetamol time to work and keep drinking water.' She pointed to the glass. 'Finish that and I'll get you more. You probably feel tired – that's down to the booze as well. Alcohol makes us spend more time in deep sleep and less time than usual in REM.'

'I thought that was an American rock band.'

'You really need to get out more, sister. Rapid Eye Movement is an important restorative stage of sleep.

You can be dead to the world and wake up shattered because the quality's been affected. The amount of time we stay in bed doesn't matter.'

'Or, in my case, the amount of time on the couch. How come you're so clued-up?'

Sam winked. 'Let's just say I know of what I speak.'

I was immediately concerned. 'Don't tell me it's become a problem again.'

'No. I spill most of it.'

After she stopped laughing at the old joke I said, 'Now, I really am worried.'

Sam reassured me. 'As far as drinking goes, I'm fine. That was a phase. It passed, though for a while it was tough. I wouldn't recommend it.'

I sensed my sister hadn't come for advice about alcohol and we returned to the silence of before. But it wasn't the same; something unsaid lay between us. Molly had been the sister without a filter. The one we took everywhere twice – the second time to apologise. If she'd been here she'd have been out of her seat, shouting, 'I need details! Juicy details! Come on, spill the beans!'

I said, 'I want to thank you on behalf of myself and my hangover. We're glad you're here. What would we have done without you?'

'You're both very welcome.'

'So why are you here, Sam? And don't insult my intelligence. You've always been rubbish at lying.'

'Not always.'

'Yeah, you have. Molly could tell the biggest fibs with a straight face and Mum and Dad believed her. But not you. What's wrong? Are you and Colin still rowing?' I shook my head. 'Honestly, being with someone shouldn't be so hard. When will both of you learn to compromise? Listen, I like Colin, always have, but perhaps the two of you don't fit any more. You're a smart, great-looking woman, you could've had any-body. Maybe marrying him was a mistake.'

'I know.'

'Then, why stay? Why keep hitting your head off the same wall?'

Sam struggled to get the words out. 'He doesn't love me, Alex.'

'What? Did he tell you that? Did the bastard have the cheek to actually tell you he—?'

'No, he didn't but it's true. Colin can hardly stand to be in the same room. This morning...'

Sam's bottom lip quivered; she couldn't go on. I forgot my hangover as my maternal instinct took over, firing questions, my tone clipped, on the edge of anger. 'What happened this morning? What did he do to you?'

Sam had come because she needed to talk. Now the opportunity was in front of her she backed away from it. 'Nothing. It doesn't matter.'

She wasn't getting away so easily. 'Tell me, Sam. I'll find out sooner or later, I always do.'

'No. Some things should stay private. Even between us.'

'So why are you here? I'm very glad you are, but why?'

'Because I'm an idiot. When people have a row they run to their family or their friends and blurt it all out. Then, they make up and the people they told are left with the resentments they've put behind them. But that isn't fair. I won't put you in that situation. Colin and I... we're going through a rough patch, that's all.'

'Another one.'

'Yes, if you like. In the long run it'll be okay.'

I took her hand. 'Oh, Sam. I hate to see you unhappy. You deserve better, you really do. You have to admit that and finish it before...'

I left the sentence unsaid. Sam seized on it. 'Before what? Go on, spit it out.'

I sighed and found the words. 'Before it gets... more complicated.'

'You mean, before I get pregnant?'

'All right, yes. It may be the last thing you want to

hear, but unless I tell you nobody else will. Millions of women have been where you are. You can walk away and start again. It takes courage. Being a Kennedy girl means that's something you aren't short of. The right man for you... he's out there, Sam. All you have to do is find him. And you can. You will. But not while you're obsessed with Colin.'

'He's not a bad man, Alex, he really isn't. I wish you could see that. He's just...'

Labouring the point wouldn't help the situation. I searched for a way to say what needed to be said without causing her more hurt.

'Nobody needs to be wrong for something to not work. Relationships only grow if the foundations are there. Otherwise, they deteriorate.' I squeezed Sam's fingers. 'That's no way to live. I meant what I said, you deserve better. Please, think about it and be honest with yourself. I'll support whatever you decide. You'll survive. I promise you, you'll survive. Better than that; without somebody dragging you down you'll discover Sam – who you really are – and flourish. A woman doesn't have to have a man by her side to be happy. I've proved it.'

Sam nodded and let me finish. 'Okay, that's me sorted. Nice speech, by the way. And well deflected.'

She lifted the empty bottle and held it in the air. 'Now, let's talk about what's going on with you. What is this?'

I swallowed nervously. From the moment my eyes had opened and Sam was frowning down at me, I'd known this was coming. With the state I was in, inevitably the focus would pivot back to me. The reply forming on my lips was far from the truth. Sam wasn't close to being ready for that. Confessing my night-time skulking around Lewis Stone's house would give away what was in my mind.

Sam waited for an answer and wouldn't be happy until she heard something that explained the scene she'd stumbled into. I forced a weak smile. 'Honestly, I wish I knew. The last I remember is bringing a glass from the kitchen. After that...' I shrugged. 'I can only imagine I'm under more pressure than I'd realised. Molly's death... turning off her life support... all of it... it's the saddest thing I've ever done.'

Sam agreed. 'For me, too.'

I wiped a tear from my cheek. 'I just miss her. I miss her, Sam. More than I thought it was possible to miss anybody apart from Freddy.'

Sam searched for my hand. 'How could you not miss Molly? She was a one-off.'

'The best of us.'

'What would she say if she could see you right now, eh? Can you hear her? I can.'

'She wouldn't be moping on a couch hungover or letting her bastard of a husband affect her confidence, that's for sure.'

'You're right. She'd be in the pub, chatting up the barman.'

'And that's where we should be. Get dressed, we're going out to get legless for a good reason.'

'And what would that be?'

'Because we can. Because we're alive and bloody well want to. Any objections? Besides, haven't you heard about a hair of the dog?'

17

The detached sandstone villa in Sherbrooke Avenue had belonged to Lewis's parents for forty years. Now, it was his. He was standing in one of the bay windows staring out; with his arms behind his back and a disapproving expression on his face, he might have been the headmaster of a private school for boys awaiting the arrival of a new boarder. He didn't acknowledge his partner and Damian was reminded they'd lost much more than a contract. He couldn't begin to guess what was going through Lewis's mind at that moment. His face was puffy, especially around his bloodshot eyes. The shirt he was wearing hung on him; he'd lost weight and when he spoke his voice was husky, as though coming from some deep well inside.

His first words set the tone and inwardly Damian breathed a sigh of relief. 'I'll do whatever you want. I don't want to fight.'

'Neither do I.'

'I don't care about anything any more.'

Damian had come fired up, expecting Lewis to resist being forced to step down as MD. The hopelessness coming off a guy who'd found positives in every business setback jarred with his partner, reminding him how far Lewis had gone down emotionally since the accident. Since a woman slipped on an icy pavement. Damian felt a flash of resentment and immediately recognised the profound selfishness of it – she'd paid for her slip with her life.

A framed steel engraving dating from 1829, titled *View of Glasgow from the Farm of Shields*, hung in the hall beyond the stained-glass entrance – a reminder of how the city had grown. The irony didn't escape him; in the end, everything was about growth. Grow or die. He followed Lewis into one of the three public rooms, each with the original brick fireplace. Damian had been here at a party to celebrate winning one of their early contracts when Lewis had hired an upmarket catering firm to supply the food and drink. Later, heartened by their triumph, they'd flirted with the idea of a chain of Stone Free outlets, only to dismiss the suggestion as running before they could walk. Although they couldn't have known it then, with what was to come it had been a good decision.

Damian said, 'You look like shit. What in God's name have you been doing?'

'Nothing. I haven't been out.'

'Have you been drinking?'

'None of your fucking business.'

'Christ Almighty!' He pointed to a bowl with crusted cereal sticking to it. 'When did you last eat something? And I don't mean cornflakes.'

Lewis ignored the question and walked to the conservatory. In the light from the floor-to-ceiling glass Damian saw even more starkly the physical toll of what he was going through. Lewis had been a handsome man, fair-skinned and boyish, fated to always look younger than his years. Not now. His features were ravaged by the demons he carried with him. And they'd done their work well – his skin had the dry translucent appearance of parchment.

He began cautiously. 'Look, Lewis, this is difficult for both of us, but I want you to know—'

Lewis held up his hand and interrupted. 'It's all right. It's okay, really it is. I'll agree to whatever you think is best. In the circumstances it's the least I can do.'

Damian was taken aback; he'd anticipated a token resistance and was caught off-guard. Stone Free was Lewis's brainchild, the company even carried his name. He said, 'I'm glad you see it that way and I apologise for speaking to you how I did on the phone. I'd just discovered my contact at L-A had blocked my calls and I lost it. Sorry.'

Lewis sat down in a rattan egg chair and shook his head. 'No, in your position I would've been harsher than that. Forget it, I have.'

'Then, let's talk the way we used to. Friends first, partners second. See if we can make something of where we are, eh?' Damian had a speech already prepared in his head; he abandoned it, took the chair opposite Lewis, and spoke from his heart. 'I've no idea what you're suffering. No idea at all. But a couple of things are obvious. As someone who knows you and cares about you, my major concern is your health. You have to let a doctor take a look at you because, clearly, you aren't well. And you need to do what you're told no matter how much you want to rail against it. Please tell me, whatever else we disagree on, we agree on that much.'

Lewis's response wasn't encouraging. Damian had

strayed into territory that was none of his concern and sensed his opposition. Some of the former strength returned to Lewis's voice and he spoke without addressing the issue. 'You mentioned a couple of things.'

Damian said what he'd come to say. 'Stone Free isn't working and it can't work until—'

'I'm out of the picture. Is that where this is heading? Don't bother, I've already decided to step down as MD.' Lewis held up his hand. 'Before you get too excited, it's temporary. I'm taking a year off. After twelve months, I'm coming back and we go on as we are.'

It was exactly what Damian wanted to hear; the best he'd allowed himself to hope for had been six months. A smile started at the edge of his mouth; he killed it. 'I think you're wise. Rent a plush villa in the South of France and soak up the sun, whatever you fancy. So long as you forget about the past.'

'I'm thinking about going up north to Loch Morar.' Lewis laughed and shook his head, as though the idea amused him. 'It's MAMBA country – miles and miles of bugger all. Does the prospect of being up there make you shudder?'

'Not at all. It sounds good; exactly what you need – a complete break. I'm confident that with a change at the top—'

Lewis corrected him. 'A temporary change.'

Damian hid his irritation. In good health or bad he was the same old Lewis. 'A temporary change, of course. That's a given. With a change at the top the deal might still have life in it. Nobody wins by walking away. Not them. Not us.'

Lewis nodded and didn't disagree. The meeting had gone better than Damian expected; no acrimonious scenes, no holding on by his fingernails, only a commitment to the business they'd created. The smile made a return and this time Damian didn't smother it.

'You'll be strolling along the shore breathing clean Scottish air, while I'll have my back to the wall, my shoulder to the wheel, and my nose to the bloody grindstone, though how somebody's expected to get any work done in that position is beyond me.'

The joke fell flat and changed the mood. Lewis said, 'You'll manage, you always do.'

The barb didn't elude Damian. It was unfair – it wasn't him who'd knocked a woman down and gone to pieces; he let it go because he understood. Giving away control of something you'd sweated blood for was hard. He lifted himself out of the chair. 'Please think about contacting your GP. At the end of the day, Stone Free is Lewis Stone and Damian Morton, two people, us. Ring the surgery and make an appointment. And whether you like hearing it or not, lay off the booze.'

Lewis didn't answer.

* * *

Damian waited until he was back in the city before making the call. He pulled into the side of the road and pressed Shawcross's number. The lawyer came on immediately. 'Damian, what can I do for you?'

'Nothing. It occurred to me that, after our conversation, it would be right to bring you up to speed. I've only just left a meeting with Lewis.'

'How is he?'

'Not great, if I'm being honest. In my opinion he needs to see a doctor. I suggested it to him as strongly as I could. It didn't go down well. Whether he will is anybody's guess. Lewis does what Lewis wants. Always has. It might be worth having a word with him yourself. So far as Stone Free goes, I've persuaded him to step down for the foreseeable future. I'll be taking over with a view to keeping Lassiter-Accardi on board.'

Oliver leaned on the table and steepled his fingers. 'I have to say it makes sense.'

'He's going up north, to his parents' place. Do you know where it is?'

The lawyer thought about his reply. 'No... but from what I've heard, there's nothing but seagulls for company. Maybe not the best place for a troubled man. Thanks for telling me. I'll get his signature on what needs to be signed before he leaves.'

18

The atmosphere in the MacLean household was unbearable. Worse than it had ever been – and that was saying something. Colin left before Sam wakened and stayed away until late, doing whatever Colin did. When he returned, the smell of drink lingered in every room. There were no words for where they were; they didn't waste their time trying to find them and ignored each other. Colin slept in the spare bedroom with the door closed. Last night, Sam had listened outside and heard him whispering. The betrayal never ended, did it? Once upon a time she would've been distraught. Not any more. Colin could go to hell for all she cared.

They weren't strangers to the situation they found themselves in; they'd been here before. So far, the D-word hadn't been mentioned, though they both knew it was coming. The alternative – living separately to-gether – had no appeal.

She was sitting up in bed reading a Catherine Cookson novel when the taxi pulled up outside. The front door opened and closed quietly; she checked the time: ten to one.

It couldn't go on. Sam wouldn't let it go on.

He was over by the drinks cabinet, pouring himself a large whisky and whatever he'd lost over the years, it wasn't his cheek. 'I saw the upstairs light and assumed you'd gone to sleep with it on. I hope I didn't disturb you.' He gestured to the bottle of Chivas Regal. 'Care to join me?'

'No, thanks. I'm surprised, Colin. You're in a very good mood for a man in your position.' He turned to-wards her and she realised he was drunk. Not quite at the slurring-his-words stage, but drunk nevertheless. 'I think you've had enough of that stuff for both of us, don't you?'

His eyes narrowed as his brain slowly processed the conversation. He repeated what Sam had said. 'A man in my position. What does that mean? What position?'

She crossed the room, sat on the arm of the couch, and tried to scare him into a reaction. 'I may as well tell you. You'll find out soon enough. I've made an appointment with a lawyer. I'm divorcing you, Colin.'

He nodded, slowly, taking it in. 'All right. Okay. In fact I've been considering the same thing.'

San threw her head back and laughed. 'Well, isn't that rich coming from you? It's your fault this marriage has broken down, not mine. God knows I've tried everything to keep it going. *You* divorcing *me*? What grounds could you possibly have?'

Colin strolled to the window and stared into the night. 'Leave it with me, I'll think of something.'

'Either way works. The sooner you're out of my life, the better.'

'Oh, Sam, do us both a favour and sing another song, will you? I've heard this one till it's coming out my ears. It's boring. Just like you. You didn't go through with it last time, and you won't go through with it now. Because I'm right. You have a life other people can only dream about. You live in this house, drive an expensive car, shop till you drop whenever it suits you, and lunch with your friends twice a week. Who do you imagine pays for it? I'll tell you – I do. Or rather the business I've built does.' He came closer, so close she could smell whisky on his breath. 'And what do I get out of the deal, eh? What's in it for old Colin?' Sam saw tears in his eyes. He knelt beside her. 'Don't I deserve to be happy?'

Whatever fairy tale her husband was telling himself, it was obvious he believed it. Sam cut through the maudlin bullshit. 'One of my sisters is dead, the other's losing it. I don't need this, Colin. You're about to get exactly what you deserve, because I'm going to make sure you do.' She stood up and walked to the door. 'You'll be hearing from my lawyer in due course. When I'm done with you, you won't have a pot to piss in and I'll still be shopping till I drop.'

* * *

With Damian gone, the house felt more empty than before he'd arrived. Lewis's footsteps echoed in the hall, even his breathing seemed loud – or perhaps his imagination was playing tricks on him – and he was reminded it was far too big a space for one person: a family should live here; parents and surly teenagers who spent endless hours on their mobile phones and treated it like a hotel as he'd done at that age. Back then, he couldn't wait to go in search of his place in the world. He couldn't know that place was Stone Free.

The meeting with his partner had been brief. The expected confrontation hadn't materialised. There had been no shouting. No screamed accusations. Damian had stayed calm, kept his emotions in check, and got what he'd come for – control of the business with the power to move it in any direction he wanted without having to consult him or anybody else. He didn't re-alise Lewis wouldn't have fought against whatever he'd demanded, even if it meant no longer being part of Stone Free.

Because there was no getting away from it: he'd fucked up.

His teeth ground together as the full extent of what he'd agreed to began to hit him. Mea culpa was all very well, but now he felt as if he'd been conned. At the Christmas party, a drunken Damian Morton had promised the crowd of employees that the business had a bright future. The same man who, just ten min-utes earlier, had suggested he relinquish his position as MD in the best interests of the company. Behind the concern, the reassuring words, was a lie. Lewis had a sinking realisation that him stepping down wasn't in-tended to be temporary. Solid reasons would be found to stretch twelve months' absence to twenty-four, then thirty-six, before a stranger in a suit was telling him how generous the compensation package was. And he'd be out. For good.

In the meantime, decisions would be taken. Irre-

versible commercial and operating decisions mor-
phing Stone Free into a slick, soulless money-making
machine, reducing it to a logo on a T-shirt. By then,
the name would be his only connection to the business he'd started. The accident and his mental state in
the aftermath had played into his partner's hands, but
blaming Damian was wrong. The responsibility, for all
of it, was his. He'd been too busy fantasising to react to
the woman falling under his wheels. Since that night,
racked by guilt, he'd been slowly losing his sanity.
Now, on top of that, he'd lost his life's work.

Damian expected him to sign whatever he slid in
front of him and disappear into the sunset like a
faithful horse put to pasture when his usefulness was
at an end.

No chance! No fucking chance!

The way to respond was to get a grip on himself
and come back stronger.

Not in a year. Not even in six months. Three
months tops. He was Lewis Stone. Stone Free was his
and nobody – nobody – was taking it from him.

The suggestion he consult a medical professional
sounded like a friend talking but Lewis didn't believe
it. In fact, the idea was a non-starter; he didn't need a
crystal ball to predict the diagnosis. The doctor would
address him by his first name and ask him to describe

the accident, nodding at the right moments to encourage him to continue, then quietly debunk the popular misconception that PTSD – post-traumatic stress disorder – only happened to soldiers in war zones, explaining that people who'd witnessed or experienced a traumatic event could suffer from it, too.

Lewis qualified, he'd no doubts about that, but he was also sure antidepressants weren't the answer. And he was damned if he was putting himself through pointless psychotherapy sessions. Guilt was the root. Guilt he wasn't prepared to admit to anybody, far less some guy in a white coat.

He showered, shaved and washed his hair, enjoying the sensation of the hot water cleansing his skin, feeling human for the first time in weeks, able to see beyond the fugue he'd been trapped in. With the crippling fatigue lifted, his appetite returned – suddenly, he was ravenously hungry. Another positive sign. Lewis put on shoes, shrugged into a heavy coat, and headed for the door.

On the mat lay a neatly folded white rectangle that hadn't been there when he'd shown Damian out; it hadn't been there – someone had pushed it through the letter box. Lewis picked it up. He read it and staggered, almost losing his balance. A shocked whisper escaped his lips. 'What the...?'

The single word printed in large black type in the centre of the page screamed at him, the good feelings evaporated as though they'd never existed, and he was plunged back into the abyss.

KILLER

PART II

19

Lewis raced into the street, frantically looking up and down the lines of expensive properties to see who had posted the note, closer to panic than at any time since the accident days before Christmas. After Damian had gone, the surge of confidence, the determination to break the downward spiral he was in, had been like a light coming on in a dark room and he'd been able to think clearly, energised by the glimpse of his former self righteously fighting back against his partner's barely disguised power grab. The damning paper on the mat with its horrible accusation had changed everything and he was back where he'd started. Except, that wasn't accurate. This wasn't that place. This was deeper and more terrifying.

From behind the wheel of a white Toyota headed towards the city, a bald, middle-aged man stared at him standing in the road unconcerned by the rain. Lewis let the car pass and walked back to the house, shoulders hunched, defeated before he'd even got started – he wouldn't be going anywhere. Not today.

In the kitchen he took off his coat, poured himself a stiff whisky to steady his nerves, and tried to process what had just happened.

Who had left the note?

What did they want?

Lewis's fingers gripped the whisky glass, shaking so badly he was afraid he might drop it, and he went over the conversation with Damian again in his head. It had been amicable, hadn't it? They'd agreed the interests of Stone Free needed to be protected and left each other on friendly terms – at least, Lewis had thought so. Perhaps he'd been mistaken. Maybe it was the bastard's opening shot in a longer play to get him out of the business completely. Morton realised better than anybody how profoundly the accident had affected his partner's mental state. Did he intend on using it to his advantage?

Had he pretended to leave and pushed the KILLER note through the letter box?

Was he ruthless enough to do something like that?

It made sense – the only thing that made sense – because no one else knew and if they did know then, surely, they'd have acted when the accident happened.

No, it was him; it had to be.

Lewis went to the window, his earlier resolve no more than a bitter memory. On another day this would be a police matter, except the last people he wanted to see were the police. Damian's accusation was eerily close to the truth, but he hadn't been in the car with him and wasn't a mind-reader.

Damian Morton didn't *know* anything.

Coming to terms with the idea that the man you'd shared so much with was actually an enemy was hard. From the start Damian had seemed happy to stand in his shadow. Only, he hadn't, had he? That had been a front when all along he'd craved his moment in the sun.

Lewis drank the whisky and decided against having another – this wasn't the time; he needed his wits about him. In a day or so he'd get a call from Oliver asking him to come in, telling him there were papers to sign. And Damian would think he'd won. Let him. While he had his back to the wall, his shoulder to the wheel, and all that bloody nonsense, Lewis would be a hundred miles away at Loch Morar working on getting his health back.

What happened in Glasgow wouldn't concern him... until he was stronger. Lewis didn't regret stepping down as MD – it was the right thing in the circumstances. Like a fool he'd assumed, given time, things would go back to how they'd been – Lewis and Damian taking on the world. Now he realised it wouldn't happen. It couldn't. Stone Free had been built on values that had nothing to do with money. His partner didn't share those values and probably never had.

Anger bubbled in Lewis's stomach, his fingers tightened on the glass and he changed his mind about another drink. As the amber liquid climbed the crystal sides, he lifted his mobile, called Damian, and was immediately transferred to voicemail. No problem, he'd try again.

20

The car bumped onto the pavement, squeezed between a Vauxhall Astra and a Volkswagen Tiguan, and stopped at a crazy angle. I turned the ignition off and got out, forcing myself to walk when every nerve in my body ached to run. The drive from Sherbrooke Avenue had been like living in a crazy dream – most of it I couldn't even remember – but somehow, I made it home. Inside the flat everything was as it had been but there was no comfort in the cosy familiarity. My head pounded, my legs wouldn't hold me. At one point I thought I was going to faint and used a hand to steady myself against the wall. Overwhelmed and dizzy, I slid to the floor and burst into tears, cursing the flaw in my personality that wouldn't let me accept that Molly's death had been a tragic accident.

Everyone else had, why couldn't I?

I knew the answer. The driver – Lewis fucking Stone – hadn't suffered a single consequence for his actions. His life had gone on unaltered. So long as he could go back to his nice house, he didn't care that a family had been devastated because of what he'd done.

That wasn't right.

During our sisterly heart-to-heart I hadn't told Sam the truth about the drinking. She had more than enough to handle coping with her husband without her role model admitting to the kind of stuff deranged bunny boilers got up to.

Stalking a stranger's home! Leaving threatening messages! Very un-Alex-like behaviour.

The long gravel-lined approach had daunted me and I'd been close to walking on by. What I was doing wasn't normal; even I could see that. Getting caught would be shameful: my face plastered on the cover of the *Daily Record*, filmed by STV and BBC Scotland hurrying away, head bowed as I came out of Glasgow Sheriff Court surrounded by reporters – assuming I came out and wasn't given a jail sentence – was my nightmare scenario. The stakes were high. I was risking my freedom, public disgrace at the very least, and the business I'd struggled so hard to build wouldn't survive. When it was over some people wouldn't forget and nobody in their right mind would employ me.

If I kept this up, I could lose the pharmacy. Lewis Stone would still be in his fancy conservatory in Pollokshields while I struggled to survive on social security.

I shuddered. It didn't bear thinking about.

In the kitchen, I removed my coat and turned on the radio. Laying out the seriousness of my actions, being brutally honest with myself about where this might lead, had brought an unreal calm and strengthened my resolve, because this was about more than me. This was about justice for Molly. In truth, I'd known what I was going to do from the moment the police had let him get back in that bloody car – off the hook, while I dangled helplessly on mine. Of course I was scared. Anybody – unless they were a psychopath – would be. But I'd walk through my fear and do what had to be done. This was only the beginning; there was a long way to go.

A knock on the front door brought me running through to the lounge. I peered round the curtain to see who was there and shrank back, panicked. Two uniformed policemen stood on the steps. How had they found me so soon? Unless they'd followed me home.

I took a few seconds to get myself under control before opening the door. The officer with three chevron stripes on his arm said, 'Sorry to bother you.'

I realised they hadn't come for me and relaxed. 'Not at all. What can I do for you?'

'There was a break-in last night four doors down. We're asking the neighbours if they heard anything.'

'What time was it?'

The policeman scratched his chin. 'The couple who live there were visiting their daughter and didn't discover it until they got home. The most obvious time would be in the early hours, though, of course, I'm guessing.'

'Usually, my lights are out by ten-thirty and I'm asleep pretty soon after that. Is it an isolated incident or have there been more?'

The officers glanced at each other. 'As a matter of fact we've had a spate of them recently.'

I feigned concern. 'In this area? I'm surprised.'

'Yes, I'm afraid so. Kids probably. Sneaking out to meet their mates when their folks think they're in bed. Young tearaways. In the meantime—'

'If I hear anything suspicious, I'll ring 999.'

'That's it, and don't worry. We'll catch them, we always do. Most criminals aren't very smart, that's why they get caught.' He pointed to my car half on, half off the pavement. 'Any idea who that belongs to?'

'As a matter of fact—'

The sergeant wasn't listening. 'Tell them to park properly in future or we'll be having a word with them. Some people shouldn't be allowed behind the wheel.' He gave a casual nod. 'Thanks for your time. Have a good day.'

21

Damian hadn't driven home when he'd left Sherbrooke Avenue. He'd gone to Sonny and Vito's in Park Road and was sitting on a stool by the window in the little deli with his second cup of espresso in front of him, eating his way through a slice of carrot cake, feeling better than he had at any point this year. Enough to give Tina a call? No, he still had too much going on for that. Fair play to her, she'd vocalised her displeasure but stuck around when plenty of other women wouldn't have.

His mind wandered back to the meeting. He hadn't been looking forward to the conversation with Lewis, yet it had been remarkably civil. Given the sensitivity of the topic under discussion and his surprise offer to step down as Stone Free MD, it was a result worthy of a small celebration. Drinking in the middle of the day wasn't Damian's style, so he'd come where the coffee was strong and the cake was sweet.

You didn't need a medical degree to realise Lewis was having some kind of breakdown; it screamed out of him. Until now, he'd resisted every offer of help and Damian hadn't a clue how to fix someone who shut him out. Time on his own away from pressure would be good for Lewis. Then he'd visit him in the north and try again. The business would cope without them – it would have to, deal or no deal. Meanwhile, as soon as Oliver Shawcross's firm did its stuff, he'd be the one heading up the company. Bringing that news to the L-A Group would put the deal back on track. And for once, the credit would be his. Wouldn't that be nice?

Damian sipped his coffee and was finishing the cake when his mobile vibrated on the table. Before he had a chance to speak, Lewis shouted down the line.

'You cunt, Morton! You bastard! Your mind games won't work! I'm on to you!'

Damian turned away in case they could be overheard. 'Lewis – what do you mean? What mind games?'

'Come off it. It was you. Who else would it be?'

'What was me? What are you talking about? I just left you. Everything was fine. What's happened?'

The laugh was forced, terse, devoid of humour. 'Don't get too comfortable in my chair, old pal. I'll be back. Stronger than before. And the conversation won't be about me. It'll be about you. I should've cut you loose long ago. Instead, I let you hang on to my coattails because I thought we were friends. Some friend. Stone Free is mine. It always was and it always will be.'

Damian was flabbergasted. 'I honestly have no idea what you're on about. Listen to yourself. Listen to what you're saying. You aren't well, Lewis, you really aren't.'

'I'm fine and I'm going to be fine. As for you – you crossed the line and there's no way back. Start thinking about how much it'll cost me to buy you out of the business. Name your price. I'll find the money, even if I have to hock everything I have. See you in three months.'

Damian put the mobile down, visibly unnerved.

He'd just been talking to a madman.

* * *

Lewis was physically and mentally exhausted, so depressed even breathing was an effort. His mouth was dry; his head hurt. Suddenly, what Stone Free had cost him was clear: he had no friends, no relationships, and without the business his life was empty. Until today, he'd considered Damian a friend; he'd been wrong. Of course he'd rejected the accusation that he'd planted the note – he would play dumb, wouldn't he? Because it was all part of the plan to ease him out. The plan that was not fucking happening.

He called Oliver Shawcross on his direct line. When he answered, something in the lawyer's tone told Lewis he'd been expecting him. As always, the urbane Edinburgh accent flowed mellifluously but there was an edge to it. Oliver tried to sound casual and failed.

'What can I do for you, Lewis?'

Lewis's reply was guarded and neutral. 'Can I take it you've spoken with Damian?'

'What? No, not recently. Did he say he'd been in contact?'

'I assumed he would. There's been a development.'

'Really? Good or bad?'

'Depends on your point of view, Oliver. We've agreed I'll step down as MD.'

'Glad to hear it. Be lying if I said anything else.

Stone Free is at a crucial point in its progress but your health comes first. Sounds as though you've realised that.'

Lewis brushed the platitudes aside; he had no use for them. 'Yeah, well, it isn't as straightforward as it might be. I told Damian I'd be taking a year off.'

'A year?'

'It won't be. Three months is as long as I'm prepared to give it. Put together whatever I have to sign and get it over to me by noon tomorrow.'

'Noon! You are in a hurry.'

'Junk the legalese for once, it isn't needed. Keep it simple. Just a statement about a change in the structure – to all intents and purposes, business as usual. Anything longer and it'll go in the bin.'

Oliver sucked air through his teeth, remembering when Lewis would have asked his advice and taken it seven times out of ten. Those days, it seemed, were gone. The lawyer was used to handling difficult clients and kept his voice even. 'Okay, except three months isn't long. I'd have thought—'

Lewis wasn't interested. 'It'll be enough, it'll have to be.'

'Have you spoken to a doctor?'

'No, and I won't be, but thanks for your concern. I

know better than anybody what's wrong with me and medication isn't the answer.'

'Diagnosing ourselves rarely ends well, Lewis.'

'Yeah, well, consider your objection noted, Oliver. Now, do your job. Noon tomorrow.'

He hung up and paced the room, pounding a fist into his palm. He'd known Oliver Shawcross for ten years. This was the first time he'd realised the man was a liar. Denying having spoken to Damian when he so obviously had threw up implications Lewis wasn't prepared for. It meant he was in on it – whatever *it* was. Shawcoss was with Morton.

Lewis went upstairs and dragged a suitcase from the bottom of a wardrobe and put it on the bed; the sooner he was out of Glasgow, the better.

* * *

Oliver gazed through his office window and across the road to the trees in the park, so beautiful in spring but when winter arrived, denuded and ugly. The metaphor for Lewis Stone and Damian Morton's relationship was impossible to miss. He stared at the mobile in his hand, astonished by the conversation he'd just had. In the circles he moved in – mostly successful professionals like himself – he was known for his measured approach and firm belief that for every problem there was a solution. That maxim was about to be tested. Finding himself between the Stone Free partners was the last place he'd expected. For as long as he'd known them, the word schism wouldn't appear in the same sentence as Lewis and Damian – they'd been like brothers, fiercely supportive of each other, determined to succeed in an industry famous for chewing people up and spitting them out. Their designs were sharp, yet it was the bond between the two that had made an impression; agreeing to represent their burgeoning enterprise hadn't been difficult. Clearly, that was no longer true and he was reminded of the folly of going into business with a friend. Experience showed that, inevitably, it went wrong. And it wasn't a case of if but when. Because people were people: old resentments, fragile egos; naked ambition and slights – real and imagined – would destroy whatever had been achieved in costly court battles. It was the way of the world, one of the reasons lawyers could take their wives and girlfriends to Antigua and St Kitts in the depths of a Scottish winter while the rest of the population were freezing their balls off.

What Lewis wanted would instantly escalate the situation. Then again, the managing director had given him an instruction, as he had every right to do;

his duty was to carry it out. Damian Morton would respond and all the king's horses and all the king's men wouldn't put what got broken back together again. He'd seen it happen; the first casualty would be the remains of their relationship; the second would be Stone Free.

Damian was a partner in the business; he had to know. Oliver was the one who had to tell him. He answered his phone right away and launched into an attack on his former friend. 'It's worse than I imagined. A lot worse. He's fucking crazy. Absolutely bonkers.'

'Calm down. Lewis isn't well. We have to figure out how to help him before he does something stupid.'

Damian was beyond empathy. 'Maybe you have to, Oliver, but I don't. I've done my bit.'

'The guy's ill.'

Damian shouted, 'Really? I'll give you an example of how "ill" he is, shall I?'

'Damian—'

'No, hear me out. Against my better judgement I went to see him. We talked. It was amicable or, at least, I thought so. He didn't put up a fight and agreed to step down in the best interests of the business. When I left everything was agreed – he'd step back. Then, he phoned, calling me names, accusing me of Christ knows what, telling me my mind games wouldn't work. What mind games? It was shocking. Real Jekyll and Hyde stuff.'

Oliver let him get it out and spoke quietly. 'As I said, he's ill. We aren't dealing with the Lewis we knew. He's going away to sort himself out.'

'Not good enough; he needs to be committed before something bad happens.'

Oliver didn't like where this was going. He said, 'I understand why, but you're overreacting. In Scotland, someone can only be sectioned if they meet very specific criteria – their mental health problem is so severe that they need urgent assessment and treatment, or they are a danger to themselves or others. Now, seriously, does that sound like Lewis to you? Because it doesn't to me. He needs professional help, no argument there, though let's not get carried away.'

There was silence on the other end of the line. The lawyer didn't know if that meant Damian agreed with him. He said, 'So Lewis told you he was going away to sort himself out.'

'Yes.'

'For how long?'

Oliver couldn't avoid answering. 'Three months. He asked me to draw something up to that effect and insists on having it in front of him by twelve o'clock tomorrow. Otherwise, he'll leave without signing anything.'

'And Stone Free can go to hell.'

'He didn't say that.'

'No, I'm saying it. If this gets out...'

Through the window, Oliver saw the branches move in the wind and loosened his tie, momentarily rattled by the implied threat. 'I've been in this game long enough, Damian. I don't need to be reminded of client confidentiality, thank you very much. Better worry about your own side and what you'll tell people when they ask why the boss isn't at his desk. I'd start drafting a press release, if I were you. Get the official story straight. As for how long Lewis is away – three months, six months – all that matters is that he gets well. Don't you agree?'

* * *

Damian ended the call without replying. He didn't agree. Not any more. He hadn't gone looking for this; nothing about it was his doing. But the idea that, somehow, Lewis could come and go as he pleased in a business that belonged to both of them wasn't on. Damian had paid his dues, played second fiddle long enough. The role of faithful retainer didn't fit any more; he'd outgrown it.

He wanted to smash the mobile off the wall. Lewis's proposal was unacceptable, beyond insulting, though it revealed something fundamental about the nature of their relationship. Lewis had conveniently forgotten his monumental fuck-up with Lassiter-Accardi, believing he held all the cards, certain he could decide when it was back-in-your-box time for Damian. The colossal arrogance of his attitude devalued his partner's contribution to what they'd built. Waiting around with his thumb up his arse for The Great Leader to put in an appearance wouldn't cut it. Whether he was ever again the force he'd been wasn't the issue today. Tomorrow, he'd be gone.

Oliver Shawcross clearly assumed it was a temporary leave of absence on health grounds – a much-needed break from the pressure. The lawyer could put his hand on a bible and swear his client had been behaving strangely – strange enough for a conversation about having him committed. And where he'd chosen to run to might not be the best place for him. Damian hadn't been to Lewis's parents' holiday home miles from the nearest village. MAMBA country, he'd jokingly called it. 'Miles and miles of bugger all.' Alone in the middle of nowhere, with only the sound of the wind in the forest and the occasional call of a bird searching for a mate, the solitude would be deafening. If that didn't tip him over the edge, perhaps something else would?

Lewis might never come back.

And Stone Free would be all his.

22

I poured a whisky – a small one this time – determined there would be no repeat of the exhibition I'd made of myself, an out-of-control fiasco nobody should've witnessed. Remembering the state I'd been in brought a flush of shame to my cheeks. This was different; I was spooked. I carried the drink over to the couch and sat down, nursing the glass between my palms. It was impossible to like the person I'd become, driven day and night by thoughts of revenge, my need for it so strong it overwhelmed even my grief and regret.

I recognised my own insanity without wanting it to stop. The note was meant to scare Lewis Stone, make him realise he hadn't got away with what he'd done. If it had frightened him half as much as finding the officers on my doorstep had frightened me, it had succeeded. I longed to tell Sam. We'd shared so much over the years, but she'd have gone mental. Insist I get a bloody grip.

And I had no intention of doing that.

Oh, to be a fly on the wall when the bastard found the little gift I'd left. It would've wiped the entitled smile off his face, for sure.

I hadn't broken the law. At least, not yet. But I'd let my own life go. Apart from odd calls to fake an interest I didn't have, I'd been MIA from the pharmacy. That wouldn't change until I'd seen an end to this. Thank God my assistant, Jenny, was able to run things in my absence. It was starting to look like she'd be doing it for a while yet.

Suddenly, the pain of losing Freddy hit me almost like a physical blow and I screamed at the heavens. 'Why? Why did you take him? I need him here. Let me wake up with his arms around me, I'm begging you!' I fell to my knees and sobbed. 'Mum, please send him back, I'm no good without him. I can't do this. Please, Mum, please.'

I must have cried myself to sleep because when my eyes opened it was dark, Freddy was still gone, and there was an emptiness in me I knew I'd never fill.

23

Oliver Shawcross wasn't happy. The papers he'd been instructed to draw up were in his briefcase though he sensed this was only the beginning of a widening chasm between the partners. Oliver disliked confrontation, the reason he'd chosen to make a career in the dust-dry arena of business law rather than more challenging alternatives. Entrepreneurs were a type, characters who danced to their own drum, ignored advice no matter the source if it jarred with their gut instinct, and never took orders. Just being around them was exciting but they could be difficult clients to deal with: big-picture thinkers low on patience for the bread-and-butter minutiae of licences and registrations or health and safety requirements.

Lewis had trusted Damian Morton to lead the L-A negotiations. Damian had repaid his faith by delivering the biggest deal in Stone Free's history, until it had stalled at the eleventh hour. A change at the top might get it back on track. What that would do for Lewis Stone's already fragile mental state was less certain.

Oliver nosed the car up the drive and pulled to a stop. Lewis was a friend. Friends were supposed to help each other. He hadn't done enough. A true friend would've done more.

The front door opened before he reached it like a scene from a horror movie. Once upon a time, the men would've greeted each other with handshakes and smiles; business would've been a secondary consideration. Today, the atmosphere was very different – they barely nodded and went straight to the dining room. Oliver laid the papers out on the table and searched his inside pocket for a pen. 'This is what you asked for. As your lawyer I have to go over it so you're clear about the implications before you sign.'

The response was as chilly as the February air. 'How typically considerate of you, Oliver. Always the model professional. Don't bother, I trust you.'

Oliver felt the corners of his mouth tighten. Lewis had managed to turn the words into an insult. 'It's not a question of trust, Lewis. If you didn't trust me, I wouldn't be here, would I? No, as a lawyer I owe a duty of care to all my clients. You'll find it in my original contract under terms and conditions. With respect, it's not something I'd make an exception with, even for you.'

'Whatever you say. Just don't make a meal of it, eh? I'm about to leave.'

Concern forced Oliver to say what he should've said weeks earlier. 'Lewis, listen to me. I'm worried about you. Even the tone of this conversation... You aren't yourself.' He came round the table and put a hand on his shoulder. 'By all means take a break from the business – you deserve it. But not like this. I'm not the enemy. Neither is Damian. Our only concern—'

Lewis mocked him. '"*Our* only concern". You can't be serious. Perform your little legal pantomime and fuck off. You haven't a clue what's going on. None at all.'

'So, tell me.'

For twenty seconds Lewis stared at him, then said, 'Or, maybe I'm wrong and I'm the one in the dark. Maybe you understand only too well, Oliver.'

'What in God's name are you talking about?'

Lewis snapped his fingers. 'Give me the pen.'

'Lewis!'

'The pen, Shawcross.'

He scrawled illegibly at the bottom of the last page and snarled, 'Now, get out of my house and don't come back. You like to give advice, well, here's some for you: enjoy the next three months with Damian, because when I come back, Stone Free will be looking for another lawyer.'

24

Sam brought the car to a halt at the kerb outside Molly's flat. On the way here, unusually for us, we'd hardly spoken, each lost in our own thoughts, staring silently through the windscreen at the rain that never seemed to stop falling.

Sam spoke for both of us. 'I hadn't ever imagined that some day we'd be doing this, did you? It's like when you wake up from nightmare. You know it wasn't real, common sense tells you it was just a bad dream, but the fear or shame or whatever hangs around for hours. Sometimes, all day. You can't shake it off.' She looked up at the window cut into the red sandstone and the closed-over curtains, exhaled loudly through her mouth, and finished the thought.

'That's how this feels. Christ, I could see this far enough.'

I shook my head. 'I'm the oldest. I assumed I'd die first and it would be you and Molly taking care of things.'

Sam shot a disapproving glance across at me. 'You always were the morbid one, even when we were kids. Any of us dying, not being here, didn't cross my mind until this. Now, I think about it all the time. Every morning it's there, waiting for me like a faithful bloody friend.'

She checked her make-up in the mirror. In the unforgiving daylight, the strain of our sister's death and her floundering marriage were wreaking havoc on a face that, not long ago, had been pretty. Now, white skin stretched like a mask over the bone and the eyes were puffy, weak and watery. Sam spoke to herself. '"Piss holes in the snow", to use one of Molly's less elegant but apt descriptions. I look like Granny.'

She faltered as sadness crashed over her and I thought she was going to break down. 'I've been trying to remember the last time I was here and I can't. My brain won't go there. As if I'm being protected, shielded from something that would destroy me. Have you had that?'

I didn't answer; Sam took that as a no.

A sigh forced its way to the surface as she dredged courage from somewhere deep and said, 'Come on, the sooner we do it, the sooner it'll be behind us. Let's get it over with.'

We climbed to the second floor, our footsteps echoing in the tenement's stairwell. Somewhere in the building a dog barked and a rough male voice shouted something I couldn't make out. On the landing, I used my key to open the door and went inside. Letters gathered in a pile on the carpet, flyers mostly, offers Molly would never take up, among them a brown envelope marked HM Inland Revenue and Customs with a Newcastle address.

Sam fanned her hand across her face. 'Better crack some windows and let some fresh air in. It's fusty in here.'

'It's damp.'

Sam wrinkled her nose. 'And turn the heating on. I haven't stayed in one of these since I got married. Can't say I've missed it. The building's probably close to a hundred and fifty years old. It needs people living in it or it shows.'

I didn't tell her I'd been to Molly's flat every other day since the accident, wandering from one empty room to another, lying on the bed, smelling Molly's clothes for a trace of the girl I'd known since the day she was born. A world without her wasn't a world I was ready to accept.

Her bedroom was dominated by the neatly made double bed against the far wall and the collection of teddy bears on top, the matching Tiffany-style lamps bought on eBay on either side. They looked real but weren't. Molly couldn't have cared less about their authenticity; the multicoloured stained-glass shades had appealed to her and that was enough. Every room had some quirky feature, no doubt picked up for pennies in some charity shop: a multicoloured Moroccan rug pinned above the fireplace; a Mandarin blue-and-white porcelain ginger jar with a chipped lid; a Jasper Conran crystal vase still in the open box. The eclectic mishmash suggesting somebody interesting lived here was soooo Molly it had always made me smile.

No one who'd been in her company more than five minutes would deny she'd been, as the humanist had described, a free spirit – a famously untidy spirit with a habit of leaving everything where it fell. When she was growing up, our mother had constantly rowed with her about it, until eventually admitting defeat and refusing to go near her room.

Molly had believed she'd struck a blow for the right of the individual to express themselves and kept doing exactly as she pleased.

Days after the accident, with our sister on life support in the Queen Elizabeth Hospital in Govan, I'd discovered that, almost a decade and a half on, not much had changed: the flat had been a mess. I'd made the bed, cleared the sink of dirty dishes, vacuumed the carpet, thrown away the blackened peaches, and emptied the fridge of milk that had gone off in preparation for Molly's return, wanting it to be a nice surprise, even if she accused me of turning into our mother.

Sam joined me in the room. Immediately I realised my mistake and hoped she wouldn't notice. Of course, she did. 'His scarf's gone.'

'What?'

'Angus isn't wearing his scarf.'

Before I could invent a story, the truth dawned on her and she turned on me. 'Oh, for God's sake, Alex! You've taken it, haven't you? Now I've seen everything. And there's a wig missing. Please don't tell me...'

Her voice faltered, the words wouldn't come, then she fell into my arms. The wig wasn't there but it wasn't missing; we'd last seen it lying in a pool of ice water in Byres Road.

When her sobbing subsided, Sam drew away from me and went to the lounge. I stayed where I was until she called me through for coffee. The scarf and the wig weren't mentioned. Instead, she started talking about Molly in the present tense, as though she'd popped out to the shops and would return in a few minutes.

'The last time I was here it looked like a bomb had landed on it, so I'm putting two and two together and guessing Big Sister has cleaned up her mess as usual. *And*, she only has instant, I'm afraid. How anyone buys Nescafé in this day and age, I'll never understand. Doesn't she realise too much instant coffee is bad for you? All acrylamide and less caffeine. Too much gives you a higher risk of cancer.'

I ignored the barb. This was tough on both of us; people reacted differently. With Sam, it manifested itself in acerbic comments best ignored.

'You know Molly wasn't health conscious. She ate and drank whatever was put in front of her. She has chocolate stashed all over the place. I even came across an unopened box of Black Magic under the sink.'

Sam snapped, 'You make it sound like a virtue. It isn't. It's stupid. I mean, Black Magic; doesn't she have taste buds? A child could tell it's rubbish, why can't she? Except, we know why, don't we? Because she thinks she's Wendy out of *Peter Pan*. In her case, the *girl* who never grew up.'

I wanted to bite back, remind Sam that, in the circumstances, her point was moot because our sister was dead. Instead, I settled for a neutral response intended to calm the storm that had blown in from nowhere.

'Stuff like that isn't important to her.' I awkwardly corrected myself. 'I mean, wasn't important.'

Sam's reaction startled me. She slammed the cup on the table and shouted, 'Well, it fucking should've been! It should've been important! Some things are! Some things...' She broke down and covered her face with her hands. 'I'm sorry, I'm so sorry. I... just wish she was here and none of this had happened. And I wish she'd bought proper coffee instead of this... processed junk. For Christ's sake, Molly!'

I let her rave on. The success of Colin's business meant Sam's opinions weren't the same as when the three of us lived under the same roof; these days she was used to better. But her outburst wasn't about better, it was about sadness. She was angry and taking it out on the coffee, which, in the absence of milk, was indeed undrinkable.

I edged closer to her on the couch. 'We both miss her. How could we not? Molly was... special... she just was. Of course we feel terrible, what other way is there to feel? I've cried myself to sleep regretting every time I pretended to be listening to her twitter on about some nonsense when I'd actually tuned her out. Little things that can't be undone tear me apart. If I hadn't decided to be a good Samaritan and stop to talk to the beggar with the dog I'd have been there. Christ's sake, he wouldn't have missed me. We're dealing in seconds. Split seconds, even. Maybe it would've made a difference. Maybe she wouldn't have slipped on the ice. Maybe she'd have been here serving us her shit coffee, and you would be making faces at me behind her back. Do you see what I'm saying, Sam?'

Sam's lips moved; she started to speak and changed her mind.

I noticed. 'What? What is it?'

Sam lifted the cup and put it down again. 'I *do* see but I think it's me. Why couldn't I have caught her instead of...?'

'Oh, come on, Samantha. Now you're being ridiculous and I won't stand for it. This is difficult enough without *inventing* wrongs.'

'I'm not inventing anything, it's true.'

'No, it bloody well isn't true. You're not responsible and neither am I.'

I wanted to add that I knew who was, but didn't.

Sam closed her eyes and kept them closed until she was ready to open them. 'You're so sure of yourself. So confident. I wish I was as certain about one thing as you are about every bloody thing. When Freddy was alive you were insufferable because life was going great. The number of times I wanted to tell you how much you irritated me...'

'Sam. I'm... I'm sorry.'

She smiled a sad half-smile. 'There, I've finally said it. And I'm the one who should be apologising. But you're wrong on this. You stopped to give the beggar money and Molly made a crack about him not being grateful. I lost it with her and we argued.'

'She always had too bloody much to say. That's no reason to blame yourself. If I'd heard her my reaction would've been the same.'

The half-smile returned and I caught pity in my sister's eyes. 'As I said... always so certain. When you slipped, I caught you, when Molly slipped, I...'

I cut her blame game short and put the responsibility where it belonged. 'You tried, Sam, that's what you did. How it turned out had nothing to do with you. How could you have known some drunken idiot would career through our lives?'

Sam's reply was weary, defeated. 'You're missing it, Alex. We were arguing, bitching at each other. She said it was the last Christmas get-together she was coming to. She said she was glad Mum and Dad weren't here to...'

I put a hand on her shoulder. 'Listen to me. Molly could be a little minx when she wanted. She opened her mouth and said whatever was in her head. That's the truth. Sometimes, she was funny and made us laugh. Occasionally, we got the other Molly, the one who said cruel things. Our sister was a wonderful human being but she was by no means perfect and we both know it. Mum and Dad knew it, too.'

Sam carried on as though she hadn't heard. 'If we hadn't been going at it like alley cats, if I hadn't been so bloody angry, I might've caught her the way I did you. The fact is, I didn't and she's dead. Christ, why does it have to be so hard? Between this and Colin, it's crushing the life out of me. It gets so bad I can hardly breathe.' She stood. 'Perhaps I shouldn't have told you. At least now you get what's going on with me and why I can't stay. I realise I'm letting the side down bailing on you like this. Let's leave doing anything. It's too soon. Too much. I can't face it.' Sam walked hurriedly to the door, anxious to be gone. 'There's a lot I need to come to terms with. Is that all right?'

I followed and took hold of her hands. 'Of course it is. There's no rush. We'll do it when you feel up to it. Just promise me you'll stop being so hard on yourself. What happened was an accident. Nobody was to blame.'

The directness of Sam's response caught me off-guard. 'What about the driver? Does that apply to him?'

Knowing how I felt, it was the wrong thing to say and she knew it the moment the words were out of her mouth. I let go of her hands, my jawline hard. 'Say his name. Give him an identity. Calling him "the driver" means it isn't personal when it's the most personal thing in the world. Lewis Stone. You didn't kill Molly, Lewis Stone killed her. And, with or without your help, he's going to pay for it.'

Sam hadn't meant for it to end like this and tried to backtrack. 'Look, I know you're hurting, we both are, but that's crazy talk. I keep telling you: the police would've arrested him if he was responsible. They didn't. Doesn't that tell you something?'

She didn't know the thoughts in my head – dark thoughts not to be shared, unimaginable before that awful night in the West End of Glasgow.

Sam said, 'Answer me. You can't, can you? Look, I don't know how to say this, but do you think this could be anger you've bottled up over Freddy? The way he died, I mean—'

She'd crossed an invisible line and exposed a truth I wasn't ready to accept.

I cut her off. 'Show yourself out.'

25

The receptionist answered immediately in a sing-song voice meant to sound professional, only managing to come across as rehearsed and robotic. 'Hilton Hotel. How can I help you?'

Colin waited a beat before replying. Moving out of their beautiful home in Newton Mearns – a home they'd built together – was an emotional wrench he hadn't factored into his thinking when he'd made the decision to leave. Despite the gulf that had opened up between them, somewhere in the back of his mind he questioned if he wasn't overreacting. After all, the problems him and Sam were having weren't unusual or limited to just them. Far from it. Many couples, especially those married a long time, went through phases where the last human being they wanted to be with was their husband or wife, and it occurred to him that this was what people were talking about when they said marriage had to be worked at. Colin almost laughed out loud; this was fear and guilt talking. If things had gone how he'd expected, he'd have been gone before this.

He said, 'I'd like to make a booking.'

'Certainly, sir. When for?'

'A week, probably longer, starting tonight, if possible.'

He heard the delay on the other end of the line as she called up the computer. 'Single or double?'

The reality of what he was doing to his wife rushed in and he hesitated. 'Single.'

'A single room for seven days, okay. Can I have your name?'

The rest of the conversation passed in a dream he'd only vaguely recall in fragments. But it was done – the first step towards ending his relationship with Sam had been taken. Colin fished an unopened packet of Benson & Hedges from his pocket, broke the seal with his fingernail, and tapped a cigarette into the palm of his hand.

Sam detested smoking and wouldn't allow it in the house. Today, that was the least of their problems.

He glanced at the ceiling and the alarm he'd had the foresight to install years before they became required by law in Scotland, wondering if he wasn't about to set it off.

Fuck that! It was still his house, too, wasn't it?

Colin inhaled deeply, blew out grey smoke and watched it drift in the air. Who could've known it would come to this the night he'd noticed Sam at a gig in The Garage? She'd got his attention and kept it – on the edge of the crowd singing along while the DJ confronted the audience as if he was about to beat the shit out of somebody because he felt like it. Sam had known every word. It was the year fashion died. Wearing a vintage T-shirt and pink jeans tucked into white platform boots making her look like somebody who'd dressed in the dark, she'd hastened its demise.

Remembering her dancing to the old Arctic Monkeys song 'I Bet You Look Good on the Dancefloor' made Colin smile; he'd loved her crazy style; and he'd loved *her*.

Somewhere along the road that emotion had shifted to someone else and his feelings for Sam were replaced by another kind of love.

Seeing the cigarette between his fingers brought a perverse thought to prove the point: how ironic would it be if she returned from wherever the hell she was to find firemen pouring jets of water on what was left of their blazing home? One less thing to disagree about.

He went downstairs to the double garage and pulled out a case. One wouldn't be nearly enough for the Armani suits, the Blake Mill shirts, and the rest of the poseur paraphernalia, the trappings used to promote the image of a successful businessman. And it was true; he was successful – very successful, in fact – but only in business. His personal life was a disaster. When the wounds had healed enough for them to talk about it, friends who'd split told of viciously squabbling over every insignificant crumb, while the lawyers – the only winners in these cases – egged their clients on from the side-lines. Colin wanted no part of that crap. He owed Sam and he knew it. Fair enough. She could have it all: the house, the cars, the clothes, the money in their shared bank accounts. Everything but the company he'd built; that was his and he wasn't giving it up for anybody.

Packing what he actually needed was a revelation – most of his fine clothes wouldn't be going with him. If he was short of something he'd buy it – a new experience because throughout their marriage, his wife had done that for him, happy to be spending his cash even if it wasn't on herself.

That was unfair, and it was unkind. Sam had been

a good wife; it wasn't her fault he'd fallen in love with someone else. But he had and the best thing to do was admit it and move on before they sucked the life out of each other.

Colin heard the front door close and scrambled to open the bedroom window to fire what was left of the cigarette onto the patio outside. His mouth twitched; he was conscious of his reaction, emasculated and embarrassed by it. Footsteps on the stairs warned him Sam was on her way. Colin zipped the case and set it on the floor; it weighed very little. Not much to show for a marriage.

He sensed her in the doorframe and turned slowly, unsure what to expect from the person who'd once been at the centre of his universe. What he saw momentarily saddened him. The woman in front of him was very different from the girl who'd taken his breath away in a Glasgow club: her hair looked like it hadn't been combed and mascara ran in black lines down her otherwise flawless skin. Colin realised she'd been crying and wanted to take her in his arms. Sam's reaction stopped him; she stared at the suitcase and back at her husband, her mouth twisting in a disbelieving snarl.

'Really? After everything you've put me through? You're running away?'

The tenderness in his heart melted. He returned her accusation with his own, delivered with a cruelty that surprised even him. 'What, Sam? What exactly have I put you through?' He waved an arm at the room, goading her. 'All I see is a life beyond your wildest fucking dreams before you met me. Before you got lucky.'

Her lunge caught him off-guard and he fell backwards, hitting his head on the dressing table. She screamed and was on him, punching and gouging, beating her fists against his chest. 'Until you betrayed me, you lying fucker!'

Colin's eyes filled with shock. 'What're you—?'

She spat the words at him. 'Did you think I didn't know? I'm your wife; of course I fucking knew! I knew about all of it! Do you hear me? All of it! Was she good? Was she a better hump than me?'

Colin felt himself harden, then he was silencing the filth pouring from her mouth with wet kisses that were returned as his fingers tore at her clothes – the blouse, the skirt, the bra, the pants, cast aside like expensive rags.

She responded, ripping the shirt from his chest, spraying buttons across the room. In seconds, they were naked on the bed and going at each other, driven by unhappiness and desperation. Sam gripped the headboard and threw herself onto him, matching him thrust for thrust. Colin thought his heart would explode, and still his wife demanded more. 'Fuck me! Fuck me! Fuck me!'

Then, as suddenly as it had begun, it was over.

For minutes they lay welded by sweat to each other, not speaking, until Colin pulled away and gathered his clothes from where they'd landed. Sam rolled her body into the C of the foetal position, ashamed and humiliated at what had just happened. She kept her eyes tightly shut, dreading what was coming, yet understanding their passion had changed nothing. She heard him moving around the room, finally lifting the suitcase, wanting him to stay as desperately as she'd ever wanted anything. A tear spilled down her cheek followed by another, and when Colin spoke his voice was a whisper, as though the words he was searching for refused to be said out loud.

'For what it's worth, I'm truly sorry. I really am. It shouldn't have ended this way. I can't make up for what I've done but at least you won't have to worry about money. The lawyer will be in touch to sort it all out. Goodbye, Sam.'

26

Lewis felt his spirits lift before he'd reached the end of Sherbrooke Avenue – he'd waited too long to do what he was doing. He pointed the car towards the M8 and the Clyde Tunnel, already feeling better. Holding on to that night had come close to destroying him. If he could turn back the clock he would. It wasn't possible to save Molly. Molly: he'd never used her name before. To survive, he had to follow what her family had done – bury her and move on.

Lewis rolled down the window. Cold air rushed in to meet him; he welcomed it and forced himself to take a different, more balanced view. Yes, he'd been distracted when he should've been concentrating on the road, but he wasn't solely responsible – nobody had questioned the victim's blood alcohol level, information that might've explained why she'd fallen in front of him. Lewis closed his eyes for a second and replayed the awful sounds of her body being crushed under the wheels.

The Golf crossed the Erskine Bridge with the river making its surly progress beneath him to the Firth of Clyde. Suddenly, the clouds parted, the sun came out, and the weight he'd carried for what seemed like forever lifted a little more, allowing him to recognise what had been in front of him all along. The breakdown, or whatever it was he was going through, had unearthed truths he'd been blind to before. Nothing was as it appeared to be: Oliver wasn't the man he'd thought he was – not by a long chalk – and the resentment Damian had so obviously been harbouring for years had come to the surface when he believed his partner was vulnerable.

Then there was the note... that had been a blow; just thinking about it unnerved him.

How could Damian have known what had been in his head? How could anyone? It didn't matter; he wouldn't let the bastard get to him. Instead, he'd use it as an incentive to drive his recovery. Lewis forced himself to say the word out loud. 'Killer.' Not a truth –

nothing like it – simply one man's sad attempt at a power grab.

He exited the bridge and joined the steady flow of traffic towards Loch Lomond, knowing he'd reached a crossroads in his life and that there was no turning back. But he wasn't afraid because the priority was clear: get his health sorted and return stronger than ever to Stone Free. He smiled and settled behind the wheel, determined to enjoy the journey through some of Scotland's most spectacular scenery.

He'd be back. All he needed was time.

* * *

Damian put his feet up on the desk and held the mobile to his ear, waiting for Oliver Shawcross to come on the line. After a minute, he hung up; the lawyer could be in a meeting or he could be avoiding him. Either way, it didn't matter. What *did* matter was where he was at this moment – in Lewis's office, his office now.

He scanned the room's bare walls that in the early days had held his partner's degree in fashion and textile design from the Glasgow School of Art in a silver frame. Lewis had an enormous ego; he'd outgrown the award and taken it down because it embarrassed him.

Damian had reminded him that at the beginning of Tom Ford's rise to fame in the world of high fashion he'd claimed in job interviews to have attended Parsons School of Design in New York City, but failed to reveal he'd graduated in architecture. It hadn't stopped him working for Gucci and Yves Saint Laurent before launching his eponymous luxury brand. Damian wondered where the certificate was, guessing Lewis had ripped it up and tossed it in a skip somewhere because it didn't fit with his ever-evolving image. Well, his image was well and truly fucked now, wasn't it? And he'd only himself to blame. Shame!

He realised what he was thinking and stopped, suddenly ashamed. Lewis was in trouble, falling apart, and here he was gloating when he should've been supporting him, getting on with running Stone Free, and hoping he sorted himself out. That's what a real friend would do.

27

There were no lights on in the house in Sherbrooke Avenue. The Victorian building stood against the night sky, a silent sentinel coldly impervious to my pain. The red Golf I remembered all too well wasn't in the drive and from where I stood across the street, panic stirred in my chest.

He wasn't there. Lewis Stone wasn't there.

Anxiety mixed with disbelief in me at his ability to leave the mess he'd caused behind and go on living as though nothing of importance had occurred. An honourable man would've admitted his fault, owned his actions, and taken the consequences. Which said everything that needed saying about Lewis Stone. And now he'd gone, or so it seemed. I felt a cynical smile twist my mouth; someone with this guy's resources could evade the legal repercussions of his reckless-ness, take off, maybe to the other side of the world, and never be seen again.

The headlights of an approaching car forced me into the shadow of a tree until it passed, giving me enough time to regain perspective and recognise I was making stupid assumptions and coming to conclu-sions driven by fear. It was midnight; Stone wasn't home. So what?

On Google I'd discovered he was single – he could be anywhere.

I crossed the deserted street and walked up the gravel drive to the front door, every noisy step roaring in my ears. I swallowed my mounting terror and peered through the bay window into a room filled with the vague outlines of chairs and a table – prob-ably where Stone entertained his entitled friends. But for sure the death of an innocent woman under the wheels of their host's car wouldn't be a topic of con-versation.

The house towered above me as I crept round it, bent low, one hand against the wet sandstone to stop me from falling. I pulled Molly's tartan scarf up over my mouth and nose and scanned the building for CCTV cameras. If there were any, I didn't spot them, though with a property like this it would be foolish to assume they weren't there. When I reached the back of the building I stopped and listened, hearing only the sound of my own ragged breathing. Darkness stretched to where I'd watched Stone through the glass of the conservatory. Not tonight. Wherever he was it wasn't here and, once again, I questioned what I was doing acting out a vendetta without a clue how it would end.

28

The drive from the city had taken the best part of five hours; Lewis was stiff and tired. He hadn't been in a hurry, drinking in the spectacular scenery as the stress fell away. Until he entered Glencoe. The forbidding 'Glen of Weeping', infamous for treachery and murder, was as intimidating as he remembered and Lewis was conscious of a shift, subtle at first, in his emotions, beginning as a growing sense of unease in the pit of his stomach. Suddenly, lightning flashed behind the steep volcanic sides of the valley, thunder growled like an angry god, and the heavens opened. He turned on the windscreen wipers and the headlights. Bad weather would only slow his progress and it would be dark before he got to where he was going.

From nowhere, the terrible sense of responsibility he was trying to escape seeped into his bones and everything he was running from was there in the car with him. In seconds, a panic attack hit, reducing him to a frightened child and he cried out. Pins and needles started in his fingers and moved up his arm, until he couldn't feel his hands, while his heart pounded so hard he thought it might burst from his chest. And through it all he caught a glimpse of the confident can-do guy he'd been before the accident and wanted him back. Lewis pulled onto a patch of scrubby grass near bright water gushing over a stony riverbed, rested his head on the steering wheel and waited for the attack to pass. When it did, he sat up straight and drove on into the storm.

Halfway across the steel-box truss of the Ballachulish Bridge, the slopes on the far side of the narrow strip between Loch Leven and Loch Linnhe morphed from dark green to a vibrant purple. Moments later, the sun, weak but welcome, lit the hillside.

Lewis saw it as a portent; all he had to do was hold it together and it would be all right.

The road, not far from the sea, bent inland the closer he got to the village. He'd emailed Flora, the housekeeper who looked after the old place, warning her he was coming up, guessing she'd need time to take care of the tasks she'd avoided; Lewis didn't blame her – he'd have done the same – and so long as the place was warm he could forgive everything else. Flora Cameron was probably in her seventies, born and bred in Mallaig, two miles from Morar. She'd been to Edinburgh twice in her life, hadn't fancied it, and never gone back. Her explanation was simple and unapologetic: 'Too many folk.' Flora claimed to be a direct descendent of Donald Cameron, the 22nd Lochiel, and was fiercely proud of her heritage. Most people in these parts told a similar story. It wasn't wise to question the truth of the tales, unless you didn't mind being snubbed and refused service in the village pub.

Lewis remembered you could sometimes see the island of Rhum from the shore. Not today. Or tomorrow, if the forecast was to be believed. As a child he'd loved walking along the paths, exploring the crystal-clear water that grew black as pitch further out, occasionally spotting otters and sea eagles, or listening to some worthy swear to have seen Morag, the monster in the loch, for a young boy's benefit. That appreciation had drastically diminished during his teenage years when a two-week visit to this remote part of the country had seemed to the restless spirit of someone no longer a boy and not yet a man like a prison sentence. But the memories were good memories.

* * *

The loch was flat-calm and silent under a cloudless sky, the morning air crisp, still heavy with the chill of night. Out on the water, a black-backed gull skimmed the surface and banked towards the sea a few hundred yards beyond the western tip. It was a few minutes after eight o'clock and in the boat at the end of the wooden jetty the boy zipped up his windcheater and rubbed his cold hands.

Lewis was eleven years old – the only child of Paul and Aileen. Young Lewis had been out many times with his father but this would be his first try at casting from the drifting boat and sensing for himself the tension in the line as a suspicious brown trout nipped the edges; he wasn't sure he'd like it. It wasn't the limbless grubs, disgusting though they were – he was used to them – but the thought of beating the head of a living thing with one of the rocks kept in the bottom of the boat repelled him, a view his father didn't share because doing this together was important. Not to Lewis – he was too young for very much to be important – to his father.

On the shore, Aileen stood on her tiptoes to kiss her husband's cheek. He whispered something Lewis couldn't hear, making her laugh, then took from her the thermos and the sandwiches in the paper bag that would be their lunch. Under his arm he held two fly rods – the smaller one brand new and less weighty than his own, bought specially for the occasion – and the plastic box of larvae. Paul Stone had no idea of his son's feelings about his hobby; more than a hobby, a passion. For him, teaching his boy to fish was a bonding experience, something they'd both remember for the rest of their lives; he wanted it to be perfect. If they were lucky enough to catch anything, the camera in the pocket of his canvas jacket would capture the moment on film. His footsteps slapped against the slatted jetty, there was a light in his eyes, and he grinned, showing straight white teeth. Everything he'd ever need or ever needed was here and if the fish were jumping, God could claim his soul any time.

Behind him, Lewis's mother waited to wave off her men, wiping her hands on her apron, face glowing with a nervous pride. Her husband handed the food and the rods to his boy and stepped into the boat. It rocked from side to side. Lewis panicked and grabbed hold of the hull. His father shook his head. 'Easy, easy. It'll take more than a wobble to sink this old tub, but if we are going down, two feet from the jetty's about the safest place we could be. Relax, you're safe, nothing's going to happen. Nothing ever does up here.'

Near the middle of the loch, Paul Stone put on sun-

glasses and gazed over the water. 'Okay,' he said, 'we'll give it a try, see what those fish are doing, eh?' He turned to his son. 'Rule number one: this isn't a test, something you have to pass. It's fun, pure and simple. If it isn't, forget about me, forget about anybody, don't do it.'

Lewis lied, 'I want to do it. I want to learn. I want to be as good as you.'

'In that case, let's get started.'

For the first half-dozen attempts, he quietly encouraged the boy to use less power and let his wrist do the work, smiling to himself as he got the hang of it. Getting him a lighter-weight rod had been the right thing. He whispered in his ear, guiding the motion of his hand. 'Remember, there's fly casting and there's fly fishing. It isn't about distance, there are trout right under us. Take it easy. Too many casts scatters them and tires your shoulder muscles. Give the fish a chance to see what we've got for it.'

Lewis's expression taking it all in was comically solemn. Paul Stone was reminded of doing this with his own father and smiled. After they'd eaten their sandwiches and drunk the sweet tea, Lewis sat in the stern, trailing his fingers in the dark water sunlight had turned liquid gold. He scrunched up his face, a sign his father recognised: a question was on the way.

'Why is it so black?'

Paul Stone answered without having to think about it. *'Because it's so deep; some say the deepest in the country.'*

'How deep is it?'

'They say it's three hundred and ten metres – a long way down.'

Lewis's curiosity wasn't easily satisfied. *'What made it?'*

'A glacier gouged out the earth. When it melted, it formed the loch.'

'And is that why it's so cold?'

'Yes.' His father laughed. *'That and the fact this is Scotland. It's always cold up here.'*

He drained his cup and emptied the dregs over the side. *'Want to try again or have you had enough for one day?'*

'Try again.'

* * *

His mother was where they'd left her, a distant figure on the shore standing on the same spot as though she hadn't moved. In the prow, a grinning Lewis proudly held the three brown trout up. When they got to the jetty he raced towards her, shouting, *'I did it! I did it!'*

She drew him to her; he felt the comforting warmth of her body and didn't resist. She glanced over his head at her husband. *'That's wonderful, darling. It really is.'*

Paul Stone matched his son's grin with his own. 'Seems we have a fisherman on our hands.'

Lewis's mother teased him. 'Will you cook them, or do you want me to do that bit?'

The boy hadn't forgotten his father tapping the trout just above their eyes to stun them with the rock, then taking a knife from his pocket and pushing it into the creature's skull to destroy the brain. Acid had risen in his throat as he'd watched him cut the gills and the tails and toss each fish into a bucket, splattering the ice at the bottom red.

'No,' he said. 'You cook them, Mum.'

* * *

Later, he'd helped her wash the dishes and put them away, happy to be involved, as happy as he'd ever been, then or since, and when his parents thought he wouldn't notice, a look passed between them, a secret only they knew. It had been years before Lewis would understand that look, or why they'd bought the abandoned property far from Glasgow and come to it so often.

It was their sanctuary. Now, it would be his.

29

The previous night had been an inflection point in the secret war I was waging against Lewis Stone, a war he wasn't aware was even going on. My midnight stalking hadn't impacted him and, apart from the KILLER note I'd pushed through his letter box, so far as he was concerned, Byres Road was in the past.

Of course, the explanation might be simple: Stone could've been at a party, out of town, or staying with a friend for a few days and be back in Sherbrooke Avenue soon.

My gut told me it wasn't so. He'd gone. The next challenge was to discover where to.

Stone Free was listed in the Scottish Business Directory as operating from Hillington Park, Scotland's largest industrial estate to the west of the city. I took the M8 towards the airport and left the motorway at junction 26. Six minutes later I was in the car park across from the main entrance. I smiled a smile that had nothing to do with humour; in the space of a few hours I'd decided to play detective, a role I was singularly unsuited for, and already the doubt that was never far away crept in to remind me how insane this was. I scanned the lines of vehicles; his wasn't there, and the already fragile belief in what I was doing weakened a little more.

In my haste to know Lewis Stone's whereabouts, I'd jumped the gun. If I truly intended to do him harm I needed to be patient; calculating and measured instead of reacting to every turn of events. Returning to the house to establish if the murdering bastard really wasn't there was the logical step. After that, I had no idea and, alone with my thoughts, I questioned everything. *Do him harm*: was that really where this was going? And if the opportunity ever came, could I actually hurt another human being? Who would I be doing it for? Certainly not Sam, and Molly was... I struggled with the word and settled for wasn't here, so not for her. That just left me.

Letting go was hard because in my mind what had happened was unfair and I was angry, wanting to take it out on the world. A picture of me as a young girl came into my head: a friend had stolen my favourite doll and refused to give it back to me so I'd hit her. Mum had seen us from the window and come rushing out. She'd taken me in her arms and whispered, 'Forgive her. Something made her do a bad thing.'

I'd started to cry. 'She stole my doll. That's not fair.'

My mother knelt beside me and lovingly smoothed my hair. 'Life isn't always fair, baby, but we still have to forgive people who hurt us.'

My mother had been wise and I knew if she were here with me now she'd tell me the same thing. But she wasn't. And I wasn't that obedient child any more.

Damian was angry and made no effort to disguise it. The man on the other end of the line hadn't bothered to get back to him, an indication, once again, of where his loyalty really lay. Stone Free wasn't a big enough concern to have its own legal department: when that day came it wouldn't be Shawcross heading it. Damian kept a hold on his temper but failed to dilute his irritation. 'I'm going to be generous and assume you didn't get the message I'd called.'

Oliver glossed over his annoyance at the implication Damian had been overlooked. Every client he'd ever worked with demanded to be at the head of the queue. Lewis had been no different; his partner was carrying on the tradition but the time to put him in his place would come. For the moment, the lawyer replied without a trace of rancour, doing what he did best: pouring oil on troubled waters. 'I've been busy, rushed off my feet, actually. I'm here now so how can I help you?'

'You can answer a question, Oliver.'

'My pleasure. What do you want to know?'

Damian gritted his teeth. 'Did he sign? Did Lewis sign?'

'Yes, he did. I have it in front of me. Shall I have a copy couriered over to you? Before you get it, remember, this is Lewis Stone we're dealing with.'

'What does that mean?'

'He did what Lewis always does.'

'Which is?'

'Exactly what he wanted.'

Damian sat up straight in his chair, already on edge. Oliver said, 'He's agreed to step down. No problem there, that part wasn't an issue with him. Really because he recognises it's for his own good as well as the business.'

'Then what was an issue?'

'The timing. He's sticking to three months.'

'Fuck!'

'Yes. And trust me, you're fortunate to be getting that out of him. It'll take more than a break, no matter what length, to sort out whatever's wrong. In my view, and it pains me to say it, you were right: he needs psychiatric help. Maybe it would've been wiser to have him sectioned. He's paranoid. Doesn't trust anybody, certainly not me. He imagines the world's against him and he's striking out. I'm afraid you and I are in the front line.'

Damian had stopped listening, still dwelling on the timescale.

'Has he actually gone? I have to know he's out of the picture and won't come bursting through the door when I'm on a conference call with the people from L-A. Please tell me that isn't how it's going to play out. Because if there's even a chance of him fucking this up any more than he already has...'

Oliver heard the frustration in the other man's voice and understood where he was coming from. 'I wish I could reassure you. Whatever I said wouldn't be the truth. In his state of mind, anything's possible. Except, he definitely won't be MD for at least twelve weeks. That should be enough to get the distribution deal back on track. After that... who knows?'

'Did he say anything else?'

Oliver repeated Lewis's threat that when he came back, Stone Free would be seeking new legal representation.

'Really?'

'The man I spoke to yesterday is untethered from reality. Unless Lewis takes some serious action to improve his mental health it will only get worse. My guess is you won't be seeing him soon. In the meantime, you're the boss at a critical moment in the company's development, and three months is a long time in business. Any business. A lot can happen.'

Damian cut the line and drummed his fingers on the desk. 'Yeah, Oliver, that's what I'm afraid of.'

31

Lewis Stone's house was no different than it had been the last time and dread stirred in me. I imagined him on a beach, in Barbados or St Kitts, a mojito in one hand, smearing coconut tanning oil on his glistening chest with the other, eyeing bronzed, scantily clad women from behind his Ray-Bans with not a care in the world, while I chased my tail in chilly Glasgow. I closed my eyes, despairing, struggling with the intensity of my anger and the need to avenge my wronged sister, physically and emotionally exhausted by it. The hatred I felt for Lewis Stone wasn't sustainable. Eventually, the thing eating me from within would force me to accept the unacceptable, that his kind rarely answered for their crimes. To me, Molly had been special. In reality, she'd been an ordinary woman whose death had already been forgotten by the system.

I lowered my head, defeat eroding my confidence, sapping my faith, Sam's words echoing in my head: '... anger you've bottled up over Freddy?'

Deep down I knew she was right. Truthfully, it made no difference. If my rage gave me closure for Molly, then so be it – I'd take it.

This visit confirmed what I'd already known in my heart: the house was a bust, which meant the factory in Hillington was all I had left. And the problem that presented was self-evident. Showing up, demanding they tell me where their boss had gone, wasn't an approach likely to bear fruit. Expecting them to give out personal information to a stranger was beyond naïve. My only option was to sit in the car and wait, trusting that eventually Stone would show up.

Bellahouston Park was a verdant oasis in the city. For the second time, I drove along its eastern edge and swung left into Paisley Road West, barely aware of where I was going as wave after wave of negative thoughts bombarded my brain. I had almost decided to turn the car round when I spotted Helen Street police station. All the resentments, all the anger against the officers who'd let Stone walk away from the accident came flooding in and I kept going.

One way or another Lewis Stone would pay for what he'd done.

The Stone Free number was already in my directory. When I dialled, the receptionist was professional, business-like and friendly, in that order. I steadied myself, trying to sound breezy. 'Lewis Stone, please.'

'Who's calling?'

'Alex Kennedy.'

Said with a confidence I didn't feel.

'I'm sorry, Mr Stone isn't available. Can somebody else help you?'

I did a passable job of feigning disappointment. 'I'm a friend so, no. When will he be around?'

I guessed what the receptionist's answer would be. 'Unfortunately, I don't have that information. If you hold I'll call his secretary, though I understand we aren't expecting him. You can leave a message. What was the name again?'

'It's okay, I'll catch up with him later.'

I opened the car window, strangely calm despite the setback.

32

Colin MacLean had never met Lewis Stone. Nevertheless, the two shared the characteristic drive of the entrepreneur. With that elusive element in their DNA, working wasn't a chore, it was a drug, a habit they had no intention of quitting. Today, that wasn't true. Colin had dragged himself through the morning, fighting to concentrate on the latest development project, struggling even to care about it, before finally admitting defeat and giving up. MacLean Property would have to get along without him for an afternoon.

At one o'clock he left the office – unheard of for him – and went to the hotel. On the third floor of the Hilton, he lay on the bed, hands behind his head, and stared at the ceiling. He didn't have to be here. Sam hadn't wanted him to leave and was willing to try again. All it would take was a phone call and he'd be back – which was fine in the moment but not a solution for the long term. This was a consequence of his choice and it was a hard one to live with.

No one needed to remind him of their history; it was burned in his brain. He'd been a young single guy, out with his mates chasing women every weekend, when he'd met a bubbly ball of female energy called Sam. Since that night he'd had highs and lows. Life had happened to him and kept on happening; he'd lost both his parents within a month of each other, moved houses, got the sack from a couple of jobs because he didn't like taking orders, eventually starting the business that now carried his name.

Sad times. Turbulent times. Through it all Sam had been with him – by his side at his mother's grave, at his father's four weeks after that, settling for an impersonal register office ceremony instead of the chapel wedding she'd imagined as a little girl and had her heart set on. Then, after they were married, suffering one rented couldn't-swing-a-cat flat after another, missing out on holidays – even a honeymoon – so he could sink money into his burgeoning enterprise.

Most women would've complained, harangued their husbands with reminders of promises made in the dark, maybe even cut their losses and ended the relationship altogether.

Not Sam. She'd understood and been there for him. Always.

Colin shrugged on his jacket ready to go down-stairs to the restaurant and eat alone, still thinking about what had been lost. He'd adored her. How could something so strong have died? But it had. Colin wasn't in love with his wife and no amount of nice memories about what they'd had would change that.

* * *

Sam hadn't bothered to go to bed – she couldn't see the point. Without Colin, what they'd built together felt like a cold, impersonal shell. A house not a home. In the early hours – the bottle and a half of Rioja she'd downed meant she couldn't be sure exactly when – she'd dragged a duvet from one of the spare rooms and buried herself, fully clothed, under it. Now it was morning, and, though she was exhausted, Sam couldn't pretend to be asleep any longer.

She sat up, stiff and sore, ignoring the pounding in her head and the queasiness in her stomach, and studied the lounge through gritty eyes. The expensive furnishings mocked her. The Boca do Lobo couch she was lying on, bought from Harrods on a mad, joyous, weekend spending spree that had ended in the Mayfair hotel with the unhurried sex of two people who understood each other's bodies better than anyone alive. She saw the hand-drawn wallpaper Colin had hated but she'd *had* to have – an arm and a leg from Abigail Edwards.

Her dry lips twisted in a sad lopsided smile. He'd been right about the wallpaper; it was bloody hideous.

How often had he given in to her? Sam knew the answer. Too fucking often.

Everywhere she looked, in every corner and cranny, were the shallow trappings of her failed marriage and the question that haunted her. Why hadn't she been enough for him?

Colin had loved her once, but he'd left because she'd driven him away.

Or had she? Was that actually how it had been? For sure, she was nobody's idea of a saint. She could be irritable, even angry, over little things. Colin caught the brunt of it, because he was there. Though it hadn't been her who'd dimmed the spark between them – he'd managed that all on his own. And when it was slipping away, she'd tried, God knows she'd tried. Sam didn't want to go there; it was too hurtful. Her cheeks burned with the memory of her last demeaning attempt to win him back. It hadn't worked because sex wasn't the answer. Their desperate coupling, driven by pain rather than love, was regretted the moment they'd rolled apart empty and embarrassed and further from each other than they'd ever been.

On the bed, Sam had closed her eyes so she didn't have to look at him and be reminded of what had been lost. For his part, he'd dressed quickly, unable to escape fast enough. His words of apology had been sincere, but like light from a dead star they'd arrived too late.

The lounge was a mess. But if it was bad, the kitchen was worse. It could've been Molly living here instead of her house-proud twin. Sam despised women who could only function with a man at their side. Weak, pathetic females. That wasn't her. Or, it hadn't been until she'd found herself alone and lonely and scrambling to make sense of everything that had happened. Opening Colin's mobile, scrolling through his texts, had been a mistake, an impulse she'd take back if she could. And for the first time in her comfortable, protected life Sam had realised there were things in the world it was better not to know: what she'd read was right at the top of the list.

She retched and stumbled to the bathroom. When the heaving subsided she stood in front of the mirror and focused on the disaster staring back. Fuck's sake! No wonder he hadn't wanted her. Would anybody ever want her again? Colin was a handsome man; he'd met someone else before and would again. Some bitch, dressed to the nines, would flash her tits and that would be it.

She bowed her head; she was wrong. This was already it.

Her husband had gone and he wasn't coming back.

33

I filtered out the distant hum of the motorway and studied the sleek lines of the steel-and-brick building with Stone Free written across it in large, dark-blue letters, not sure why I was here again. Except, no, that wasn't right, I understood exactly why: the factory was the only connection I had to Lewis Stone. Sooner or later he'd pull into the car park and my plan would be back on track. My lips parted in a cynical half-smile – calling it a plan was a massive exaggeration. There was no 'plan'.

I hadn't felt good about leaving my colleagues at the pharmacy and taking an extended leave of absence, though it was for the best. Those last months with Freddy had been heart-breaking but I hadn't given up, even when I'd known it was hopeless. I wouldn't be giving up on my sister, either.

Sam felt differently about it and for the first time I saw the tragic coincidence we shared: we'd both lost our sister and our husbands, except there was no chance of my Freddy coming back and she already had Colin to hate. There had been no word from her and guilt rippled through me. I had two sisters. Two! Not just one. All my focus was on Molly. It didn't take a genius to suss the other twin needed help. Sam was desperately unhappy but at least she was alive.

I yawned and checked my watch: 3.25 p.m. Stone could show up any time. The cynical smile returned – who the hell did I think I was kidding? My fantasy about him sunning himself on a beach was probably more accurate than I knew.

A wiser lady would do as Sam had done: move on. I yearned to be that woman. And I could be – the car key was in the ignition. All it needed was a flick of my wrist to switch it on, drive away, and not look back. Perhaps, as time passed, I'd realise it had been the right decision and let Molly rest in peace. If God existed – and I was far from certain – he'd judge Lewis Stone and find him wanting. I caressed the stubby black barrel, closer than I'd ever been to quitting.

A mobile catering van appeared in the rear-view

mirror and rolled to a stop across from the factory. Workers who'd been expecting it emerged from nearby buildings and formed a queue, chatting while they waited to be served. Clearly, for some, the van was the highlight of their afternoon. I sat up straight, pulse racing, eyes on the Stone Free building.

The glass doors pushed open and two females came out into the light, one wearing black trousers and a white blouse tied at the front, the other a jacket and matching skirt. I leaned forward to get a better look, unsure if I could believe what I was seeing. The figure was fuller but the face had hardly changed. I dredged my memory for a name – Rose, Roberta; it wouldn't come. The woman stood in line with her colleague, counting coins into her palm, brushing her long auburn hair over her shoulder.

Maybe it was the gesture because, suddenly, I remembered: Rachel – last seen near the back of the class in a chemistry lecture at Caledonian Uni. The girl must've dropped out and no wonder: the MPharm degree was a demanding four-year slog I'd only just survived.

Obviously, Rachel hadn't.

By five o'clock, the temperature had plummeted, a sheen of frost covered the road, and the sky above Hillington was a black void: Scotland in February. I sat behind the wheel, scanning the faces coming out of the factory into the night. The rest of the afternoon since the catering van's visit had passed quickly, and, though my hands and feet were cold, I felt better than I had outside Stone's empty house. My plan had shifted from emotional notions of revenge and threatening notes. Now, it had a form. That it depended on a woman I hadn't seen in years and didn't know from a hole in the wall wasn't something I allowed myself to dwell on.

Rachel – I couldn't remember her second name – wore a three-quarter-length fawn coat. At the door, she stopped to say goodnight to a colleague, waved her on her way and turned, for a second staring directly at my car before giving her attention to pulling on gloves. I acted on reflex, ducked, and cursed my stupidity. What an idiot! Get a grip!

Unaware she was being spied on, she crossed to the car park, still fiddling with the gloves, and got into a Mazda. The headlights came on and she settled herself, checking the mirror, fastening her seat belt, letting the windscreen clear before moving. I watched her go through her routine, revelling in the small triumph blind faith and perseverance had brought me. The Mazda edged out, tyres crunching on the frozen asphalt. I followed, keeping my distance. The disappointment of Sherbrooke Avenue and the realisation that Stone had left felt a lifetime ago.

A difficult day – a hard day to go through – was coming to an end. Emotionally, I was exhausted – there would be no trouble sleeping tonight – but it wasn't over just yet. There was one last thing to do and I was confident I'd finish the day more hopefully than I'd started it. This stranger from the past could give that to me. I gripped the wheel with both hands, slipped in behind her, and joined the line of rush-hour traffic crawling towards the city.

34

For Lewis Stone, returning to the house on the shores of Loch Morar was like coming home; the nearer he got, the better he felt. With every mile, the events in Glasgow faded. He let the sea air in, taking one deep breath after another into his lungs, shaking his head at his stupidity, silently chiding himself for not having done this sooner. Why hadn't he? Lewis knew the answer: his life had been dedicated to the business; everything else had come a poor second behind Stone Free. But what was done was done. Here, in the place his parents had loved, he'd rebuild his strength, realign his priorities, and return stronger than ever.

Two miles beyond Arisaig, a sign for the hamlet of Portnaluchaig told him he was almost there. He left the A830, bypassing Morar village with night falling like a cloak around him, hugging the north shore through the tiny settlement of Bracora to Swordland. He smiled at the memory of the boyish imaginings that had conjured demons, magicians, and warriors to inhabit these places with such evocative names. When the road turned towards Tarbet on the southern edge of Loch Nevis, Lewis parted company with it and followed the line of the water along a dirt track, bumping over rocks and broken pieces of birch and rowan, able to see only as far as his headlights allowed. The twin beams cast shapes and shadows as the Golf bounced and bucked over the hard ground. Lewis tightened his grip on the wheel, his concentration absolute. It had to be.

He wasn't alone: a tawny owl swooped low across his windscreen, pounced on something scurrying on the forest floor in a precision strike and carried it off between its talons. Lewis had just witnessed a master predator at work. Further on, he startled a pair of red deer, a large stag and a smaller hind, quietly grazing in a stand of pine. The male raised its great antlers, regarding the intruder with curiosity, before crashing deeper into the safety of the trees followed by the female.

After what seemed an eternity, the track opened

into a clearing and he saw the house. Flora Cameron came to the door, wiping her hands on her jacket, and for a moment Lewis was reminded of his mother. The highland woman had gained weight, the pleasant face fuller than Lewis remembered, her dark hair faded to grey. She eyed him critically up and down and spoke, her accent lilting and soft, unlike the guttural consonants of Glasgow.

'So, you made it. I was starting to worry you'd changed your mind. We haven't seen you in a while.'

'I took my time.'

'How was the drive?'

Lewis unloaded his cases and closed the boot. 'Fine. It was fine'. He grinned. 'Apart from the last bit. I'd forgotten how isolated we are up here.'

Flora tilted her head the way the stag had done. 'Isolated? That's a lowlander speaking. Folk round these parts don't think there's much to miss in a city. Otherwise, they'd all live down beside you, wouldn't they?'

Wisely, he let it go. This part of the country had a rich history; whatever else was lacking, pride wasn't in short supply.

'I must say your email surprised me, Mr Stone.'

'Why?'

'Your mother and father came here all the time. How long has it been since they passed?'

'Almost ten years.'

Flora shook her grey head. 'We assumed you'd forgotten us.'

'Not at all; I've been busy.'

'I thought the weather might be keeping you away.' She drew her arms round her and Lewis caught the glint of a wedding ring on her finger. 'Winters can be hard. Too hard for most people from the south. The tourists tend to wait for summer.'

Lewis smothered a smile. Flora Cameron hadn't liked his 'isolated' comment. Calling him a tourist was her subtle way of evening the score. His family had owned this house for two and a half decades. Pointing that out wouldn't alter the opinion of a woman whose ancestors stretched back 250 years and lived beside a loch formed by a glacier. In her view he was and always would be an outsider. It wasn't a battle Lewis could win and he didn't try.

She gestured over her shoulder to the house. 'The roof was leaking. I had it repaired. And rain was coming in under the back door. That's been sorted, too.'

'Thanks, how much do I owe you?'

She frowned. 'I haven't counted it up.'

Lewis didn't believe her. A cousin – they were all cousins up here – would've done the work for next to nothing. Flora hadn't decided exactly how much to overcharge him. When she had, she wouldn't be slow to tell him.

She hurried on. 'I've lit the fire as you requested. You'll find coffee in the cupboard – only instant, I'm afraid. We don't do the fancy kinds you get where you're from. There's half a dozen eggs and milk for the morning in the fridge along with a beef stew. If you're staying longer than a week, you'll be needing more wood. I can arrange that, if it suits you. Or, perhaps, like your father, you'd prefer to cut your own?'

The second reference to his parents in as many minutes struck a chord and, suddenly, Lewis wanted her to go. He said, 'I'll attend to it but thanks for the casserole, Flora. Much appreciated.'

'Och, it's no trouble. Can't have you telling those Glasgow people we don't know how to treat our guests. That would never do.'

35

Keeping Rachel in sight wasn't difficult, even in the darkness. She drove cautiously, never more than 50 mph, happy to stay in the inside lane. At the approach to the Kingston Bridge her Mazda left the M8 for the M74 until junction 2A, when she took the exit for Cambuslang. Ten minutes later she pulled into the driveway of a whitewashed house across from the park. I watched her get out and go inside as self-loathing washed over me. Spying on Lewis Stone, the man who'd killed my sister, wasn't normal. Hurt, confused and half mad with grief, I had found it easy for me to justify, at least to myself, but this...

There was no other word for it.

This was *insane*.

I pressed my fists against my temples, angry at myself and my ludicrous behaviour. Putting notes through a letter box and running away had been crazy enough. Rachel whatever-her-name-was had nothing to do with Molly's death. Her only crime was working for Stone Free. Invading her privacy wasn't right and was probably a giant waste of time – the chances of her knowing where her bastard of a boss had gone were so low as to be not worth considering. Yet, here she was, the unwitting victim of a stalker.

It couldn't go on. It wouldn't go on. And if, as I suspected, Rachel hadn't a clue about Stone's whereabouts it would be time to pause and consider the wisdom of continuing with this one-woman vendetta. The police were satisfied no law had been broken and Sam believed they were right. The truth I was reluctant to face was that, with or without Molly, the world kept turning. I engaged the gears and started for Shawlands. Tomorrow was another day but if it didn't take me nearer to finding Lewis Stone I'd accept what everybody else had accepted – that Byres Road had been a tragic accident for all concerned and get on with the rest of my life.

Wherever she was, Molly would understand and maybe time would erase the memories for me.

...coming down the steps laughing, Molly and Sam

winding each other up; slipping on the ice and Sam catching me; the beggar's empty red-rimmed eyes and his mongrel wagging its tail as my fingers ran through its coat; Molly falling into the road and Sam's outstretched hand trying to save her like she'd done with me; the screech of brakes...

36

The sound of a car door slamming wakened Sam from a troubled sleep. Headlights strafed the wall above the fireplace, illuminating the Linda Charles limited-edition prints Colin had bought for her three years ago as a surprise birthday present. There were two of them, in matching frames: the first, *I Bet You Look Good on the Dancefloor*, was from the Arctic Monkeys' song the DJ had been playing when they'd met in The Garage at the bottom of Sauchiehall Street. The second, *Lucky Man* – a title borrowed from The Verve – was her favourite. In it, a guy in a white tuxedo knelt behind a beautiful woman, kissing her neck, while she leaned back and offered herself to him. The chemistry between the lovers mirrored the lust they'd slaked later that night in Colin's cramped Hillhead bedsit and countless nights since.

Out in the street, the unknown driver ground the gears and accelerated, returning the room to darkness. Her addled brain struggled to process what had become of her and Colin. How could something so rare and fine have died? What had she—?

Sam cut the inquisition short as clarity arrived in a blinding flash of anger.

'Stop! Just fucking stop it! I didn't do anything! He did! I'm not a perfect wife. All right, I admit it.' She fell to her knees, sobbing uncontrollably. 'But what have I actually done wrong?'

Her question went unanswered, yet she knew. It was Colin who'd been unfaithful, not her. He'd walked out on the marriage when she'd been prepared to fight to save it. And, yeah, okay, he was a man. Men thought with their dicks, she got all that, but... did he have to have been such a bastard?

More than anything, Sam wished she didn't love him.

She ran the shower, thought about a drink and changed her mind. Seconds later, she was frantically sloshing amber liquid into a glass, her hand shaking like a hopeless alkie on the verge of the DTs. Getting drunk wasn't wise. Fuck it! It was a night for burning bridges; she'd deal with the consequences tomorrow. What was sauce for the goose...

Wherever her soon-to-be ex-husband was, he wouldn't be crying about his broken relationship or racking his brain about how it could be fixed. No chance. He'd be back to his old ways. Living it large. Out on the pull: Paul Smith suit, Armani shirt, Salvatore Ferragamo shoes; the full fucking bhoona! And the fortunate girl, because for certain there would be one, wouldn't be going back to a tatty bedsit in a West End tenement at the end of the evening.

Sam gulped down the whisky, desperately wanting to be that girl.

She let the hot water cascade over her skin, stinging her shoulders. It helped. Or maybe the booze was starting to work. When she'd towelled herself down, she threw on the silk dressing gown lying over a chair and refilled her glass halfway to the top. Whisky wasn't her usual poison; it would do the job. She studied her reflection in the dressing-table mirror: a slack-jawed, puffy-eyed hag twice her age stared at her, the history of a hard life written on her face.

Sam didn't spare herself. 'Christ Almighty! You're not going anywhere looking like that, lady.'

She lifted her mobile and punched in a number. A

disembodied voice on the other end of the line said, 'Mearns Taxis.'

'I'd like to order a car.'

'What time?'

'Nine, nine o'clock.'

That should be long enough to do something about the trainwreck in the mirror.

'Where to?'

'Into the city.'

'The city, fine, but where?'

'I haven't decided. When I do, I'll let you know.'

37

In the office in Hillington Park Industrial Estate, Tina sat in a chair, quietly fuming. She wasn't used to being kept waiting – even by the boss. She sighed loudly for the umpteenth time to let Damian know she was bored. He didn't lift his head from what he was doing and she went back to examining her nails, cursing him under her breath. Since their embarrassing public performance at the Christmas party, he'd had no time for her. A girl like Tina didn't need to put up with that. Lately, he'd been preoccupied with everything Stone Free. If it hadn't been for the kudos she'd earned from her workmates, she'd already have binned him and moved on.

She threw her hands down into her lap. 'What're you doing?'

Damian answered without taking his eyes off the task in front of him. As well as not being bright, Tina had the attention span of a fourteen-year-old. An explanation would be wasted on her so he didn't bother and said, 'Stuff.'

'What kind of stuff?'

'Stuff that needs to be done so everyone can keep getting their wages. Maybe you'd prefer I didn't bother?'

'It's Friday night. How much longer are you going to be?'

He felt his patience drain away and tried to call it back. 'Listen, Tina. If you imagine this is my idea of a good time, you're wrong. I can think of ten things I'd rather be doing.'

Tina realised she obviously wasn't one of them and felt angry at the insult. He might've been talking to the cleaner.

He said, 'You can head off home if you want. Call a taxi. Charge it to the company. I'll sign for it.'

'No, no, I'd rather stay.'

'Then, content yourself. Go on Tok Tok or whatever it's called and let me do my job.'

'TikTok.'

'Yeah, that. I'll be finished as soon as I can. Promise.'

The atmosphere in the office he'd started to think of as his lifted the moment the door closed behind her. Damian had expected the fling – because, as far as he was concerned, that was all it was and ever would be – would flame and burn and die a natural death without too much drama; he had enough to cope with handling the L-A situation.

A worm of anxiety slithered in his gut; something wasn't right. The conversation with Lassiter-Accardi's London representative had been strange, the reaction down the line not what he'd expected. Lewis's departure had been – there were no other words for it – coolly received, almost as though it was no longer a significant factor in getting the business they'd been discussing for months over the line. He went to the window and gazed through the glass at the night sky. The thing inside him moved; he felt sick. This wasn't how it was supposed to be. The deal had run aground at the eleventh hour on rumours about the stability of Stone Free's management. That doubt had been resolved. For Christ's sake! He was the one who'd resolved it. The Americans had nothing to worry about; they ought to have been delighted. So why weren't they?

The worm in his gut became a full-grown serpent as he tried and failed to unearth what had changed. Because something definitely had. Damian had spent most of the morning printing out the email trail between L-A and Stone Free, laying the pages on his desk, examining each of them to discover when exactly the tone of the correspondence had altered. The initial contact had come from Stone Free, introducing the small independent Scottish company to the retail giant, expressing the hope they might be able, at some unspecified point in the future, to do business together. Without serious capital injection, Stone Free had gone as far as it was going to go; they needed a break to take it to the next stage. He remembered the email well; he was the one who'd written it, drafting and redrafting the text until it hit the right note – the confidence of a brash young business aligning itself with the huge power of the American retailer.

Damian had expected a reply, though not so quickly. Three days later he'd found it in his inbox, signed by an L-A vice president called Marsha Winter. In a few brief, brisk paragraphs she'd told him Stone Free was one of several companies on her radar, congratulated him on the job they were doing over in Scotland, and echoed his hopes for the future. He hadn't allowed himself to get too excited. Americans liked flashy job titles. Every third person in the organisation was some sort of president; on its face it meant very little. A quick Google search filled in some of the details: Marsha Winter was Marsha Alicia Winter from Albany, New York, with more than a passing resemblance to a young Gladys Knight. She was forty-three and unmarried, a graduate of Columbia Business School, and, clearly, Marsha had been raised in a household that valued politeness, though, reading between the lines, he didn't sense a real interest from her end. He'd wondered if she could sing and forgotten about her.

He hadn't heard from the vice president again but five months later somebody called Franco Conti – another VP, of course – had written to him, and it had been obvious L-A had done their own research. The tone had sharpened. Damian Morton had begun to believe.

In Lewis's office he'd spoken that belief out loud. When asked for his gut feeling, he'd replied, 'I think they see us as innovative, ethical, and great from a marketing perspective. "Saving the World One Stitch at a Time". That kind of crap.'

Lewis had played devil's advocate. 'Okay, except there's a downside. Lassiter-Accardi's a big fish in a big pool. They didn't become that by giving anything away. They'll seduce us with figures, wave spread-sheets and projected global-volume sales we can only imagine under our noses, while they screw our margins to the floor. We could be the most successful business on the planet and have zero in the bank.'

'So, you're saying... what are you saying, Lewis?'

'Getting into bed with them could be the best and the worst thing for us. Overnight Stone Free clothes would be in thousands of outlets worldwide from Cardiff to Cape Town.' He'd raised a hand at the building they were in. 'This factory won't cope; we'll need new premises. Maybe down south. Maybe Vietnam, for fuck's sake. Immediately, we'll be in hock, more debt than we've ever dreamed of.'

'That's inevitable if we're to grow.'

'Agreed. Won't stop us waking up in a cold sweat at two o'clock in the morning, though, will it? Do you think it'll be worth it?'

Damian had hesitated. He'd done his homework; none of this had taken him by surprise. Lewis had been asking him to commit himself, to put his name behind it, and that wasn't something he'd been prepared to do alone. He'd qualified his reply. 'Worth it if two circumstances align and stay aligned, yes.'

'And those would be?'

Damian had paced the room, gathering his

thoughts. He'd said, 'In 1626 the Lenape Indians sold the land rights of an island to the Dutch for sixty guilders' worth of trinkets, a jar of mayonnaise, two pairs of wooden clogs, a loaf of wonder bread and a carton of Quaker oats.'

Lewis hadn't been in the mood for a history lesson. 'Get to the point, Damian.'

'The island was called Manna-hata. Today, better known as Manhattan. And my point is, we wouldn't be the first to be dazzled by shiny beads. Let's not be sweet-talked into becoming busy fools.'

'And the second?'

'A guarantee they won't back out without at least a year's notice. Otherwise, they could stop doing business with us any time they felt like it. We'd be landed with stock we can't sell, premises we don't need, and a mountain of debt we can't pay.' Damian had sat on the edge of the desk and toyed with a pen. 'Effectively, we would have put all of Stone Free's eggs in one basket. Their basket. L-A would be our biggest, maybe even our only, customer. We'd need them more than they needed us.'

Lewis had nodded. 'Spot on. A weak position in anybody's book. I totally agree, so if that's their proposal it has to be no. You and I could be back where we started, drinking on the slate in the Horseshoe, proving we were the losers everybody always thought we were. One more thing – the story you just told.'

'Yeah, what about it?'

'It isn't true. That version of history is designed to make us believe the Europeans were smart and they weren't. The Dutch made a mistake. They did a deal with the Canarsee people – probably the first Native Americans they came across. The problem was, the land didn't belong to them; they were just passing through it. And, in the long run, it didn't turn out cheap. The Dutch spent years in a series of battles with the tribes who actually *did* own Manna-hata.'

'Now it's my turn to ask what *you're* saying.'

'Simple. Never underestimate who you're doing business with.'

The door opened, bringing Damian back to the present. Tina had her coat on, her expression telling him everything he needed to know about their faltering relationship.

She said, 'Unless you're ready to come with me right now, I'm leaving.'

'I'm sorry, I really am. Lewis isn't here. I'm running the whole bloody show. Honestly, I'd much rather be spending the evening with you.' He kissed her cheek, pulled notes from his trouser pocket and pressed them into her hand. 'You enjoy yourself. I'll make it up to you. And while I'm slaving over this rubbish I'll be thinking of you.'

It was exactly what Tina had known he'd say and she didn't believe him. She took the money and gave a weak 'you're forgiven' smile. Except, he wasn't. Far from it. Her revenge would go unrecorded – he'd never know – but his neglect was going to cost him a helluva lot more than cash. Two hours from now, he'd still be here. By then, she'd have soaked in a hot bath, done her hair and her make-up, and be squeezing into the new 'little black number' she'd bought from Massimo Dutti in Buchanan Street. Later, a new lover would be between her thighs, somebody with his priorities straight. Tina smiled to herself – a lot more than his priorities.

Over Damian's shoulder his computer pinged; he had mail. He glanced at it, anxious for her to be gone, and hurried her out. 'I'll call tomorrow. Maybe we can do something. Lunch in the Ubiquitous Chip in Ashton Lane would be nice.'

She hesitated. 'The Chip? Yes, maybe. Just don't make it too early. A girl needs her beauty sleep.'

As the office door closed behind her, he opened the email. When he read the sender's name, his earlier frustration dissolved.

Marsha was back in touch.

38

Sam smoothed her dress, turned side on and admired the result in the mirror. Not bad, not bad at all. If that didn't do it, Scottish guys had lost it. Seeing herself lit up, she found it impossible to believe Colin had passed when it was there for him. The Colin MacLean she'd married would've had her on the floor, then carried her upstairs to their bedroom to finish the job. Foolish boy. He wouldn't get another opportunity. 'Plenty more fish in the sea,' her father used to say and, cliché or not, he'd been right. Tonight, his daughter intended to hook one of them.

She topped up her wine glass and drank half of it. In the early days, Colin had been happy with a few pints of lager with his mates. Her idea of a 'good time' was a couple of Carlsberg Specials while she was getting ready and vodka and soda water in the club. Sam had never liked the taste, but she'd read somewhere that the low sugar content got you drunk quicker, a major consideration back then. The success of the business had taken them from an ordinary couple to people who could afford the finer things in life: they lived in a house that was far too big, drove top-of-the-range gas-guzzling cars; Colin had acquired a taste for Johnnie Walker Blue Label and bought wine by the case from the Sunday Times Wine Club. Very posh. At a party, she'd overheard him discussing soil composition, the vine-growing advantages of long hot summers and rainy winters, and south-facing blah, blah, blah, with a tosser who knew less than he did.

Sam laughed and took another sip. What a fake. What a bloody poseur. What an absolute *loser* of a man. His 'knowledge' could be written on the back of a fag packet. Red or white or fucking rosé; chilled or unchilled or straight from the bottle. She knew all she needed to – how to drink the stuff.

That was what it was for, wasn't it? Everything else was insecure folk trying to impress each other.

She emptied her glass, refilled it to the brim, and took another look at her figure in the long mirror in the corner. Yes, oh yes, wherever Colin was tonight he wouldn't pull better than this. This was prime. Guys were thick, that was the truth. Out chasing hamburger when there was steak at home. For them, the grass was always greener, or slimmer, or younger – the idiots didn't realise when they were well off.

Hopefully, that criticism didn't apply to all of them. Because, although he didn't know it yet, some lucky bastard in Glasgow was about to hit the jackpot.

* * *

Colin pressed the TV remote and watched the screen on the wall fade to black. He'd lost the plot of the movie half an hour ago and hadn't tried to pick it up again. A semi-bright twelve-year-old could've written the script the D-list cast of no-talent nonentities delivered with the personality of a paper cup. Wooden and predictable. It was always the best friend or the brother who'd harboured a grudge for decades. Knowing that considerably narrowed the suspects and significantly spoiled the enjoyment.

He considered having another beer from the minibar and decided against it, but a couple of whiskies sounded good. Colin rolled off the bed and checked out the options. The selection wasn't great: two bog-standard blends and one of the cheaper malts he wouldn't have in the house. Except, he wasn't in the house, he was in a hotel room in Glasgow, bored and depressed, about to drink shit whisky. Colin broke the seal on one of them and went to the window. From the sixth floor, he had a clear view of the red tail lights on the M8 before the Kingston Bridge straddled the river. The last time he'd spent a Friday night as pointlessly as this he'd been in his teens, mooning over some girl he'd imagined he was in love with, and whose name he'd forgotten.

The bush telegraph was alive and well – it seemed his split with Sam was a hot topic on the wire. God alone knew how because he hadn't told anybody. Earlier in the evening three of his mates had called asking him to join them in the pub, offering to help him drown his sorrows. 'The best way to get over a woman,' one of them had suggested, 'is to find a replacement as soon as possible.' He'd confidently voiced his macho-idiot philosophy. 'Look at it like trading in a car. At first you're happy to have something to drive. Any old banger will do. Don't get me wrong. Not saying Sam's an old banger. Far from it.' He'd sniggered. 'You were punching above your weight that night, son. To tell the truth, when I saw she was with you I was jealous. But on the car thing, eventually you raise your expectations and go for something with a bit more under the bonnet, if you know what I mean.'

Colin knew what he meant and had wanted to deck him.

'In the end it comes down to what you're after – comfort or performance.'

That clown had been divorced three times and hadn't learned much from the experiences. According to the rumour mill, his fourth marriage was coming apart after seven turbulent months and his latest wife was back staying with her parents, which spoke volumes about *his* performance. Colin had his own problems without taking marital advice from a serial failure.

He put the miniature to his lips and drank. The alcohol tasted raw and burned his throat, a harsh reminder of why he didn't rate it. Colin pictured the barely opened bottle of Blue Label on the cabinet of the lounge in Newton Mearns – was it still there, or had Sam emptied it down the sink in a fit of rage?

A pang of regret passed through him; maybe he'd been wrong not to meet up with the boys. Anything would've been better than spending the night in this box. At least it would've been a laugh. He smiled a grim smile. Who was he kidding? No, it wouldn't. They were his friends and always would be but what they had in common was the past, not the present, and certainly not the future. If they were thrown together now, Colin wasn't sure he'd even like them. An hour or two in their company he could stand... just about. After that, he'd be faking it, looking at their faces, some he'd known from his school days, seeing them as they really were: sad bastards living lives of quiet desperation, working jobs they hated but couldn't afford to quit, married to women they didn't speak to most of the time, or divorced and visiting their kids every other weekend, while some fucker called Darren or Billy or Sean played happy families with the woman they'd once loved. When the booze started to take effect and the old jokes that hadn't been funny the first two dozen times were trotted out yet again, walking down memory lane would be more than he could stand, and he'd be forced to invent an excuse to leave, to get away. Despising himself for despising them.

A car raced across the bridge. Glasgow Airport was only ten or eleven miles further on. How easy it would be to fly somewhere, anywhere, and leave the mess he'd caused behind. And it had been him who'd caused it.

In a night of truths Colin didn't hold back from taking responsibility for his actions. Sam was the innocent party; the damage had been done by him. She'd been a good wife, a great wife even, supporting his dreams and mad ambition in the early days. Settling for less so he had more money to put into his business.

Her reward for standing shoulder to shoulder with him was to be despicably betrayed.

To claim in his defence he'd never meant to hurt her only added insult to the injury, even though it was true. The affair had started so innocently, but by the time he'd realised where it was leading he'd been in too deep and it was too late. Because, the worst thing – the very worst thing – had happened: he'd fallen in love. From that point on he could hardly look at himself in the mirror without wanting to be sick. Living a lie was cheating all of them. It couldn't go on.

Colin had planned to let Christmas go by before he told Sam it was over between them. The accident in Byres Road had changed all that. After it, she'd clung to him, needing more than ever to believe in *them*. Confessing would have finished her. So he'd done the only thing left – buried his feelings, and tried to move on. A flawed strategy, because falling in love with one person meant falling out of love with another, and no matter how much he denied it to himself, the flame had died and couldn't be rekindled.

Colin opened a second miniature and emptied it in one go, the cheap liquor spreading through him, clearing his brain, prompting a question he should've already asked himself.

How did she know?

The answer was shockingly obvious – she'd got hold of his mobile.

A blinding flash of clarity found Colin and he felt ill remembering exactly when it had happened. Thinking she'd already left, he'd taken a shower. When he'd come out wrapped in a towel, Sam had been in the room, yards from where he'd left his phone unguarded – something he never did. Her expression had been set in stone, her mouth twisted. At the time he'd put it down to the angry words they'd had earlier. But he'd been wrong; it hadn't been just another row in a long line.

Rage at his own stupidity erupted in him. Colin fired the empty bottle across the room, exploding it against the wall in a shower of glass shards, and fell onto the bed, head in hands, imagining the horror on his wife's face as she read the horny threats and graphic promises of lovers who couldn't keep their hands off each other.

He ran his fingers through his hair, closer to panic than he'd ever been. What had he done to her? Those exchanges were straight out of the bloody Kama Sutra.

His parting shot, reassuring her she'd be okay financially, returned to complete his shame. How very fucking generous of him. Everything he had he owed to her – the house, the business, the money in their joint bank account. And the deeper implications of the doomed affair rose to greet him. If she wanted to, Sam could ruin him.

* * *

Sam got out of the car and paid the driver. It had been years since she'd been alone in the city at this time. The booze she'd downed before leaving the house – three glasses; more than half a bottle – relaxed her enough to quell any anxiety she might otherwise have felt. Without it, she would've been nervous and on edge. Her and Colin's idea of a night in town was dinner – he liked Indian so probably that; Swadish in Merchant City was one of his recent favourites – then, a couple of drinks in Waxy O'Connor's or Gin71 in Renfield Street, and a taxi home before midnight to make love in the dark. In Waxy's, Colin would drop the wine-connoisseur malarkey and order Guinness, carefully drawing the creamy top into his mouth, leaving a white moustache on his top lip. Sam would laugh. He'd grin and make a funny face at her over the rim of the glass.

That was the real Colin MacLean, the most attractive man she'd ever met.

Impossible not to love.

Where had that guy gone?

She was wearing Christian Louboutin ankle boots, black calf leather and cotton, so extravagantly expensive she'd hidden them in the back of her wardrobe without telling Colin she'd bought them. The boots were sensational to look at, no doubt about that. Walking in four-inch heels on Glasgow's cracked pavements without falling over required the skill of a circus performer. Added to the wine they were an accident waiting to happen.

The stewards on the door watched her teeter towards them. Sober, this lady would have no problem finding a man, but beginning the night well-oiled was asking for trouble and begged the question: what kind of man? The inner city was a dangerous place for a female who'd started the party early. Dangerous and deceiving; the threat didn't always come from a hopped-up druggie in a back-street alley; sometimes it wore Armani or Jo Malone and paid with an Amex Black Card.

They let her pass. Saving lost souls wasn't the business they were in – if they turned away every woman with a drink in her, the place would be closed in a week and they'd all be out of a job.

Sam checked her coat at the cloakroom, went through a door and into a wall of sound. On the far side of the room people were on the dance floor, slow-motion mannequins in a rainbow of strobe light. She let her eyes adjust and made her way to the bar. The young guy behind the counter wore a white shirt open at the neck, sleeves neatly folded and rolled up to the elbows, and a gold crucifix on a chain round his neck.

He noticed Sam and smiled. 'What can I get you?'

'A white wine.'

'One white wine coming up. Sweet or dry?'

'Dry. No, wait, vodka and soda. In fact, make it a double.'

39

The flash of a thousand cameras froze the dancers in time. In the middle, Sam swayed to the music, eyes closed, arms outstretched, tears smudging her mascara and running down her face. The defiance dredged from the wreckage of a broken heart had ebbed away; pain and alcohol overwhelmed her. She pushed through the crowd to the booth in the corner and a bald-headed guy in a black T-shirt busy setting up the next sequence. The DJ's name was Gary. Every weekend – Friday, Saturday, and Sunday – this was his gig. Punters telling him what to play pissed him off. Requests were never welcome, although, to be fair, it depended on who was making them.

Sam shouted above the noise to get his attention. 'Hey! Hey!'

When he didn't hear, her fingers tightened into a fist and punched his shoulder. Gary's reaction was instant and angry. 'What the hell do you think you're doing?'

The question went unanswered as Sam said, 'Play the Arctic Monkeys.'

The words – as much of them as he could make out – were thick and slurred. The DJ saw the wild eyes, the black track lines on her cheeks, and realised she was wasted. Wasted women weren't his scene. Too much hassle. Far too much.

'What?'

'The music's crap. Put the Arctics on.'

'Who?'

Sam leaned closer. 'The fucking *Arctics*!'

He laughed dismissively. 'They're ancient. You're joking, aren't you?'

'No. I want the Arctics.'

Said like a petulant child.

'Yeah, well, you're the only one. Where the fuck have you been? Don't you know? Nobody listens to them any more.'

* * *

The music was like a blanket thrown over the room, blocking out everything but the insistent beat. Sam half staggered onto the floor and started dancing with a blond guy wearing Chelsea boots, black chinos, and a mustard V-neck who looked as if he was in his mid-twenties. She stabbed an accusing finger in the air and shouted to her new partner.

'You're drunk!'

He moved closer and spoke in her ear with a trace of accent in his voice. 'Are you sure it isn't you?'

Sam threw her head back and laughed. 'Must be, because I see you twice.'

She hadn't noticed the man next to him, also blond, dressed exactly the same.

'That's because there *are* two of us. We're twins.'

'You're twins! Wow! So am I.'

'What a coincidence. Are you younger or older? I'm Anders. Edvin beat me by fourteen minutes and never lets me forget it.'

'What?'

'I'm asking if you're younger or older than your twin.'

The question instantly brought memories even the booze couldn't shield her from. Sam didn't reply. Anders sensed the change in her and stepped away. 'Have I said something wrong?'

'No. I'm not used to dancing so much, that's all. I need a drink.'

'Of course. I'll get you one.'

'Vodka and soda.'

Back at the bar he snapped his fingers at the barman in the white shirt, an approach guaranteed to get him nowhere in Glasgow; the man ignored him and served two women at the far end. He said something, they giggled, and Anders gritted his teeth. In Stockholm the service was better, the females were blonde, their tits spilling out of their tops. In fact, in Stockholm everything was better.

The club was busier than when Sam arrived, filled with stylish men and glittery women on the town and up for it. Suddenly, she felt depressed and out of place. Edvin caught her staring at them and said, 'Silly, isn't it? All dressed up, pretending they're movie stars. In the morning they'll still be themselves.'

He leaned closer. Sam noticed his eyes, piercing and blue; the bluest she'd ever seen, and felt a flutter in the pit of her stomach. Edvin spoke as though he didn't want to be overheard. With the music blasting there was no chance of that. 'Has my brother upset you?'

'No, he hasn't.'

He seemed pleased. 'Good. He can be too direct,

especially with ladies. I'm sorry to admit he's a bit of a Neanderthal. Hard to believe he's studying medicine at the Karolinska Institute in Stockholm. I've told him to do something about his attitude. Of course, he doesn't listen.'

Sam was lost in those eyes and hardly heard him. 'What did you say you were called?'

'Edvin.'

'Edvin. Nice name.'

He bowed. 'Thank you. Contrary to popular belief not everyone in Sweden eats herring, drives a Volvo, and is called Björn.'

'Or Benny?'

'Yes, or Benny or Agnetha or Anni-Frid. Abba has a lot to answer for.'

'Is it true the whole country's sex mad?'

Edvin hesitated, then nodded. 'Erm... I can't lie. It's those long winter nights. What else is there to do?'

Sam was sobering up. She said, 'It's amazing, you're—'

'Twins, yes.'

'I told your brother I had a twin.'

'Had?'

'She died.'

'I'm sorry. Maybe I shouldn't ask. Were you close?'

'Yes.'

'You must miss her.' Edvin glanced towards his brother. 'Perhaps boys are different. I'm not sure I'd miss Anders.'

'I can't believe that. You look the same, you dress the same – how could you not miss him?'

Edvin ran a hand over his smooth chin. 'If you get to know us better, you'll understand. Physically, we're identical. As people, we're different. Very different.'

'In what way?'

'In every way. Since we were children we've fought over the smallest things. Still do. Sometimes we don't speak to each other for months.'

'Then, why're you here in Glasgow together?'

Before he could reply, Anders squeezed between them with the drinks. Edvin scanned the crowd and put a protective hand on her shoulder, drawing her attention to the dancers on the floor. 'You know,' he said, 'this isn't the right place for a woman like you. You shouldn't be here.' He wagged an admonishing finger. 'Especially if you insist on drinking so much. Make this the last one you have tonight or you'll regret it in the morning. Agreed?'

The strobe reflected in his blue eyes, making them sparkle like sapphires on a sunny day, turning his blond hair to gold. In the light, Sam saw a young Norse god. She didn't notice his brother tip the white crystalline powder into her glass behind her back and stir it with his finger.

'Agreed.'

'Call me Edvin.'

'Agreed, Edvin.'

'One last dance. But only with me. And I'm sorry, I haven't asked your name.'

'It's Sam.'

'Short for Samantha?'

'Nobody except my sister calls me that, just Sam.'

'Then tell me... just Sam. After we have our dance, do you want to go to a party?'

40

Sam listened for a voice, a sound, a clue – anything to tell her where she was – and heard only silence. She opened her eyes and blinked at the light coming from the window. There was blood on the bedclothes. Her blood. Under the crumpled sheets her fingertips gently traced the source of the pain. Her left nipple pulsed with a steady ache. Sam touched it, felt indents in her skin, and understood. She'd been bitten.

She drew the clothes away and forced herself to examine her body. What she saw made her gasp: her belly and the insides of her naked thighs were yellowed and purple with bruises. Nausea crashed over her in sickening waves; Sam thought she was going to throw up.

When the spasms passed she lay still, praying she was in her own bed. Some sixth sense, some nameless dread, whispered it wasn't so. Sam lifted her eyes to a scene from a nightmare: her clothes were scattered across the floor, the contents of her handbag spilled on the carpet, and the boots she'd paid stupid money for lay by the wall, one of them minus a heel.

Part of her was horrified and reached for answers. Another part held back, afraid of what those answers might reveal.

A door closed in the hall outside; wherever she was, she wasn't alone. Fear leapt in her chest. Her last clear recollection was of defiantly swigging from the bottle while she waited for the taxi to arrive, acting like a rebellious teenager. Her husband had deceived, discarded, and finally deserted her; she'd intended to hurt him. A reckless, futile, ambition. Because Colin would never know. And even if he did it would only drive him further away.

There was no Mr and Mrs MacLean. He was done with her.

Christ! She was falling apart – the previous night was almost a total blank. Maybe that was for the best. Except, her conscience wasn't about to let her off so lightly. The images were out there; she sensed them – blurred shapes prowling like marauding sharks in the deep uncharted waters of her subconscious, biding their time. For a second, the fog cleared and she heard a voice with barely a trace of accent speaking to her.

want to go to a party

Sam scrambled off the bed, raced to the bathroom, and vomited in the toilet, only just getting to it in time, retching until her stomach hurt and lime-green acrid bile burned her throat. She rested her brow against the cool porcelain bowl, hugging it, terrified of the truths ready to show themselves. Because there was more. A lot more and she collapsed on the floor, paralysed by fear and shame.

* * *

Behind the reception desk, the night manager was busy filling in his timesheet. He didn't lift his head when the three people passed through the hotel foyer in the early hours of the morning, giggling and shushing each other – he'd been in the hospitality game for decades and seen it all before. People were messed up; he wasn't the morality police. So long as they didn't disturb other guests they could do as they pleased.

The woman hung between her two male companions, eyes fluttering, a lazy smile on her lips, suntanned arms draped over their shoulders. She was older than them.

Sober, she probably wouldn't have given them the time of day. The men holding her up were almost identical – maybe that was the attraction: tall and blond, wearing the same clothes. Weird. That alone should've been enough for her to give them a body swerve. They nodded reassuringly to him as they crossed the atrium to the bank of lifts. He watched until the doors closed, then went back to what he'd been doing. In seven hours, his shift would be over; he intended to spend the whole day in bed.

In the room, the two Swedes dumped the female on the bed and undressed her; she slipped in and out of consciousness and didn't resist. When she was naked they took turns with her, then rolled her up onto her knees and had her again. They laughed about what they were doing together in Glasgow. The same routine as weeks ago in Amsterdam, and Dusseldorf before that.

This was their thing. This was what they did. They could've had any number of women. That was too tame and didn't interest them. They were booked to stay until Sunday. Pulling on their first night in the city meant a change of plan. Later this morning they'd be on a plane to London. After that, a budget flight to Stockholm would get them home in time to go for a drink. They might even go clubbing.

* * *

Sam tried to stand; her legs wouldn't hold her. She crawled to the shower and sat on the floor with her back pressed against the tiles, letting the hot water soothe her. After a while her mind cleared. Slowly, it came to her. Edvin and Anders – probably not their real names – on the surface, handsome and charming. Underneath, sexual predators working as a team. And she'd made it easy for them. The world was awash in gullible females. Until last night, Sam hadn't thought of herself as one of them.

* * *

Damian tipped two sugars into the cup and watched the crystals disappear beneath the muddy liquid. The coffee was a brand Tina insisted on and hadn't been great even when it was fresh; reheated it was metallic and bitter. He stirred and took a sip; it was still ghastly, except, now it was too sweet.

Of course, it might be nothing to do with the coffee. It could be him. He hadn't slept, there was an unpleasant taste in his mouth and his tongue felt thick. The contact from L-A late on a Friday afternoon, when most people had drawn a line under work and were planning their weekend, had been unexpected. The mail popping up on his screen had guaranteed him a night of anxiously pacing the floor, and for the first time he was sharply aware of the responsibility he'd so willingly assumed. Since their modest beginnings, every decision about Stone Free had been taken together. As a team. Now, he was *it*.

His mobile rang: Tina. He sighed and didn't answer. It was Saturday; she'd expect him to take her to lunch and mooch around like a spare prick while she searched for something to buy. Usually Damian didn't mind but today he'd more important things on his mind than accommodating a female demanding attention he didn't have to give. Lewis had been right about one thing: office romances were not good news, doomed to end badly.

He'd been livid with him for having a 'thing' with an employee and they'd come as close as they'd ever been to an actual fallout.

'I really believed you were better than that, I really did, Damian. Life's complicated enough.'

'It's nothing, just sex, we're having a bit of fun. You're overreacting.'

'Am I? Ever heard the saying "Don't get your honey where you get your money"?'

Damian had bristled and defended himself. 'Relax, it's harmless. Tina's solid gold. She's looking for the same as me.'

'You'd better hope she is. Stone Free on the front page of the *Daily Record* in some industrial tribunal isn't the kind of publicity the Americans would welcome. Please tell me you aren't taking her to the Christmas party.'

Damian had understood how what he was about to say would go down. 'Of course not. She'll be there – she is a member of staff, after all – but she won't be with me.'

Lewis had leaned back in his chair and studied him. 'I hope you're telling the truth. Shafting the help isn't a good look. Lassiter-Accardi work with brands who use sweatshops in Bangladesh, the Philippines, all over the place. Modern slavery in some cases. They turn a blind eye to child labour in Manila yet an allegation of sexual harassment from a female employee in Glasgow would have them running for the hills.'

It was a lecture and Damian hadn't liked it. 'What're you on about? Nobody's harassing anybody. Credit me with some sense.'

'All I'm saying is – that it's going on at all isn't great, but it's something else again to publicly flaunt it.'

'Oh, for fuck's sake! I'm not "flaunting" anything.'

Lewis had been determined to make his point. 'Playing with matches is fine so long as you don't burn the house down with me inside.'

The exchange had irked Damian then and still did, probably because Lewis had been right. With Lassiter-Accardi's misgivings about the stability of Stone Free's management resolved, they didn't need more drama. Damian hoped they'd return with a fresh proposal – one they could both live with. The American giant was well capable of turning an already tight screw and, worryingly, there had been nothing from their end. Now, on a Friday night of all times, when every self-respecting person had been heading out to get rat-arsed down the pub, they'd made contact.

If he could pull a fresh deal off, it would be good news for everyone in the company. His first instinct had been to call Lewis. Old habits and all that. Worn out, he'd managed to snatch a troubled hour only to wake in a panic, sweating, convinced he'd forgotten something important. The pressure was getting to him and when the first pink light of dawn had streaked a grey sky he'd been there to greet it.

He ought to be exhausted. Instead, he was energised, talking to himself out loud like some speeding druggie. His PC lay on the table in the kitchen; he booted it up and pored over the email for the twentieth time. It was short, the tone friendly, ending with an invitation that had his heart beating faster in his chest and his gut churning every time he read it.

Vice President Marsha Winter wanted to meet.

The turnaround – from ignoring his calls to this – set off alarm bells for him and, once again, he wished Lewis were here. With these people, two heads would be better than one.

At face value it was reason to celebrate: Lassiter-Accardi were courting Stone Free again; the massive opportunity appeared to be back in play. Twelve months from now the brand could be known world-wide. If it was, they'd be rich, the jobs of everyone who worked for Stone Free secure. But the nagging doubt, the lurking disquiet, finally surfaced. Why Marsha? Apart from the initial reply to his email, she hadn't been involved. So, he asked himself again, why her? And why now?

Meeting in person wasn't necessary if it was thanks, but no, thanks.

Was it?

* * *

Tina tried Damian's mobile and couldn't reach him. She considered leaving a message and decided not to bother. Damn him! But, coming after the previous evening, it didn't bode well for the future. In the office he hadn't been able to get shot of her fast enough, practically running her out of the door. She'd watched him, bored out of her skull, sifting the sheets spread on his desk, his face tight with concentration, too pre-occupied to remember she was there. The corner of Tina's lip curled in a sneer. Well, somebody had a short memory – when she'd been spread on that desk and his trousers were round his ankles, his priorities had been very different.

She tried Damian's number again, her patience slipped, and she swore to herself.

'C'mon, c'mon. Answer the bloody thing. Where the hell are you?'

She'd laughed off the incident at the party as the entirely predictable result of a free bar; the drunken misadventure of people with more Prosecco inside them than was wise. In reality, it had added fuel to the flames of her rising status and she'd smiled at her new nickname: Queen Bee. If Damian binned her, she'd be seen, not as a liberated woman with the nerve to do the boss, but as a sad little tart who'd got what she'd deserved. Behind her back her colleagues, especially the females, would be merciless.

He picked up and she spoke into the phone, her tone brittle. 'I'm assuming you're taking me for lunch. And, yes, I had a very nice time last night. Thanks for asking.'

'Sorry about that. Couldn't be avoided. I'll pick you up at twelve-thirty and we'll go somewhere, you choose. There's a street-food place in Partick called Rickshaw that's supposed to be good.'

Damian was animated, trying hard to be nice, talking too much. Tina sensed he was faking it. She said, 'What aren't you telling me? And don't lie. You're rubbish at it. Are you really sure you want us to be together?'

The hesitation lasted only a second. Long enough to confirm what Tina suspected.

He said, 'Of course I do. What are you talking about?'

Tina didn't hear him; she'd already hung up.

41

Sunlight streaming through the window brought Lewis out of a dreamless sleep. The journey from Glasgow had been exhausting, capped by the final drive through the forest; he'd expected to be out of it until noon and was surprised to find himself wide awake. After the city, the silence was deafening. He made coffee and sat by the window. Out on the loch, two sea eagles skimmed the surface searching for breakfast.

Lewis drained his cup and let his eyes roam over the modest room, trying to visualise how it had looked in his parents' time when the three of them had spent as much of the summer here as his father's business commitments had allowed. Lewis couldn't picture it. It was too long ago; he'd been too young. Of his visits as a teenager his memories were mostly of him lying on his bed, willing the days to pass until he returned to his friends in Glasgow. The bond with his mother and father loosened as their son inevitably outgrew them. Lewis felt his mood dip – it didn't take much these days – a reminder he'd come to this place to get himself well. The way forward was to be active instead of digging up old bones.

When he'd dressed he went outside. The jetty was about the same age as the house but hadn't fared as well, its wooden slats rotten and dangerous. Now he'd arrived, Lewis understood that, without a purpose, time would hang heavy on his fragile mind and days would be as long and fruitless as those teenage days. Repairing the landing might be just the project he needed.

He walked along the sandy shore as far as the overhanging branches would let him and back again, at one point hunkering down to gaze at his reflection in the clear water. An Arctic char swam into view a yard from the bank, its red underbelly brilliant in the light. Lewis wondered if the rods his father had bought all those years ago were still around and if he'd got rid of the boat. Back in the clearing, he discovered it under a tree to the side of the house, resting on a lightweight two-wheel trailer covered by a dark-green tarpaulin. Lewis had no idea how long the old tub had been lying here or what condition it was in but there was only one way to find out.

The tarp was secured by ropes, tightly fastened through brass eyelets. He untied them, threw back the oilskin, and stumbled away; an adder lay curled in a ball in the bottom of the hull, its distinctive black-and-white zigzag markings instantly recognisable, hibernating until a rise in temperature roused it from its months-long torpor. He remembered reading about a Yorkshire terrier, on a walk in the Highlands with its owner, having its leg amputated after being bitten on the paw by a snake, a timely warning of how far he was from anywhere if there was an emergency.

The adder hadn't moved; leaving it where it was wasn't an option. His father had carefully wrapped the oars in canvas and bound them together with duct tape. Lewis used them to lift the creature out and tip it into the undergrowth well away from the house. He'd seen more wildlife in the last fourteen hours than he had during a lifetime in the city.

The paint was crumbling and faded though the hull seemed solid enough. Some of the panels were rough and unvarnished and relatively new, replacements for ones that had finally given up the ghost. Lewis dragged the trailer to the shore, eased it into the loch, and pushed the boat off it into the water. He fixed it to the jetty, satisfied with his work, and went to look for the rods.

42

Six miles south of the River Clyde, the sun was shining but it was bitterly cold. I huddled behind the wheel of my car across the street from Rachel's house, cradling a takeaway latte between my palms. Recognising Rachel had been a huge piece of good luck, only I didn't feel lucky. In the almost two months since the accident, my life had spiralled out of control; my determination to see justice done was destroying me and there was nothing I could do about it. Incredibly, Mrs Sensible had morphed into a self-appointed vigilante willing to sacrifice everything, even the livelihood I'd worked so hard to get. Following a stranger, a woman I barely remembered, was a new low, as unhealthy as it was bizarre. Freddy would have taken me aside and spoken in that quiet voice I missed so much, then gently led me to a better place. And because it was my soulmate speaking, the man I loved and trusted above all others, I would have let him. But that could never be. Freddy was dead. He couldn't help; the choice was mine and mine alone, and swapping one fantasy for another wasn't a solution. The madness of what I was doing had been revealed; there were no more excuses.

From this point, it was all on me.

The morning passed excruciatingly slowly, cars and people coming and going along the busy road glazed with frost; nobody noticed me. To lift my mood I switched the radio on and soon turned it off again, irritated by the presenters' vacuous cheerfulness and music that to my ears was just noise. At ten minutes to twelve, just as I was considering giving up and going home, Rachel appeared – no kids in tow, no husband or even a boyfriend – a single girl going into town, probably to hit the shops. Yesterday, she'd worn a fawn three-quarter-length coat. Today, she'd gone for black and added a scarf tied under her chin. She'd need it; it was bloody freezing.

The previous night on the motorway into Glasgow, Rachel hadn't looked the world's best driver. Now, she proved it. Without checking, she fired the ignition and reversed out into the path of a blue Astra bombing down the street. The Astra braked and skidded on the icy surface, but couldn't avoid crashing into the Mazda in an explosion of bending metal and shattered glass. I saw Rachel thrown across the car, the seat belt rescuing her, jarring her arm and neck, preventing more serious harm.

I was already out and running.

The back had buckled under the Astra's impact; the front had escaped. I dragged the door open. Inside, Rachel was ashen, not fully aware of what had just happened.

'Are you hurt? Are you all right?'

Her bottom lip trembled. I realised this was an opportunity and took her hand. 'Don't worry. I saw the whole thing. It wasn't your fault. Can you get out?'

'I... don't know. I think so.'

'Good but don't. Stay where you are. The police will be on their way. Let them see a helpless female behind the wheel. They'll expect you to be distraught; don't disappoint them.'

A man shouted, 'Why didn't you check if the road was clear before you moved? What the hell were you playing at?'

I faced him, feigning anger. 'You were going far too fast. She didn't have a chance.'

'What? Me? What're you talking about? I was on the main road. I had the right of way.'

Rachel spoke to herself. 'I didn't see him. I didn't see him.'

I heard her, hunkered down and whispered, 'Listen to me. You didn't see him because when you looked he wasn't there. Do you understand? You looked. He wasn't there. Say it.'

Rachel did as she was told. 'I looked. He wasn't there.'

'Right. That's the story, stick to it and you'll be fine. He's chancing his luck. Don't let him bully you.'

The Astra's owner walked round his vehicle, examining the damage from every angle. It didn't get better. He took his frustration out on a tyre that had blown, kicking it with his foot. 'First accident in twenty years. And all because of a stupid bloody woman.'

'No, it wasn't. I saw what happened. You caused it.'

The man's fist balled at his side. 'Then you're as fucking blind as she is.'

The anger inside me that had been there since Freddy died stirred. 'Really? Let's see who the police believe – the guy who was going too fast or the witness who saw him.'

Lewis pushed with his legs and pulled with his arms, bending into every stroke, using his whole body to lean forward then all the way back. He felt the strain on his abdomen; his fingers cramped, but he kept going. Finally, well out from the shore, he lifted the oars from the water and rested his elbows on his knees as the fire in his chest lessened and his breathing returned to normal. He wiped the sweat on his brow with a tired hand, exhilarated by the sheer physical effort he was so unused to. When was the last time he'd done anything like this? Certainly not in years; he was well out of practice. Like so many lessons in life, his father had taught him to row and Lewis thanked God for it; the sense of freedom was overwhelming. In the timeless surroundings, his mobile phone was an incongruent, ugly reminder of everything he wanted to run from. He took it out of his pocket and dropped it over the side; it disappeared, never to be found.

Now he was alone. Lewis picked up a rod and cast his line, watching it glide through the air, dip, and drop on the surface, truly centred for the first time in months. The darkness had retreated but it hadn't gone – there was still work to do before he'd be free of it. Here, in this tranquil place, he'd be able to confront his demons for the imposters they were.

44

In Cambuslang, I'd given a statement to the police and waited until the damaged car was towed away. The devastated look on Rachel's face had said everything about how she was feeling and I'd seen my chance slipping away. Coming to the café in Great Western Road had been my suggestion. If we'd gone into the house, Rachel would have stayed firmly stuck in the drama of her own making and talked about nothing else. Persuading her to go into town under the guise of cheering her up was a necessary deception. Something a friend would do. I wasn't that – my interest in this stupid woman extended to getting her to reveal Lewis Stone's whereabouts and no further.

The old Alex, nice Alex, would've felt bad but she didn't exist.

All that mattered was finding him.

On the drive into the city Rachel had stared out of the window, too shaken to speak, turning with tears in her eyes as the reality of how close she'd been to serious injury hit home. 'If you hadn't been there, hadn't seen it...'

I breezily swept the coincidence away. 'Right time, right place. I'm only glad I was, otherwise he'd have blamed you.'

Doubt clouded Rachel's mind. 'I can't remember much. I wish I could.'

I kept it light, reinforcing the fantasy, skilfully guiding her away from the truth.

'Because it happened so fast and you weren't expecting it. The street was clear so you reversed. That middle-aged boy racer came out of nowhere. Lord knows what speed he was doing.'

'Will they charge him?'

I made a disbelieving grunt in my throat. Rachel didn't hear the bitterness in my voice. 'I wouldn't hold your breath.'

'Yes, but—'

'Nobody was injured. You're both insured. I expect that'll be it.'

'You seem to know a lot about it.'

'Not really. It's what tends to happen. The police are too busy catching real criminals to be bothered with car accidents.'

'I could've been killed.'

'You were lucky.'

'But, I mean, it's still a crime, isn't it?'

I had an answer for her but agreeing was the easy option. 'Yes,' I said, 'it's still a crime.'

Rachel watched me and I knew a question was coming. My passenger shifted in her seat, studying her guardian angel, seeing me for the first time. Eventually, she said, 'Have we met before?'

'I don't think so.'

'There's something about you. Where do you live?'

'Shawlands.'

'Shawlands? What were you doing in Cambuslang?'

I had my story ready. 'I work almost every weekend. When I have a Saturday off it's good to get out of town. I was heading for the Clyde Valley.'

'Why did you stop?'

I feigned a laugh. 'I thought I'd forgotten my phone. Turns out I was sitting on it.'

Rachel smiled. 'Well, all I can say is thank God for your dodgy memory.'

In Kothel, we squeezed between two women and a couple of female college-types lost in their own world, trying to impress each other with banal chat. I tuned them out and ordered coffee from a slender waitress deftly moving between the tables. When it arrived, Rachel lifted her cup with both hands, as though one wouldn't be enough to stop her spilling it, eyes darting fearfully around the room, and I knew she was reliving the accident.

I patted her arm. 'Put the crash behind you as quickly as you can. You'll be shaken up for a few days. Tomorrow you'll be sore in places you didn't realise you had and don't be surprised if sleeping is difficult for a few nights. Par for the course, unfortunately. Although, if that's the worst of it you won't complain. It's tempting to go over it again and again. My advice: don't allow yourself to dwell on it.' I sipped my coffee and carried on. 'You said "I could've been killed" and you were right. When his car ploughed into you that might've been it. But it wasn't, you aren't dead. You're here. With me. So, let it go – the fear, the anger – let it all go. The insurance companies can argue the toss about the damage. Fine, that's their job. Yours is to get your peace of mind back. Cars are metal and rubber and glass; they can be replaced. People can't.'

'Has something like this happened to you?'

'No.'

'Because you sound like you know what you're talking about.'

'Well, it's common sense, isn't it? I'm imagining how I'd be.'

Rachel pulled away to get a better look at me. 'This is weird. Are you sure we haven't met? I mean, absolutely certain?'

I played the game. 'Not absolutely, no. I'm a pharmacist. I meet lots of folk. Maybe I filled a prescription for you.'

Rachel snapped her fingers. 'Got it! Caledonian. You were on the MPharm course. Always top of the class while I struggled to keep up. I hated you for being so clever.'

I roared with phoney laughter. 'Nobody's ever accused me of that. You were wrong then and you're wrong now. The MPharm is a heavier workload than a BSc Honours degree. For me, it was four years of hell. I almost packed it in half a dozen times. So, why don't I remember you?'

'Because I did, pack it in, I mean. And if you're filling prescriptions you must've stuck with it.'

'To the bitter bloody end.'

'So, if I can't sleep I'll know who to come to.'

I was the last person Rachel should ask. That wasn't what I told her. I said, 'The best I could do is a sedative antihistamine, I'm afraid. It's recommended for people working night shifts. Where did you go after you quit? Did you transfer onto a different course?'

The conversation was helping Rachel; she seemed brighter. 'No, no. I'd had enough.' She glanced at the students. 'Further education wasn't for me. I got a job, then I got another job and it slowly dawned on me that the world hadn't been waiting for Rachel.'

'Sooner or later we all come to the same conclusion. What're you doing now?'

'I'm in fashion.'

'How exciting.'

'Not really. I work for Stone Free. Have you heard of it?'

I gushed. 'Heard of it. Lewis is a friend – well, he *was* a friend – I haven't seen him in a long time. How's he doing?'

'Not good. He used to be in his office when I arrived in the morning and still there when I left at night. Not any more. Hasn't been seen since the Christmas party.'

'Why? What's happened to him?'

The two women were paying their bill and the students were leaving; nobody was listening. Rachel bent closer and I felt my pulse race. 'The rumour is he's suffered some kind of breakdown.'

'Oh, no, that's awful.'

'Damian Morton is running things.'

'Who's he when he's at home?'

'You must know him – he started Stone Free with Lewis.'

I tried to cover my slip. 'Oh, right, I do. Never liked him much.'

Rachel didn't pick up on it and inwardly I sighed with relief. She said, 'I saw them round the factory. They acted like friends. Well, until they had a big bust-up.'

'A bust-up?'

'Apparently. That's the story.'

'A bust-up about what?'

'Nobody knows, except, at the party, Damian was pissed and got caught with a girl from Production. They were both out of their heads. Then, he made a drunken speech about a deal that was in the pipeline.'

'Really?'

'Yeah, he got up in front of the entire workforce and blurted it out. Lewis left in a rage and that was it. He dropped out of sight.'

I filed that little gem away. When he'd slipped behind the wheel of his car, Lewis Stone had had other things on his mind.

'Business partners have disagreements every day of the week.'

'Yeah, perhaps they do, but from being involved 24/7 to nada is strange, especially if it's your name on the door. That's how the breakdown gossip started.'

Rachel stopped, concerned she'd said the wrong thing. 'I'm sorry. You and Lewis... you weren't... were you?'

I searched for words to describe what had never been. 'What can I say? Ships that pass, no more than that, although it took me months to get over it. He was a nice guy. I liked him even if he did dump me.'

'His loss.'

'That wasn't how it felt at the time. I was gutted because we might've had something. If he's in trouble I'd want to know.'

I'd helped this woman; Rachel was keen to return the favour. She said, 'All I can tell you is the deal hasn't materialised. Everybody's scared to ask if it fell through. And in the morning it's Damian in the office first where it used to be Lewis. Who knows what's going on?'

'Maybe I should call him.'

'It's worth a try. My guess is you'd be wasting your time.'

I pretended to take her assessment badly. 'We were close once upon a time. That counts for something – it has to. You're saying Lewis might be ill. I can't just leave it.'

Rachel responded to my distress. 'Like I said, Damian has a girlfriend called Tina, one of the machinists. The little tart acts as though she's the Queen of Sheba because she's going out with the boss. As for him, he's besotted, a typical man. She's got him under her thumb. I could ask her.'

'Really? That would be so great.'

'With what you did for me today…'

'All I did—'

Rachel didn't let me finish. A sly grin started at her mouth and reached her eyes and I realised I'd been conned. The scared-little-girl performance had been while she wasn't sure about me. Now she'd decided I was all right it wasn't needed any more.

'All you did was lie for me. I didn't see that car. Didn't see it because I wasn't looking. He might've been going too fast. That was just his bad luck; the crash was my fault. Whatever you thought you saw, you were wrong. But I'm grateful. Maybe I can do something for you. Our Tina will relish the opportunity to boast how much she knows about Stone Free. She'll do it to show me she's in with the bricks. Circle of trust and all that crap. Give me your mobile number. I'll call if I get anything.'

45

The oil was in a battered plastic bottle underneath the sink, and it was old. Lewis poured the viscous liquid into the hot cast-iron frying pan, watching it spread across the bottom. Two dead-eyed brown trout, around three quarters of a pound each, lay gutted, descaled, and washed on the draining board beside the sink. He'd forgotten how many times he'd seen his mother take what his father had caught, dredge it in flour and shake off the excess. There was no flour, so he lowered them as they were into the pan and turned the gas back a notch. The hot oil sizzled; the skin crackled and caramelised. After three minutes, he flipped them over, cooked the other side, slid them onto a plate, and sat at the kitchen table. Later, he walked down to the jetty with only the sound of his footsteps and the gently lapping water for company. The old boat was where he'd left it earlier in the day when the grey loch stretched out before him. Now, it was black and endless. Lewis took in a lungful of air, then let it out slowly, savouring the almighty silence, suddenly in tune with Flora Cameron's jaundiced view of lowlanders and their overcrowded cities. While he'd worked sixteen-hour days in Glasgow striving to 'get somewhere' in the fashion world, this was here as it had been in his parents' day and countless millennia before.

Everything he wanted. No need to search for it somewhere else.

Lewis thrust his hands into his trouser pockets and came across a crumpled piece of paper. He smoothed it out. In the darkness it was impossible to read it. He didn't have to – he knew what his partner and former friend had written.

One damning word: killer.

And in that moment all the good feelings evaporated. He tore the vile thing into shreds and hurled it into the wind, screaming his fury across the loch.

'Liar!'

46

Asda in Toryglen was ten minutes from my house and open twenty-four hours a day, but I rarely came here. As I pushed the trolley around the deserted aisles, I wondered who actually used late-night supermarkets. What kind of people bought teabags and fish fingers at midnight? The answer was obvious: lonely people; people with nothing better to do on a Saturday night.

People like me.

Rachel's admission in the coffee shop had taken my belief in the human race to a new low – something I hadn't believed possible. She was responsible for the crash. I was there; I'd watched it happen. Until she'd admitted it, I hadn't realised she knew it, too. Her shock and innocence had been a self-serving act to avoid the consequences of her actions. And I'd fallen for it.

'I didn't see that car. Didn't see it because I wasn't looking.'

Spoken without a hint of remorse.

When I'd dropped her back at her place, the middle of the road had been sprinkled with broken glass. Rachel had glanced at the tiny shards glinting in the light as though they had nothing to do with her and opened the door. 'I really need to start using those mirrors.'

'That's what they're for.'

'Yes, I keep forgetting. Idiot female driver 101. Thanks again for being in the right place at the right time. I'll be in touch as soon as I can.'

A mile further on I'd pulled in and tried to make sense of a world I didn't understand. I had my own brand of fakery going on; my motives for being there weren't pure. Rachel was grateful, yet her attitude jarred. What if somebody had been injured? Maybe seriously hurt? Would it have made a difference to her or, for that matter, to me? Would I have been deflected from my objective? I didn't think so. If I'd told the police what had actually happened, she might have been charged with reckless driving and any faint hope of learning where Lewis Stone was would've disappeared. I'd been lucky. On another day I might've had to choose between victims – Cambuslang or Molly. Speculating which would get the vote wasn't somewhere I wanted to go.

In Aisle 4, an older man with thinning white hair, horn-rimmed glasses and a creased beige raincoat peered at a line of tinned peas, comparing prices. He came to a decision and added the winner to the packet of biscuits in his basket. His eyes darted in my direction, saw a woman by herself, and he walked the other way.

'I'll be in touch as soon as I can,' she'd promised only hours ago. Rachel wasn't friends with Tina. They wouldn't talk until they met at work on Monday, perhaps not even then. Stupidly, I checked my messages in case I'd missed her. On the screen, the picture of Freddy in his red cagoule when we'd gone camping on Arran had been replaced. Instead, cropped from a photograph I'd found at the bottom of a drawer, a twenty-year-old Molly smiled up at me.

My dead sister was my new wallpaper.

How screwed up was that?

47

Damian lay in the dark listening to Tina quietly snoring beside him, hating her almost as much as he hated himself. It had been a day of huffs and silences that had ended in disaster. When he'd finally managed to get hold of her and talk her round, she'd picked Mamasan in Ingram Street for lunch, pointedly ignoring him from beginning to end, toying with the Pad Thai she'd ordered, pushing it languidly around the bowl. Given the atmosphere, a movie seemed a decent idea. Damian had taken her blank expression when he'd suggested it as a yes and gone to the Odeon Luxe Glasgow Quay. Twenty minutes into the film he'd tried to hold her hand, been rejected, and drawn a line under the whole sorry fiasco.

Life really was too short.

It was time to end this thing.

In his flat, Tina had thawed, made coffee and sat next to him on the couch. He'd soon realised why: she was horny. Sex had been the last thing on his mind. But when she'd kissed his neck and started to unbutton his shirt, getting out of it wasn't on the cards and he'd faked arousal, hoping animal attraction would do the rest. Tina was one of those rare creatures who looked better with their clothes off than most people did with them on. But his body had refused to go along with the lie and what had followed had been humiliating beyond belief for both of them – he couldn't get an erection. His partner, already unhappy with him, hadn't hidden her annoyance. After the third miserable attempt, Tina rolled from under him and turned away. He'd sat on the edge of the bed, too embarrassed to look at her, aware she was judging him. In a relationship based on love and mutual respect, his failure wouldn't be spoken about again. This wasn't that. It was a fling; loyalty didn't come into it. On Monday morning, women in the factory would whisper as he went past, sniggering behind their hands, because they had it on good authority the Big Boss wasn't so big after all.

Apologising made it worse. Damian had said, 'It isn't you, nothing to do with you, it's me.'

The affair was doomed, the accusation in her reply hastening its demise. 'Well, of course it isn't me. Me? You cheeky bastard – what the hell are you talking about? Why would you even think it is?'

'I don't want you worrying—'

'Worrying? What have I got to worry about? You're the one who can't perform.'

He'd closed his eyes and let the recriminations wash over him. 'What I'm saying—'

'I get what you're saying and you can shove it.'

'I assure you it hasn't happened before.'

She'd screamed at him, 'And that's supposed to make me feel better, is it? You sad little man. Surprise surprise, it doesn't.'

'I'll make it up to you.'

'Will you?' Tina had eyed his nakedness and sneered her contempt. 'That'll be interesting. Though somehow I doubt it. You won't get the chance. At least, not with me.'

In a few months they'd gone from making a public spectacle of themselves, eating the face off each other, to not being able to be in the same room. The drunken passion at the Christmas party that had enraged Lewis might've been a dream. Losing Tina would be no great loss. She'd been a distraction, one he could do without, especially when his focus needed to be on the business.

Except, she was a distraction with a big mouth and he'd prefer to limit the damage before she told anyone who'd listen about his erectile dysfunction.

He slipped into a dressing gown and went through to the kitchen, careful not to waken her. The PC was where he'd left it before the day had gone to shit. Tina's anger and frustration weren't misplaced; in fact, she'd been right to complain – his attention hadn't been on her and she'd reacted. What had affected his ability to perform was tucked away in the Lassiter-Accardi file under the heading 'Marsha'. Any company in the country would've jumped on it, drafted a response, and sent it immediately. Damian had waited impatiently for the email and been gutted when it hadn't come. Maybe because this would be his first important decision since taking over from Lewis, but he found himself holding back and wasn't sure why.

He picked up the printout and read it again.

Hi Damian. Sorry to have been out of touch. I trust everything is good at your end.
I am arriving in the UK on Monday for four days and would like to schedule a meeting with you to discuss

the future. Of course, I appreciate the short notice but it's important we hook up. If you can't come to London, I'll fly to Glasgow.
Let me know.
M

The email hadn't changed; neither had his reaction to it. The first time he'd read it he hadn't known whether to laugh or cry and still didn't. He shut down the voice inside him whispering disquiet and focused on what was in front of him. Lewis wasn't around to share in the good news. Ironically, if he hadn't stepped away there would be no good news to share. Over his shoulder, he heard Tina stir in the bedroom. Things between them were bad enough without her waking up and finding him missing. To hell with her, she'd soon be history; only a fool would allow such a huge opportunity to slip away when it was so close. Tina had been a mistake – he wasn't about to make another one.

He kept the reply brief, aware of the gnawing in his gut that was probably nerves but could be something else. If the Americans were going to shaft him, he was determined not to just roll over and take it.

Hi, Marsha, I can do Tuesday afternoon but you'll need

to come to me.

Lassiter-Accardi were based in Atlanta, helping to make it the tenth largest economy of cities in the US and twentieth in the world; Damian knew because he'd researched them on Google back at the beginning of the email chain. Of course, that didn't mean Marsha Winter was in Georgia: she could be on the road; she could be anywhere. But wherever she was, she wasn't asleep. Before he could close the PC down it pinged.

The mail was short and very, very, sweet.

Tuesday's fine. Let's do it.

48

He stood by the window and looked out over the tree-lined Victorian terrace, yards from the traffic on Great Western Road. Hotel du Vin in the West End was informal, understated, and elegant – a good place to meet. He'd gone with a black jacket, T-shirt and cords, in keeping with the image he wanted to project. Stone Free was a young, ethically aware company; suits, shirts and ties weren't what it was about. His palms were sweating; he was nervous and with good reason. This was arguably the most important discussion of his life, and since the early hours of Sunday morning in the kitchen, when he'd overcome his inexplicable resistance to the breakthrough and tapped a one-fingered reply to the email, he'd thought of little else.

The fast response had encouraged him to believe fortune was, indeed, knocking on the door.

Outside, the sun was shining, although the temperature was a chilly eight degrees. So much had gone on. So many changes. But the Americans had come back to the table and it looked as though the deal was still possible. How ironic to be in the hotel where the Christmas party had been in, this time to meet Marsha Winter. The memory didn't warm him. He'd made a complete arse of himself that night and hoped he wasn't about to do it again.

Damian checked his watch – her plane from Heathrow would've landed at Glasgow Airport; she'd be in a taxi and on her way.

L-A was a challenge, of course, but there was an element of predictability to it. Marsha Winter would expect to leave with an in-principle agreement that nailed Stone Free's margins to the floor for the privilege of visibility in their outlets; the fine-print details would come later. Unless Damian was on his game, Stone Free's costs would increase dramatically in line with the anticipated new level of sales, but the bottom line wouldn't make great reading.

More than once he'd asked himself if he was prepared to walk away. The answer was yes. For the reasons he'd laid out with Lewis, he had to be.

Tina was a different problem.

The affair was dead though not yet buried. There were two ways to approach it, neither with much appeal. Sacking her under some pretext would get her tight little arse out of the building, except the deserved repercussions wouldn't be pleasant; the fallout would be damaging. A lawyer would mount a compelling argument for unfair dismissal and take the case to a tribunal where, almost certainly, Stone Free would lose. The second option was to pay her off. Give her cash to shut up and go away. Risky. The vindictive bitch might turn it down just to get back at him.

He tried to clear his mind; today wasn't the day to kick that particular hornets' nest. He'd speak to Shawcross about setting up a non-disclosure agreement so she'd have to keep her mouth zipped if she wanted to walk away with the prize.

A taxi pulled up at the front door. Three people got out, two men and a woman with more than a passing resemblance to Gladys Knight, wearing a multicoloured mink coat that must have cost more than Damian's car. One of the men held the door open deferentially, then fell in behind her up the steps. Without a word being spoken, Damian had learned something.

Marsha was the boss.

49

Somehow I'd made it to Tuesday and there was nobody more surprised than me. Sunday had been the longest day of my life. Wanting a result so badly was destroying me and while my head said it was too soon to hear from Rachel my gut demanded it. In the coffee shop I'd been careful not to lay it on too thick. She was devious but she wasn't stupid. My intervention when she'd reversed into the road had never been properly explained; in the heat of the moment she'd been happy to accept my help. The story was simple unless I tripped myself up and complicated it: I was an old friend of Lewis Stone who'd like to get back in touch. No more than that. Not exactly an emergency.

When Monday morning came around, I was restless and tired, my nerves were shot and I had to get out of the house. It occurred to me that if Stone had returned from wherever he'd been I wouldn't need Rachel, or anybody else for that matter. On a whim, I drove to Sherbrooke Avenue and sat outside the house. The red Golf wasn't there, which didn't necessarily mean its owner wasn't. After a while, I screwed up my courage, walked up the gravel drive and peered in the big bay windows.

The bastard hadn't been home the last time and he wasn't home now.

Back in the car, images rushed in: Gupta – Dr, Mr, whatever the hell he called himself – turning off the machine keeping Molly alive. There were figures standing by her bed. Me and Sam and Colin, listening as our sister's breathing faded and she finally left us. The numbing disbelief I'd felt returned and I was overcome by the most profound sadness. I broke down, wailing with grief, totally gone. When the storm passed, I dried my eyes, but I was still filled with a hatred I wouldn't have thought myself capable of for the man who'd caused this.

If Rachel didn't get me what I needed I'd find some other way.

50

The meeting rooms had names – the Glenlivet, the Rosebank, the Ardbeg. Damian had booked the smaller, more intimate, McCallan, assuming, because Marsha hadn't told him otherwise, that it would be just the two of them getting to know each other before the real talking began. When he saw the men get out of the taxi, he realised he'd made a rookie's mistake. Three to one. Lewis couldn't be there but Oliver Shaw-cross should've been, even if it was only to make up the numbers. If this had been a war, he'd have lost the first battle.

Marsha came through the door like Diana Ross singing that Bee Gees song – Damian couldn't re-member its name. One of the men slid the fur coat off her shoulders in a move kept for moments like this. They said you only got one chance at first impressions; clearly, Marsha was a believer. She held out her hand, smiling, eyes dancing as though she was genuinely pleased to see him. He took it and she said, 'We meet at last, Mr Morton.'

'Indeed we do.'

Up close, orange, bergamot and frangipani, evoking balmy nights on the French Riviera, wafted between them. Two things immediately struck him about her apart from the scent, the tailored cream suit, and the diamond ring on the third finger – she was better looking than Gladys Knight and thirty-five years younger. When they were seated, she screwed the top off a bottle of Perrier and poured herself a glass without introducing her colleagues.

Across the polished mahogany table, the smile snapped off; it had served its purpose. Marsha said, 'This is where I'm supposed to tell you Scotland is one of my favourite places in the world and ask stupid questions about the Loch Ness monster, right? I'll leave that for the tourists and get to why I'm here. What I will say is, you've created something cool, something we can work with. Stone Free is a brand that can and should go places.' She took a sip from her glass. 'You're a smart guy, Damian. May I call you

Damian? I prefer to be around smart people. It saves time; they figure things out for themselves without having to be spoon-fed.' She paused. 'You've done a good job; we like it. Actually, we like it a lot. So, let's cut to the chase, shall we? Lassiter-Accardi wants your company. I'm here to buy Stone Free.'

51

Sam hadn't had a drink since the club in the early hours of Saturday morning but still wasn't right and wondered if she ever would be. When she closed her eyes she had flashbacks, monochrome pictures of being violated by the blond predators that shamed her. It was easy to blame the evil perverted bastards who assaulted and abused women because they could get away with it. But her own recklessness had played a huge part. On another night she'd have avoided them. Two men dressed the same was like a neon sign saying We Are Weird. Her desperate attempt to get back at Colin had been fated to end in disaster from the moment she'd lifted the whisky to her lips.

Everything after that had been inevitable.

Tears threatened to come; Sam resisted them defiantly, muttering, 'No. No. I won't be beaten by this.'

Friday night had only been the latest in a long line of missteps. Falling for Colin hadn't been one of them, although maybe she was telling herself what she wanted to hear. When it came to the man they loved that was what women – weak women; foolish women – did, because it was better than having to face the truth. And what was the truth? In her case she'd been in so much of a rush to be Mrs MacLean she'd forgotten she'd been Sam Kennedy long before Colin had appeared on the scene. A doubt as old as any cliché crossed her mind: perhaps if they'd had children...

Sam shook her head. Perhaps this, perhaps that, perhaps the fucking next thing.

Even if she'd known how it was going to end, she'd still have danced with him, still let him take her home, still kissed him.

She loved him, loved him enough to do anything he'd asked. Like giving up her career. Sam had enjoyed nursing and hadn't been keen to leave it behind. Colin had wanted to play the alpha male and have his wife at home. Me Tarzan! You Jane! To please him she'd agreed, a decision that had come back to bite her because she'd sacrificed more than a job – she'd given away her identity, her place in the world, and now, without her husband, she was nothing; worth nothing, a boring waste of space he didn't even want to fuck.

Her mobile rang. Sam read the caller ID and sighed. It was Alex on to make sure she was all right. Well, she wasn't all right. A million miles from all right and in no mood to pretend otherwise.

So, no thanks, sister. Not today.

52

I had it all laid out nice and neat in my head: Rachel
would call me during her lunch hour and tell me
where Lewis Stone was. I'd thank her and never see or
hear from her again. Then, I could begin in earnest to
hold the killer to account.

It couldn't come soon enough and I was restless
and anxious, the waiting playing on my nerves. Sam
wasn't answering her phone, probably because she
didn't fancy a lecture from her big sister on positive
thinking. If she only knew! From the first time she'd
introduced me to her new boyfriend I'd liked Colin
MacLean and knew he'd be good for her. Sam could
be a handful when she decided to be. He was the

calming influence she'd needed; the break-up of their marriage had shaken my faith. It still didn't feel real.

Around three in the afternoon, I realised my imaginary scenario was just that and felt myself go down. Rachel might have forgotten about it; it wouldn't exactly be important to her. Sooner or later, Stone would come back to Glasgow. When he did, I'd be waiting.

Ending his life was all I thought about. How wasn't something I'd considered. In my mind's eye, Stone was on the ground looking up at me. There was blood everywhere. His face was twisted in pain and disbelief, his final moments on earth squandered trying to understand who had done this to him and why.

I'd run the confrontation in my head more times than I could count during long, tormented nights when rage and resentment had kept me going. Now, I saw it for what it was – the delusional fantasy of a silly woman.

Despair closed round me like sea fog.

Crying would've helped, but I couldn't. I was all cried out. Instead, I lifted my car keys and headed to Molly's flat.

53

A waiter stuck his head in the door and apologised when he saw him sitting alone.

'Sorry, I thought everyone had gone.'

Damian glanced towards him, too shell-shocked to reply. Marsha Winter's perfume lingering in the air confirmed it had actually happened. On the table, an envelope lay open, a single sheet of letter-headed paper beside it. In the centre of the white page a number had been written in pen. Pounds or dollars; it didn't matter. It was more money than he'd ever seen or ever hoped to see and he felt numb.

The meeting had lasted less than twenty minutes. Beyond taking her coat, the men with her had made no contribution. She'd done the talking with an economy honed by years of experience. 'I'm aware this isn't what you were expecting.'

Damian had answered honestly. 'No, no, it isn't.'

The vice president had made an admonishing noise in her throat. 'It should've been. Businesses grow or die. There's no third choice. Standing still isn't an option.'

'We don't want to sell. To you or anybody else.'

Marsha had pursed her lips, steepled her hands in front of her, and he'd known she'd been here before. Many times. 'Of course. In your position my reaction would be the same. For you, Stone Free is more than projections on a spreadsheet. It's your life, who you are. But the marketplace doesn't give a damn about sentimentality. Without serious capitalisation, the Stone Frees of the world shine bright, flame and burn out. It's inevitable. The big chains will either beat your margins down so low you'll be working for pennies, or deny you access, shut you out completely. Either way, it'll be over. Two years from now – if you make it that far – somebody, maybe even us, will pick up the pieces for a fraction of the potential value.' Marsha had smiled. 'And that's the key, the word people don't get. Potential.'

She'd put the accent on the first syllable and pronounced it Po-tential.

'Something that can be, might be, should be but isn't, at least, not yet.'

Damian had jutted out his chin. 'That won't be us.'

Marsha carried on as though he hadn't spoken. 'L-A can take what you've created to more customers than you can even dream about.'

'What about the people who work for us?'

She'd shrugged. 'Their contracts will be renegotiated but they'll have jobs if they want them.'

'And me?'

'Acquisitions are tricky. Having the previous management involved in the first year can steady nerves and helps continuity. A familiar face and all that. It's all about perception, so we'll require you to stick around for a while. Consider it a condition of the sale.'

'What about Lewis?'

Marsha's expression was impassive; that decision had already been made.

'Your partner isn't in our thinking.'

'Lewis is Stone Free.'

'Was. We don't need him.'

She'd seen the look in his eyes and moved to neutralise it. 'I wouldn't worry about him, he'll be rich. You'll both be rich.'

'Stone Free is about more than money for us – you said you understood that.'

'And I do. But, at the end of the day, this is what it comes down to.'

Damian had listened to enough. 'I'm afraid you've had a wasted journey.'

On cue, one of the men slid a sealed envelope into her manicured fingers; she'd pushed it across the table. 'Our offer reflects the respect we have for the work you've done in taking the business this far. Don't tie yourself in knots with details. There isn't anything that can't be sorted. Believe me, I know. You'll find it's generous.'

Marsha had stood so she was looking down on him. She had all the moves. 'We recognise the complexities at your end. It's good for twelve days. After that, if we haven't heard from you, we'll go elsewhere. That isn't a threat, Mr Morton, it's a fact.'

* * *

At seven o'clock in the evening Oliver Shawcross was still at his desk, an Anglepoise lamp casting shadows on the walls of his office. For the dour lawyer, working late wasn't an imposition – there was no one waiting for him at home, no harassed wife or noisy children to climb over him delighted to see their dad. It filled the gap where relationships should be and stopped him noticing how lonely he was. Financially, he'd done all right; money wasn't a concern, and likely never would be, though it wouldn't help if he lost Stone Free as a client. His last conversation had ended with Lewis promising to fire him as soon as he returned to the business. Wild talk. Or was it?

Damian Morton calling him so late was surprising. He sounded anxious, maybe angry, the lawyer couldn't tell. 'They want to buy us. Can you fucking believe it? They want to buy Stone Free.'

Oliver spoke quietly to calm him down. 'I'm not with you, Damian. Start at the beginning. Who's they?'

'Lassiter-Accardi.'

'You've spoken to them? I thought they'd lost interest.'

'Until a couple of days ago they had. Now, they're back and they want it all.'

'You mean...?'

'I mean buy us out and clear us out.'

'Have you contacted Lewis?'

'Not yet. I called. His phone's turned off.

'He needs to be told.'

It sounded like an order and Damian couldn't control his frustration. 'And you think I don't know that? Right now I'm running the business, not him. And if I remember correctly, it's my signature that's required.'

'True, but not on something like this. Lewis is your partner; he deserves to be in the loop. Look, get him back down here and we'll do some PR leak to the media that Stone Free has rejected a massive offer along with a picture of the two of you together. It'll be great publicity.'

It was Damian's turn to be surprised. 'I'm afraid I haven't made myself clear, Oliver. We don't need him. Lassiter-Accardi don't want to work with us – they want to buy us out, push us out, and are offering an obscene amount of money for the privilege. Real money. I was as shocked as you but it's too good to turn down. As far as I'm concerned, they can have it.'

The lawyer stared at the phone in disbelief. 'Sell? Sell the company? Surely you don't think you can do that without him?'

'As I already said... my signature. And you have a short memory. He fucked me, you, the cat, the dog, and the gardener, so, yes, if I have to do it without him, I will.'

The lawyer felt his patience slip. 'Then, he'll fight it and he'll win. Even a sniff of legal complications will have the Americans heading for the hills. You know it, I know it, and Lewis will, too. Bring him onside or forget it.'

54

Damian rearranged the sheets of paper on his desk, still rattled by the events of the previous day. He hadn't expected the offer to buy Stone Free and wasn't prepared. Calling Shawcross had been a knee-jerk reaction but it had been a mistake, he could see that now. Oliver was an insufferable fucker at the best of times and Damian had made a bloody fool of himself on the phone with angry bluster about pressing ahead without Lewis. Nonsense of course, any sale needed the agreement of both partners, but the lawyer had been right – if Lassiter-Accardi got wind of legal difficulties they'd walk. Relations between him and Lewis were at an all-time low, irreparably damaged; no way back even if they wanted one. He could guess the reception the idea of selling would get and had been tempted to ask Oliver to go up north instead of him, then remembered the two of them were old friends and let the idea go.

Lewis's number was still unobtainable, which made a long drive to the Highlands unavoidable – the offer to buy would be gone in twelve days. Marsha Winter was a well-dressed shark; her job was to identify companies ripe for acquisition, move in, and swallow them whole. Stone Free fitted the bill. Her offer was undeniably generous. It represented freedom, the chance to start again, to build something without having to accommodate another opinion, another ego. Getting Lewis to see it like that was something else entirely.

Tina hadn't contacted him since the sex fiasco. Damian wasn't unhappy about that; he really didn't have time for it with all the shit going down. He needed to offload her without damaging the business – this one or whatever project came next. His best hope was some new man – some Jack the Lad with a nice car, money in the bank, and a cheeky line of chat would catch her eye and that would be it: she'd finish with him. Of course, he'd play his part, pretend he was gutted. Inside, he'd be cheering. But till the lucky guy swept her off her feet and off his hands it would be unwise to forget Tina was a loose cannon capable of causing him all kinds of trouble.

He heard a noise and looked up. Tina closed the door behind her and stood with her back against it, as though she was afraid to come nearer. She flashed a weak smile. 'We need to talk.'

Damian's heart jumped in his chest. He was elated. This was it; she was going to call him a limp-dick loser and dump him. He flattened his palms on the table, ready to go into his act. Her voice was a whisper, raw with remorse. 'I owe you an apology. How I behaved... it was unacceptable. Disgraceful. If you never want to see me again...'

Damian couldn't speak.

She said, 'You've probably had an awful few days. So have I. And I deserve it.'

'Tina...'

She held up her hand to stop him. 'No, this needs to be said. I'm ashamed of myself and so I should be. What I did was unforgivable. You'd be within your rights to throw me out of your office – and I wouldn't blame you if you did.'

She rushed towards him and pressed his fingers to her breasts. Under the material he felt the soft smoothness and imagined his lips on the dark areola in the centre.

His if he wanted it.

'Please forgive me. I needed you so much and re-acted badly. I was selfish, only thinking of me and what I wanted, I admit it.' There was a cry in her tone, a genuine regret – this was a Tina he hadn't met be-fore. She hurried to explain herself before he could misunderstand. 'That isn't an excuse. There is no ex-cuse. What happened to you on Saturday night can happen to any man. I should've been sympathetic. You're a wonderful lover. Come to my place after work and let me make it up to you.'

He hid his disappointment she wasn't ending it. 'I'd love to, Tina, I really would, but I can't.'

Her eyes widened. The question might've come from a child. 'Why? Why can't you? I've said I'm sorry and I am. Truly. Isn't that enough? I love you, Damian.'

No, she didn't. Tina loved Tina and nobody else. This wasn't the moment to tell her. He said, 'Of course it's enough.'

'Then why hold a silly mistake against me?'

'I'm not. I have to be somewhere.'

She squeezed his fingers so hard it hurt. 'Take me with you. We could...'

Tina let go of him and slowly drew away, her contrition short-lived. 'You're lying. You're fucking lying to me. There's someone else, isn't there? That's the reason you couldn't do it. You didn't want me, you wanted her.'

'No, no. You're wrong. I'm not.'

'So why can't I go with you?'

'Because I'm going to see Lewis.'

'Lewis?'

'Something important's come up.'

'Where is he?'

'His parents had a house on Loch Morar. Now it belongs to him.'

'Loch where? Never heard of it.'

'Morar. It's near Mallaig.'

'Why not just call him?'

'I've tried. He must be in an area with poor service. Trust me, Tina, driving for four or five hours isn't my idea of fun.'

'I don't mind.'

A long journey trapped in a car with Tina had to be avoided at all costs. Every time he lied to her it got easier. He lowered his voice, faking concern. 'But I'd mind. There's nothing for you to do up there. You'd be tired and unhappy, and that would make me unhappy. So, no, you can't come. If I leave today, now, I'll be back tomorrow. You can make it up to me then.'

'I don't get it. You're running the show; you're in charge, aren't you?'

Damian faltered. 'You know I am – for now, anyway.'

'Well, what's so important you have to chase after the guy who used to be here?'

'Business.'

It was true but it didn't sound true – it sounded hollow and phoney and made up. Tina's mouth twisted, a hard light came into her eyes; suddenly, telling the truth had become more difficult than telling a lie. She jabbed his arm. 'Excuse me if I don't believe you. You couldn't get rid of me fast enough on Friday. Saturday night you're rubbish in bed, then I don't hear from you for days, and now you have to be somewhere else?' She stepped back and stood con-frontationally, hands on her hips. 'You really must think I'm thick. A meeting with Lewis Stone. Really? Is that the best fairy story you can come up with?'

'It isn't a fairy story.'

'Come off it. You were delighted Lewis wasn't around because it let you strut your Big Boss stuff. Now, you're telling me you have to speak to him urgently.'

'Tina, please don't take this the wrong way. It's complicated – you wouldn't understand.'

She laughed mirthlessly. 'The little lady wouldn't understand. Fuck off, Damian! I'm not a fool; don't treat me like one! Who is she?'

'Don't be stupid.'

'It doesn't matter. She's welcome to you. For her sake, I hope she's easily pleased and isn't expecting much in the Nat King Cole department.'

Damian checked his watch. 'I haven't time for this crap. We'll continue the conversation when I get back. Or not. Your decision.'

'It is my decision and we won't. Your jacket's been on a shaky nail for a while. I'm binning you. You hear me? We're history!'

He lifted his coat and his car keys off the desk and brushed past her on his way to the door. 'Whatever floats your boat, Tina. Tell the whole fucking world if it makes you happy. I don't give a damn any more.'

Damian fired his coat into the back seat and pointed the car in the direction of the Erskine Bridge twelve and a half miles away. All of a sudden, getting away from Glasgow seemed like a very good idea. Tina was an unstable woman who'd say or do anything to get what she wanted. Her apology had sounded sincere but just minutes later she'd been taunting him about his last performance in bed. The crazy cow had somehow managed to shoehorn a lie about loving him in there. He concentrated on the road and tried to clear his head. It was over with her and thank God for that. She'd been bad news from day one. He'd hooked up with a bunny boiler; what the hell had he been thinking?

Damian was a decent-looking guy who'd had his share of women, though none so unashamedly wanton as Tina, and Lewis's warning echoed in his brain.

'Don't get your honey where you get your money.'

Wise words that had fallen on deaf ears.

He couldn't recall who'd made the first move but from the beginning the affair had been on fire. They'd recklessly seized every opportunity that presented it-self to go at each other like animals. If Lewis had known they'd done it in the middle of the day up against the wall in the office with his PA outside the door and eighty employees twenty-five yards away, he'd have gone berserk. They hadn't even bothered to lock the door. Risk added to the excitement in ways he couldn't explain. Madness, all of it. He'd been insane but the fever had broken.

Damian's first problem was waiting for him at Loch

Morar. When that was settled he'd deal with Tina. And to hell with buying her off; she'd get whatever severance pay she was due and not a penny more. Attempting to blackmail him wouldn't end well; he'd call in the police if he had to.

55

The dark clouds that had chased him from the city finally caught up as he was passing Cameron House Hotel and Duck Bay Marina. The heavens opened, heavy rain and a spectral mist settled over the water. Damian turned the wipers on and reduced speed. He still had a four-hour drive in front of him through some of the finest scenery Scotland had to offer, but if the weather closed in any more it would take longer. How much longer was anybody's guess. Oliver Shaw-cross had denied any real knowledge of Lewis's place – all he knew about it was what Lewis had told him: it was off the beaten track on the northern shore. Not much to go on and a load of crap. He'd been the family's solicitor, for fuck's sake! Damian got his anger under control – he'd call the lying bastard when he stopped for a break.

The further he got from Hillington, the more he understood why Lewis had chosen to run to the banks of a remote Scottish loch to re-find his balance. The report from the Glasgow meeting would send that spinning again. He realised now that calling Lewis wasn't a good idea and was glad his partner had switched his phone off. Even if he could get a hold of him, only some conversations worked over the phone – this wouldn't be one of them. Not if he wanted a result. Marsha Winter's offer needed to be sold face to face otherwise Lewis would reject it out of hand.

The rain eased to a steady drizzle falling from a grey sky close enough to touch. A yellow-and-white sign informed him he'd entered the Loch Lomond & The Trossachs National Park; he was skirting one of the most famous places on earth. Today, anything that wasn't related to the deal didn't matter; he could've been anywhere. Damian took a right towards Crianlarich, totally focused on navigating the twisting narrow road, resigned to losing hours of his life he wouldn't get back. Under pressure, Shawcross would tell him the location of the house. He'd find it and watch Lewis's face crumple in disbelief – the last man on earth he'd expect or want to see; he wouldn't be welcome.

He felt an ache in his shoulder, stiffness in his neck, and the stirrings of tiredness behind his eyes but pressed on. Imagining Lewis's objections wasn't difficult; there was a fair chance he'd turn the proposal down before he even heard what the Americans were offering. Persuading him to sell his 'baby' would take something else, something they both wanted more than money.

A clean break. A chance to go it alone.

In a word, freedom.

* * *

A mile beyond Ballachulish, he pulled into the village of Glencoe and ordered coffee in the café from a smiling waitress. The place was busy; given the time of year he had assumed he'd be the only customer.

His anger when he'd realised Shawcross hadn't told him the truth had abated, though it hadn't gone. The lawyer couldn't be trusted; he was Lewis's man. Whatever the future held for Stone Free, Oliver Shawcross's time was up – he wouldn't be involved in any new business Damian started.

Shawcross answered on the first ring and Damian

said, 'I'm guessing the Scottish Legal Complaints Commission takes a dim view of lying to clients, Oliver.'

Shawcross was immediately defensive, nervous, a far cry from his usual urbane self.

'I've no idea what you're talking about.'

Spoken without conviction.

'Really? You do surprise me. Isn't there something in the rules about not acting when there's a conflict of interest? Or have I got that wrong?'

'I honestly don't—'

Damian didn't hold back. 'When I asked where the Loch Morar house is you told me you didn't know.' He laughed a grim laugh into the receiver. 'And like a bloody fool I believed you. Until I remembered you were the old man's lawyer. Of course you knew. You were the one who broke the news to Lewis that his parents were dead. Drove all the way up there to do it, as I recall. A nice touch that. Better hope the Law Society thinks so, too, otherwise they'll suspend you for acting improperly. Might even take away your licence and you'll be out of a job. I'll be writing to them as soon as I get back to Glasgow. In the meantime, don't make it worse than it already is. Give me that fucking address!'

56

I was at Molly's flat when Rachel called, lying on top of the bed with my arm drawn over my eyes to keep out the light. I may even have been half asleep. She sounded far away, or maybe it was me. When what she was saying finally registered, I couldn't speak and she hung up. I felt no elation, no sense of success, not sure whether to laugh or cry. In the end, I managed a little bit of both. It had been the longest of long shots, yet it had paid off and I couldn't take it in.

Like most women I found stalking sinister and creepy – something only perverts or the mentally un-stable did. But that was the old me. The new version had watched Lewis Stone in sub-zero temperatures, stuck a damning note through his door, walked up the drive and peered in the windows of his house. After that I'd befriended an unsuspecting female, made a false statement to the police about the car crash she'd caused, and bought her coffee and carrot cake in the West End.

Disturbing. Unhinged. And it had worked.

Because now I knew where the bastard was.

How I felt defied description. Numb was an adjective I'd used a lot recently. Empty was more accurate. I'd lost sleep thinking about this moment, cried till my eyes were red and swollen when I'd feared it wasn't going to happen, and got on my knees by the side of my bed, praying to a god I no longer believed in for the chance and the strength to kill Lewis Stone.

Rachel had delivered. So why wasn't I happy?

I knew the answer and it scared me. In the Highlands, the man who'd murdered my sister was probably sitting in a comfortable old armchair in front of a roaring peat fire, savouring a glass of ten-year-old Talisker or Glenmorangie, unaware he'd reached the end of his life.

PART III

PART III

57

He opened his eyes and lay still, waiting for his brain
to catch up with his body. In the darkness, his fingers
cautiously searched the bed, half expecting to brush
Tina's warm thigh and hear her stir in her sleep. Except, that was the past; she wasn't here; he was by himself in a strange room. His mobile was on the floor
where he'd left it. Damian checked the time. Twelve
hours ago, he'd been hunched over the steering wheel,
hugging the coast road on the final leg of his journey
north, while lightning flashed in the black clouds
gathered like an angry crowd out at sea and a solitary
boat ploughed a course through the choppy grey water, headed, no doubt, for the shelter and safety of
Mallaig harbour. Day had faded from the sky when

he'd read the sign for Morar in his headlights and turned right off the A830, exhausted because he hadn't wanted to be doing this. After everything they'd achieved, it didn't seem real it was about to end.

Lewis hadn't been just a partner, they'd been friends, brothers in arms in an alien world; two guys dreaming the same dream. Now that dream was about to be realised, he'd come to the arse-end of nowhere to bring the curtain down on a collaboration that had taken them from a dimly lit lock up in the East End of Glasgow to the cusp of international success.

Apprehension mixed with regret in Damian's chest; he tasted acid in his throat and swallowed hard to rid himself of it. Maybe the bloody accident had been to blame or maybe this was how it was doomed to go from the beginning, but for sure Lewis hadn't been the same man since. The interests of Stone Free hadn't been his priority as he wrestled in a losing battle with his demons. The poor bastard may even have brought them up here with him. It no longer mattered because Damian intended to discover where he was and present Lassiter-Accardi's offer. But an impasse was on the horizon unless he could find the words to persuade Lewis to sell to the Americans.

The previous evening the whitewashed Morar Hotel had been his only option in the village. The room on the second floor was clean and cramped. He'd given it a cursory glance, got in the car, and driven two miles further on to Mallaig, surprised to find he had an appetite. The Fishmarket Restaurant close to the pier hadn't been busy – at the height of the tourist season it would be a different story. Damian had ordered Mallaig haddock and chips from the menu card, gone back to the hotel, and fallen asleep, exhausted.

That had been yesterday.

He made himself coffee – instant, but better than nothing – cupped it in his palms and took it over to the window. Before his eyes, the mist lifted and Loch Morar slowly materialised with the dawn. According to Google, he was looking at the deepest body of fresh-water in Britain, millions of years old, a tranquil land of natural beauty teeming with wildlife.

Lewis's parents had loved this place and passed that love on to their son. When he'd needed to escape he'd come to where they'd been happiest, to the house on its shores. In better days, Damian and Lewis had talked about walking on the famous silver sands together.

It hadn't happened. Now, it never would.

Their time as partners and as friends was over.

* * *

Colin MacLean was discovering the single life wasn't all it was cracked up to be.

He'd slept badly. Again. The bed was too big, the bedroom too warm and, of course, the sodding window wouldn't open. Why did hotels do that? Were they afraid people would hurl themselves out? No, the reason was less dramatic and more practical. As a property developer, he knew fixed windows, with no tracks or hinges and very little maintenance, tended to be less expensive and more energy-efficient; guests' comfort wasn't a factor.

Some time in the middle of the night he'd got up and switched the air conditioning on so there would, at least, be airflow. It hadn't helped; he felt irritable and dehydrated, his head thick, heavy on his shoulders, as though he'd put away too much whisky and was suffering the consequences. Ironic, because last night he'd decided not to get drunk.

Work had been a nightmare – one fucking problem after another – the best part of the afternoon spent shepherding two planning officers round a site, answering questions from one of them that were self-evident to anybody who'd bothered to look at the drawings for five minutes, while his mate had stood in the mud taking photographs of the location and the nearest buildings.

They were leaving when the spokesman had dropped his little bomb. 'It's fair to say you can expect objections to this development. Not uncommon, as you'll no doubt appreciate, Mr MacLean.' He'd shared a smug insider's laugh with his colleague. 'Always some disgruntled buggers waiting in the wings, aren't there? Anything in the city centre attracts the public's interest. As a matter of fact, we've already had a couple.'

Colin remembered grinding his teeth. In a few jovial sentences they'd moved into brown-envelope country. 'How many is a couple?'

'Mmmm, two or three.' He'd slapped his clipboard against his thigh. 'Then again, it's early days. Won't be surprised if more come in. Just giving you a heads-up. One professional to another, so to speak. These views can influence the outcome, though I suspect you know that.'

In his room, Colin had poured himself a glass from the bottle of Laphroaig bought in a Tesco Express in Hope Street, damned if he was paying the mini-bar prices for bog-standard booze. The bastard from Planning had got under his skin; he'd been fishing, shooting a line to see if it got a nibble. Subtle unless you were able to read between the lines and decode what was actually being said. On its face innocent banter and all completely deniable.

Colin had turned the cork stopper in his fingers, thought about having another drink, and hadn't; he hadn't been in the mood. Instead, he'd run a bath and stayed in it until the water cooled. Then, he'd put the whisky in his case in the wardrobe where it wouldn't be discovered by the cleaning staff, and gone to bed depressed.

At 1.50 a.m. he'd sat up. His throat was sore and his head hurt. If Sam had been with him she'd have gone to the medicine drawer in the kitchen and come back with two paracetamol and water to wash them down, then stood over him until he took them. But, she wasn't. The planning guys weren't the issue; in his time, Colin had dealt with scores of them. Jumping through hoops, greasing the wheels where necessary, came with the territory.

He was heading towards forty, thickening round the waist, skin that had been tight starting to sag. There was salt in his dark hair, lines at his eyes. His life was passing, he would never be young again, and he'd made a right royal mess of it.

His mind threatened to take him to what he'd lost. A part of him wanted to go, to wallow in the pain he knew was waiting. If he did, he might never find the way back.

Instead, he settled for a lesser hurt and pictured Sam discovering the graphic texts, reading them as her world shattered around her. Forcing herself – God alone knew how – to carry on, knowing her husband, the love of her life, had betrayed her.

Where had she found the strength when every fibre of her being must have raged at his deceit? Yet, she had.

They'd ignored the elephant in the room and avoided each other, the conversation about their marriage going unsaid as they'd struggled to breathe the same air, while the tension between them had grown like a living thing. Even then, she hadn't confronted him, perhaps telling herself that until one of them actually spoke the words out loud there was hope.

For his part, knowing how much she'd needed to lean on him after Molly's death, he'd put his own feelings aside and tried to give his wife the comfort she needed and deserved. Yet, though she wanted it more than anything she hadn't been ready to let him in and they'd drifted even further from each other to where they were now.

Colin stumbled to the bathroom and looked at his reflection in the mirror, detesting the face staring back at him. In the room, his mobile vibrated on the bed-side cabinet. He checked caller ID, saw it was Sam and sighed; he wasn't ready to talk to her. After a minute, she rang off and he sat on the edge of the bed, head down, studying his hands.

Could it get any worse? Colin didn't think so. She was worth five of him. Ten! After everything he'd put her through Sam was still fighting to save them. If the past could be eradicated, rubbed out like chalk on a blackboard, would he go back and spend the rest of his time on earth making it up to her?

The truth was, he wouldn't.

Because it hadn't been some cheap one-night stand; he'd fallen in love.

Madly, gloriously, recklessly in love.

And there was a price to pay for that kind of happiness.

This was it.

* * *

Sam listened to the number ring out and told herself Colin would be in an early-morning meeting with an architect or his site manager. When she'd met him, he'd been a handsome young smart arse with corny chat-up lines that made her laugh. And for most of their time together that was exactly what they'd done. Somewhere along the road it had stopped being enough for him; she'd stopped being enough and he'd betrayed her. Sam could put what he'd done behind her and get on with the rest of her life, or get him to realise it didn't have to end like this. They'd been strong before; they could be strong again. Men were men. Expecting the one she'd married to be different was a pathetic exercise in self-deception. Women were the glue that kept long-term relationships going – everybody recognised that.

So long as she didn't allow herself to focus on the lies he'd told about working late when he'd been with her, she'd be okay. Thinking about them, imagining them naked and melded together, changed nothing. The affair had been wrong, but it was over – she knew that. And yes, forgiving him wouldn't be easy but she had to try, because the thought of a future without him was unbearable.

Sam put down the phone. Her husband had done a bad thing, a very bad thing. Other marriages wouldn't survive. Theirs would; she'd be the glue that kept it together and Colin would come back home where he belonged.

58

Oliver Shawcross was clever, no argument there, but he didn't realise what was at stake. Lewis certainly would if Damian could get him to listen to reason.

He paid his hotel bill and left. Outside, the temperature was in low single figures and a spider's web of frost covered the windscreen. Damian fired the ignition and waited for the heater to do its work. When the screen cleared, he edged into the deserted street and felt himself tense. He'd made mistakes – of course he had, and didn't need reminding – but the rift in their partnership was Lewis's doing, not his.

He followed a sign for Bracora, skirting the shore almost on top of the water, the only vehicle on the road. The ominous clouds he'd seen over the Sea of the Hebrides the previous evening had moved out over the Atlantic. In summer, with a flaming sun dipping beneath the horizon and grazing sheep dotting the hills, this would be a very beautiful place to be, and for a moment he understood why Lewis had come here. Further on, the road cut inland past the tiny settlement of Swordland and rose towards Tarbet and Loch Nevis. He carried on straight, over a rutted dirt track that disappeared in a forest of Scots pine.

Bushes and branches scraped the sides of the car, obscuring the sky, and he was forced to use his headlights. He kept going, doubt he was on the right path growing in him, until the treeline thinned and he saw it; the original building, probably the property of some rich landowner, was set back from the stony shore fifty yards from an ancient wooden jetty. Damian guessed Lewis's parents had sunk a small fortune into preserving and extending it. The porch was certainly a later addition and he easily imagined them sitting there, sharing a glass of wine, watching the sun sink over the hills on the other side, while their wee boy searched for tiny fish in the rock pools.

Lewis's red car was parked at the side but there was no sign of him. Damian shouted, 'Lewis! Lewis, it's me!' and got no answer. The anxiety he'd felt earlier returned; his chest tightened. So much for solitude.

Somebody could die out here and not be discovered for weeks, months even. He rapped the window with his knuckles and called again, louder this time, 'Lewis! It's Damian! Are you in there?'

The door was open – why would it be locked? Damian turned the handle and stepped inside, immediately catching the smell of cooked fish in his nostrils. He checked the bedrooms and found nothing. Wherever Lewis was, he wasn't here.

Back outside he crossed to the jetty, its posts studded with rusted iron rings, and scanned the grey loch; a large white-tailed sea eagle swooped low over the water, tilting its massive wings in an exhibition of grace and speed before it was joined by its mate. Damian shielded his eyes and watched them fly in a wide arc around a small boat, scavenging for scraps, hoping to get a meal without working for it.

Damian raised an arm and waved. Whoever was in the boat might not have seen him, or maybe they had and preferred not to respond. Instinctively, he knew it was Lewis out there and felt a fresh rush of anxiety.

* * *

Lewis saw the figure waving to him from the jetty but couldn't make out who it was; they were too far away.

His first thought was Flora Cameron, though why would she be here? She'd been paid. Lewis didn't expect to see her until the following week, when the canny old highland woman would be clutching tradesmen's invoices in her wrinkled fingers for the maintenance she'd had done to the property. And visitors were a non-starter – who in their right mind fancied driving over rough ground from the Tarbet road through the woods? To his knowledge, the last person had been Oliver Shawcross bringing the news about the crash in India.

The figure waved again. Lewis rewound his reel and carefully rested the rod in the bottom of the boat, dipped the oars in the water and started to row. From the jetty, Damian followed his progress, dreading the conversation he'd driven the best part of five hours to have, anticipating how fractious it would be.

Lewis slipped a rope through one of the iron rings and secured it, ignoring him till it couldn't be avoided. He turned and Damian saw his face, ruddy from exposure to the open air. Lewis had always been in decent shape, though at the height of his breakdown the weight had fallen off him; now, he was still thin but, even in such a short time, seemed fitter.

His opening question set the tone for what was to follow. 'What the hell are you doing here?'

'I've come to see you.'

'Okay, you've seen me. Now, fuck off.'

'I can't. We need to talk.'

'You might, I don't. I said everything I had to say in Glasgow.'

'Lassiter-Accardi have come back to us.'

Lewis hesitated but only for a moment. 'Have they, indeed? Then, you've had a bloody long journey for nothing because I'm not interested in doing business with them or you. How did you find me?' He held up his hand to stop Damian answering. 'Let me guess – Shawcross. Fucking lawyers, eh?'

'I didn't leave him much choice, Lewis.'

'Not good enough. Not nearly. There's a reason he's in a position of trust. Clearly, he's forgotten what it is, which means he needs to be removed before he can break any other confidences. He's fired. When you see him tell him to consider he's working his notice.'

'I threatened him.'

Lewis laughed. 'With what? That you'd write something nasty on a piece of paper and put it through his letter box? That's your party trick, isn't it?'

'Is that what you were on about? I don't know anything about any piece of paper.'

'Well, I don't believe you.'

'Lassiter-Accardi—'

'Don't own the whole world, at least, not yet.'

'They want to buy us out.'

The ruddy glow left Lewis's face; he faltered. 'They want... to buy...' He turned away and came back again. 'And what have you promised them?'

'I haven't promised them anything. Get a grip. A concrete proposal's been made for Stone Free. It deserves our consideration. That's why I'm here.'

Lewis sneered. 'Well, they can have my consideration right now. Not happening. Not fucking happening under any circumstances.'

'Why? You haven't even heard what they're offering.'

'No need. I'm sure it's generous. I'm equally sure you have a side deal going. My concern is what comes after we've taken their money. They'll ruin what we've created. Guaranteed!'

'There's no "side" anything, you know me better than that. And it isn't that simple. We reject them and they'll shut us out of their markets. Stone Free will have nowhere to go. The business will stagnate. As for guarantees, that one's nailed on. Big fish gobble up little fish – it's what they do, Lewis.'

'Yeah, and sometimes the little fish bite back.'

'Not in this case. We sell or we go under. Not today. Not even tomorrow. But soon.'

He gazed across the loch; the words didn't come easily. 'Let's be honest with each other instead of trading insults and resentments. Lassiter-Accardi isn't the problem. You and I have gone as far as we can go together. With or without the Americans, we're finished. This gives us a chance to walk away with something to show for the work we've put in. Start again with nobody else's opinion to consider. What we had was good, but it's over. How it ends is up to you and me. And you're right, the offer is generous. More money than we've ever had. Let them have Stone Free. We may even be able to squeeze a bit more out of them.'

Lewis had heard enough. He lost his temper and turned on his partner. 'Is that it? Is that all this means to you: bloody money? Listen, when we started we didn't have two coins to rub together but we had values. Values, Damian, remember them? We were committed to the idea of ethical fashion and were determined to make a difference, no matter how small. Fifteen years ago people didn't care where the stuff they bought came from. Now, they do. Ethical sourcing has gained ground massively. Lassiter-Accardi is a moral dinosaur, totally the wrong fit for Stone Free. Six months after we sell to them they'll move production to sweat shops in Bangladesh, the Philippines, or some other child-labour hellhole. The factory in Hillington will close. Everybody working there will be made redundant. That's the future you're racing towards.'

'You're exaggerating. I don't believe any of that.'

'Don't you? Dig into their record and see for yourself. They shouldn't be anywhere near our business, not unless we're there to make sure they withhold our values. If they get hold of Stone Free they'll reduce it to just another low-quality disposable-clothing manufacturer guilty of a slew of human rights violations against the poorest people on the planet, and nobody will give a fuck.' His eyes blazed. He grabbed an oar and jabbed it at Damian's chest; Damian felt a stab of pain above his heart and gasped. Lewis shouted, 'You're a soulless fool and always were. I was an idiot for not recognising it sooner!'

His former friend matched the anger directed at him with his own. 'Really? Allow me to refresh your memory, can I? Since you knocked that woman down you haven't been worth a damn, to Stone Free or to yourself. Even your old pal Oliver has given up on you. Ask him. While you've been busy feeling sorry for yourself, I've been running the business. And don't pin it on the Americans. They are what they are. If we'd been strong they would've stayed in their lane – they would've had to. We could've got the deal done on our terms. Protected everybody's rights. But we weren't, the door's closed on it, and that, my old chum, is down to your misguided "poor me" shit.'

Lewis's rage boiled over; he lunged at his partner again and missed. Damian punched him hard, connecting with his jaw. He went down, hitting his temple off one of the jetty's thick wooden supports and lay still. Damian thought he might be dead. When his eyes fluttered and opened, the fire had gone out of them. Damian wanted to help him but it would be a mistake. Lewis sat up; there was blood on his face. He seemed not to notice and spoke quietly, the Lewis he remembered. 'I've signed a legal agreement to stay out of Stone Free for three months and I'll honour it. After that...' He left the sentence unfinished. 'You claim it wasn't you who put the paper with its sickening accusation through my letter box. Well, apart from Oliver Shawcross, who else was aware of my state of mind? You were the only one.'

Damian was tired, tired of all of it. 'For God's sake man, it wasn't me. Why in God's name would I?'

'To tip me over the edge, that's why. With me out of the picture, Stone Free would be all yours. You could do what you liked with it.' He ran his hand over his jaw. 'Don't insult me any further by denying it has crossed your mind. Of course it has, anything else wouldn't be you.'

'So why come all the way up here to talk to you?' He shrugged, defeated. 'Lewis, this is madness and it isn't getting us anywhere.'

Lewis shook his head and stood up. Damian tried to take his arm; he wearily shrugged it away. 'It's too late. Too much water under the bridge and all that. A shame, really. We were a great team. We created something we can be proud of, and that can't be taken away from us. This isn't what you want to hear, I know. Anything else would be selling my soul. It seems the Americans have us where they want us. Either way, they'll end up owning Stone Free. But they'll have to scoop it out of the gutter because I won't be selling to Lassiter-Accardi or anybody else. So you can tell your friends they can go to hell. As for you and me... we have nothing more to say to each other. When I come back to Glasgow, I'll expect you not to be there. Shawcross will handle the details – the last thing he'll do before he joins you.'

On the dirt track in the woods, Damian had to reverse to let a woman he assumed was Lewis's housekeeper pass. She glanced suspiciously at him and drove by. He'd wanted out, wanted it to end, but not like this. This was sad.

59

Rachel's call should've lifted me; it hadn't. Listening to her deliver the information I'd ached for was strangely unsettling and I understood why. This was it: no more excuses, no more spying, no more brave talk or childish notes pushed through a letter box. I'd been in a lonely place, feeding on my loathing for Lewis Stone, telling myself when the chance came I wouldn't hesitate – I'd take it and rid the world of him. With the opportunity for revenge staring me in the face, the fever had broken and I was overwhelmed by fears I hadn't been aware existed. If I'd had a gun, my choices would've been simpler – shoot Stone, then turn it on me.

Clean, tidy, and absolutely untrue. Because, at the

end of the day, more than anything, I wanted to live. Not sharing my intentions with anyone had left me an option – I didn't have to go through with this. Nobody would know.

Nobody except me.

Foolishly, I had assumed I'd be able to put my humanity to one side and kill Lewis Stone for what he'd done to my sister. Now, I wasn't sure. In the final seconds before he forfeited his life, would I have the moral or even the physical strength to see it through? I didn't have an answer to that and I desperately needed to find one.

We were strangers; that gave me an advantage. He'd briefly seen me on that bitterly cold night in the West End when I'd lost it and gone for him. In the circumstances I doubted he'd remember. Other people might. I caught myself considering what kind of disguise to wear and laughed out loud. I'd been watching too many TV dramas. According to urban myth, women preferred to poison their victims. Given my career, getting my hands on something to do the job would be 'shooty-in' to use a Mollyism. Fine, so far as it went, except an autopsy would show what had killed him and, all of a sudden, it would be an investigation into the murder of a prominent Scottish businessman. Some keen-eyed detective hell-bent on making a name for himself would pore over the victim's past, turn up the report from Byres Road and his involvement in the death of a woman, and realise he'd stumbled on a motive.

'Victim'. The word made me want to vomit.

There was a victim – no argument about that – but it wasn't Lewis fucking Stone.

To get away with it his death had to look like an accident.

I'd gone through to the lounge, still holding the mobile in my hand, feeling stupid and useless. How often had I thought about a plan without actually doing something about it? This latest obstacle made me seriously wonder if it wasn't already too late.

Sitting on Molly's couch surrounded by her bizarre collection of 'stuff' with Rachel's news ringing in my ears had only added to my sense of inadequacy. Far from simplifying the task, knowing Lewis Stone was in a house on the north shore of Loch Morar exposed the gaps in my thinking. From the beginning I'd assumed he'd be alone – that it would be him and me, facing off against each other, like the final scene in a movie. And the good guys would win because the good guys always won in the end, didn't they?

Childish bloody nonsense. What if he wasn't? What if he had a woman with him? I hadn't considered that. Or worse: what if he was with people, part of a crowd? Getting to him would be impossible. Suddenly, I was drowning in problems without solutions as the monumental discrepancies in my thought process were revealed to me. I'd been blind and deaf and dumb. Especially, dumb.

Yet, a spark inside wouldn't die. In Molly's room I opened her wardrobe and tried on her clothes. None of them fitted; a wine-coloured polo neck was so tight it almost choked me and I couldn't get her blouses to button. Everything was too small but our heads, give or take, were the same size and, really for the first time, my mental fog cleared and I saw a way forward.

Sam had hated Molly's wigs. I loved them.

60

Lewis stood at the end of the jetty with his fists defiantly clenched at his sides, staring out over the loch. He didn't watch his soon-to-be former partner leave and only turned to face the house when the sound of tyres crunching over fallen leaves had faded and there was nothing but the soft lapping of the water and the breeze rustling through the forest. The fight had lasted seconds but the meeting had been ugly and solved nothing – the differences between the men ran deep, deeper than Lewis had appreciated; neither wished to save what had been lost.

Damian had shown his true colours. He'd sell Stone Free to the highest bidder in a heartbeat, the ethical values they'd discussed when they were starting out merely an eye-catching USP. How had Lewis not seen it? He should've killed the idea of any association with the Americans the minute it was raised. That he hadn't showed how far even he had drifted from their mission in the quest for success. Lassiter-Accardi was bad news, the name reviled wherever people were forced to toil in cramped and unsafe conditions, breathing in toxic substances or inhaling fibre dust. All for a few dollars a day, barely enough to live on.

Lewis shielded his eyes from the glare of the sun reflected on the water. He could've gone anywhere. Instead, he'd chosen to lose himself here in memories of simpler days. Until Damian arrived it had been working; he'd slept well, cooked what he caught and ate it, cut the booze down to a glass before he went to bed, and felt his perspective slowly returning. But the peace he'd found had been breached and as Lewis looked at the house he saw it as it really was – run-down and forgotten, the exterior crumbling, eroded by decades of winter wind and rain. Without someone living in it permanently it would eventually return to the state of disrepair it had been in when his father discovered it.

He screamed across the loch, 'Fuck you, Damian Morton! Fuck you!'

Lewis felt his mood sink back into the darkness

he'd escaped; he couldn't go there, not again. Fuck that, too.

* * *

The big house in Newton Mearns had been a statement, a tangible expression of what she and Colin had achieved, something they could both be proud of, and it had become Sam's prison.

Her husband had warned her not to get too attached to it or too friendly with the neighbours because they wouldn't be staying for long. It was a stop on their journey, a stepping-stone, nothing more. Bigger and better was coming down the line. A villa in the Algarve was mentioned. Another time it had been a luxury flat in Dubai. This was the electronic age, he'd said: offices, desks, fixed workspaces were yesterday's thinking. Location wasn't an issue. She'd reminded him how much he enjoyed pulling on wellingtons and trudging through wet mud, while his site manager explained progress or lack of it on a build.

During a mad weekend in London they'd gone to William Evans in St James Street and paid silly money for two pairs of bile-green – Molly's description – Le

Chameau boots. When she'd foolishly told her sister how much they'd cost, her reaction had been vintage Molly.

'Why does God insist on giving money to stupid people? I bought mine at Matalan.'

Sam had reacted angrily. 'You don't get it or you don't want to get it. They're unique, made by a master bootmaker.'

Molly hadn't been impressed. 'So, no more wet socks, then?'

Funny if it hadn't been sad. Nobody could give Sam lessons in that. Colin wasn't taking her calls – not willing to move even an inch when she'd offered to forgive him and start again – and she felt isolated, alone, and depressed. She couldn't give him up and it was tearing her apart. This house was *their* house. To-gether, they'd agonised over every piece of furniture, every picture, every bloody ornament, returning to a shop three or four times to look at something they were considering buying for it. When they'd moved in they'd had a cleaner, a local woman recommended as doing an acceptable job. Until Sam had found a chip in the skirting and sacked her on the spot. From then on, she'd taken care of the place herself.

But not any more.

It looked as if a bomb had hit it. Everything was everywhere. In the kitchen, the dishwasher was full and the sink wasn't far behind, like the permanent chaos in Molly's flat. With one fundamental difference – Molly had been fine with it. Molly had been happy.

There were crates of lager and beer, wine and spirits, in the double garage. On the concrete floor Sam noticed a bottle of Chivas Regal a supplier had given Colin next to the precious bloody wellingtons they'd worn just once.

Seeing them brought her sister's caustic comment to her mind. 'So, no more wet socks, then?'

She choked back a tear, swearing quietly. 'Damn you, Molly. Damn you for making me cry.'

In the lounge, Sam wiped dust from the neck of the Chivas and gave the label a cursory inspection. Colin hadn't touched it – his tastes had moved on; these days, he was used to better. The thoughts, more apt than intended, hit like a blow. If she'd been on her feet she would've fallen.

his tastes had moved on

She couldn't accept that. For it to be true, everything she'd believed about them would be a sham. They were Colin and Sam. Sam and Colin. Mr and Mrs MacLean!

Sam unscrewed the top and hesitated, reluctant to give in, telling herself, 'One more try. Just one.' No answer from him would be the excuse she needed – oblivion would be waiting to swallow her up and carry her to a place where there was no pain.

She tapped redial and heard the number ring... once, twice, three times... then stop.

The silence made her want to be sick. Colin had rejected her and was still rejecting her, certain he didn't love her any more. But he was wrong. What they'd had didn't just die. It couldn't, it was too deep, too strong. Why couldn't he see that?

Sam put the bottle to her lips as tears ran down her cheeks, moaning softly to no one. This wasn't right. She wasn't the one who'd betrayed them.

* * *

On the outskirts of the city, Damian pulled into a petrol station and filled up. He'd driven non-stop from Lewis's house, yet didn't feel tired – he was too angry. No coffee or comfort breaks meant he'd shaved forty minutes off the journey, but it hadn't been a good experience; the stunning scenery had flashed past without him noticing as he'd raged against Lewis.

Damian understood where his partner was coming from. In fact, he agreed with him and always had – Lassiter-Accardi and its ilk were a disaster for the environment – but, at the end of the day, they were just two guys from Glasgow trying to make their mark. Righting wrongs was somebody else's responsibility. It had to be.

Damian went to Hillington rather than go home. In his office, he sat behind the desk with his head in his hands and tried to think, although what was there to think about? Lewis had made his position clear – on Stone Free and on them as partners. Without his agreement, the offer would expire and Damian had believed Marsha Winter when she'd said they'd go elsewhere; it was in her eyes.

The sound of the door opening brought him into the moment. He looked up to see Tina quietly closing it behind her and braced himself for another tirade.

Damian held up his hand. 'Tina, before you start, this isn't the—'

She didn't let him finish and there was something different about her, a sly confidence that hadn't been there before. 'I've spoken to a lawyer who specialises in cases like mine.'

'Cases like...? You don't have a case.'

'Not according to him. He says I do, and a very strong one at that.'

'Tina…'

'Tina nothing. Don't "Tina" me. You abused your position and coerced me into having sex with you.'

This was all he needed. He snapped, 'Don't be ridiculous. That's not true and you know it.'

Tina's lips pressed together in a smirk. She said, 'Here's what I know, Mr Morton. I turned you down but you kept on and on at me until I gave in. And that's what I'll be telling the police. Sexual harassment's a crime – you could go to prison.'

A butterfly of anxiety fluttered in Damian Morton's chest. He'd been distracted by Lewis and Marsha Winter and hadn't seen this coming. 'Tina, that's just not true. You threw yourself at me.'

She ignored the accusation and took her fantasy a step further. 'Maybe I'll remember how you raped me and made me promise not to say anything about it.' She drew her shoulders back and lifted her chin. 'I wonder how much it's worth to keep that from getting out.'

He couldn't believe this; his fingers gripped the edge of the table. 'You want money?'

'For what you did to me I deserve it. A lot of money.'

Twice in one day he'd found himself arguing with a crazy person. Suddenly, it was all too much. Something inside him snapped and he screamed, 'In six months nobody in this place will have a job! So, go ahead! Call the police! Call anybody you like! But get out of my office before I fucking strangle you with my bare hands.'

61

In months I seemed to have aged years: my skin was rough and wrinkled – the skin of a woman who'd lived hard – and my eyes were dull. I'd read somewhere that the colour of the iris was like fingerprints, unique to each individual. Mine were almost black. And then there was the wig. Molly could 'do' wigs. On her they'd been stylish and 'out there': quirky, zany and mad don't-give-a-bugger-what-anybody-thinks. Clearly, I couldn't. Whatever it took, I didn't have it. On me the wig looked stupid and fake and, for a second, I considered taking it off, then remembered why I was wearing the damned thing in the first place.

More and more often, Freddy was in my thoughts. Nothing unusual there. I'd talked to him every day since we met; his death hadn't changed that. But it had been Freddy I'd spoken to – my handsome husband, the funny guy who made me laugh all the time. Now, it was the hollowed-out husk he became in the months before he passed when just looking at him had been almost too painful to bear. Time was supposed to heal. To ease the hurt. In my case, it hadn't. I'd used my widowed status to more or less withdraw from the world and protect myself emotionally. A blind man could see I'd failed and was still failing.

I crossed the room and stood at the window. In the daylight, Mallaig's little harbour might've been a still life painted by a gifted artist. Small boats crowded the water, two of them orange-coloured dinghies moored near the pier. Further out, three larger craft with bright-red hulls berthed in a line together with others of their ilk. In one, a man in yellow overalls bent to his task, oblivious to his surroundings. No pleasure craft these. Not some fund manager's tax write-off hobby registered in the Cayman Islands. Working vessels braving the elements searching for shellfish and prawns that would appear on the menus of expensive restaurants in London and Paris.

It was beautiful yet it gave me no joy; it wasn't why I was here.

The previous afternoon on the other end of the

phone the landlady had asked how long I'd be staying. I hadn't had an answer because it was impossible to know; on the first day I could run into Lewis Stone on Mallaig Main Street – if a ferry port and fishing village on the north-west coast was big enough to actually have a main street – or I might never find him.

The farther away I'd got from Glasgow, the more I'd understood the enormity of the task. Dwelling on it would've had me giving up, turning the car around, and driving home, so I hadn't, yet I was powerless to stop the small quiet voice whispering its truth. There was more chance of me winning the bloody lottery than finding Lewis Stone. Sam hadn't been slow to share her theory about why I was in so deep and perhaps she was right. Either way, I was powerless to stop it by myself. She'd phoned four or five times. I hadn't returned her calls – not how a big sister should behave. She needed me and I'd shut her out, too concerned with juggling anger, hate, despair, self-pity and every other negative feeling under the sun.

Inside, I knew Molly's passing had been the excuse I'd been looking for to hit back. And it was destroying me. Life wasn't fair; where had I got the idea it was supposed to be? Bad things happened to good people. It was time to try accepting that. What I was doing couldn't go on – I couldn't go on – it had to end and I had to be the one to end it. In the towering majesty of The Great Glen, I made a sacred promise to my husband. 'Three days, Freddy. Three days and, one way or another, it'll be over.'

I believed he'd heard me and would hold me to it. Somebody needed to, because I was far from sure I'd be able to.

My brief acquaintance with Rachel had shown me she wasn't the most trustworthy person in the universe. That was a laugh! I'd conveniently forgotten the lies I'd told the police – not on her behalf, on mine. In service to *my* agenda. To be fair to her, she'd delivered what she'd promised and I was grateful. But her information was second-hand – or maybe third-hand was more accurate. Stone might already be on his way back to Glasgow or boarding a flight at Edinburgh Airport for London while I chased in the opposite direction.

The implausibility of it all finally won out and I drove with my old friend the black dog in the car and sank back to that dark place I'd never really escaped. Avenging Molly had become more than a righteous quest. It had taken over, possessed me like an evil spirit. Grief had morphed into something more, almost as if I were slowly adopting piece after piece of her, making it my own.

The evidence was everywhere: I'd packed my stuff into a canvas bag found at the bottom of *her* wardrobe, slept the night on top of *her* bed, and started north the next morning wearing *her* blonde wig and the tartan scarf I'd taken from Angus.

The realisation of how far it had gone unsettled me, that was true. But I wasn't ready to pull to the side of the road and sit sweating and scared behind the wheel, glad to have seen the awful truth of my actions before it was too late. None of that. Changing course wouldn't come into it. I'd asked Freddy to give me strength, told him I would do the rest, and driven on towards Loch Morar with the calm of an executioner in my heart.

* * *

Mrs Gillies could have been fifty-eight, eighty-three, or any age in between; her hair was grey but she had the smooth unlined complexion of a much younger woman, and I was reminded of the ancient face in the mirror upstairs. She stayed behind a door of the B&B at the end of the hall where I guessed she kept tabs on the comings and goings of her guests. She'd heard my steps on the stairs and was waiting for me at the bottom. I felt obliged to be friendly. 'Good morning. I'm off for a walk round the harbour and to get myself a coffee. Where would you recommend?'

She laughed. 'That won't take long. There isn't much in Mallaig. It's hard even for me to imagine what it was like in its heyday. The kippering yards were where the petrol station is now. They used to say you could smell the smoke out at sea before you even saw the village.'

'It's lovely.'

She sighed. 'Aye, maybe it is and maybe it isn't. I'm thinking you'd see it differently if you'd been looking at it all your life. If it's a walk you're after, you'd do better on the sands. Did you see the film *Local Hero*?'

'Yes.'

'Well, that's where they did the beach scenes. The Silver Sands, they're called. Not difficult to understand why.'

I hadn't seen the movie, though – thanks again to Google – I knew about the sands.

'How do I get there?'

'Go to Morar. Start there. As for coffee, I don't drink the stuff myself, but I hear talk The Bakehouse & Crannog on the Old Quay is very good.'

* * *

I walked along East Bay into the centre, skirting the harbour, more workaday from this level than the panorama I'd seen from the window. The fisherman in yellow overalls was still at it; he didn't look up, completely focused on whatever he was doing. I understood how that felt and wished I didn't.

Mrs Gillies had told the truth. Mallaig was small; the nearest place of any size was Fort William forty-odd miles away. I'd been polite and didn't tell her I already knew what her home town had to offer because the previous night I'd trawled every restaurant and checked out The Marine, The Steam Inn and Chlachain pubs in case the man whose miserable existence I'd sworn to end was standing at a bar buying single malts for the locals.

He wasn't – at least, not while I was there. To be certain, I'd even included the car parks in my search – only one, as it happened, the West Bay – but saw no sign of the red Golf GTI that had killed my sister.

Not a great beginning and I'd tossed and turned in the strange bed, picturing what Stone would do and where he'd go in a place like this: he had to eat and fill up with petrol. That meant the Co-op on Station Road and the garage at the harbour. Perhaps, sometimes, even monsters got lonely and yearned to reconnect with people, ergo, my tour of the bars and restaurants.

It felt logical and I was keen to believe Lewis Stone would come here – eventually.

How it would help was what had kept me awake.

There was a sharpness in the morning air that stung my cheeks and made my throat raw. Herring gulls scavenging for the easy pickings of scrap fish and seafood readily available around the harbour swooped and soared in the sky. From nowhere, a tiredness that wasn't physical descended on me and, for a moment, I heard the black dog padding at my heels and felt his warm fetid breath on my neck. I closed my eyes and mentally screamed at him to leave. When I opened them, he was gone – a victory, tiny and no doubt temporary, but better than nothing; I'd take it.

The Bakehouse was a surprise – a real bakery, heavy with the smell of yeasty fresh bread in wicker baskets and sweet pastries in a glass display cabinet reminding me I was hungry. I bought coffee and an almond croissant and sat on one of the two weathered wooden seats overlooking the water. It was time to do what I'd come to do and I was so uneasy about it I was forced to hold my cup with both hands to stop it spilling over.

There were worse things than not finding Lewis Stone. Like finding him.

The sand was running through the glass. I finished

my drink and walked back to Mrs Gillies' house and my car. Halfway round the harbour I stopped and leaned on the grey-metal barrier to watch a CalMac ferry arrive from the islands.

If Freddy had been here, sailing to Skye or Rum with him would've been wildly romantic and impossible to resist. But he wasn't.

It was going to be a long three days.

62

Shawcross wasn't getting it, or perhaps he didn't want to get it was more accurate. He was missing the urgency of the situation. Damian tried again. 'Okay, one more time, Oliver. Against my better judgement I went up north to see Lewis and – to answer your first question *again* – he wasn't fine. In fact, I'd describe him as very far from fine.'

'He disagreed with you and you argued. What did you expect?'

Damian wanted to scream. 'I expected him to recognise I hadn't driven all the way there for the good of my health. I expected us to try to have some semblance of a discussion and come to a decision based on the imperatives of owning a business that has gone as far as we can take it and needs help from outside. Also, and excuse me for being a nit-picking arsehole, but we didn't *argue*, as you put it, we fought. And I do mean fought. The bastard tried to do me a serious injury.'

'This is Lewis we're talking about. He wouldn't hurt a fly. You're exaggerating, surely?'

Damian heard himself breathing hard into the mobile. 'Tell me the truth. You told him I was coming, didn't you?'

The lawyer rejected the premise. 'Absolutely not. I give you my word.'

'The word of a lawyer – how much is that worth?'

Oliver let the insult pass him by. He said, 'Why would I?'

'Because you're his man, his father's lawyer from way back; you're old mates.' Damian chuckled. 'Not that that will do you any good, Oliver, he intends to fire your arse out the door as soon as he comes back.'

'I know, he told me. Which makes a mockery of your nasty insinuation, don't you think?'

Damian backtracked. 'Okay, you've convinced me. So here's our dilemma: the Lassiter-Accardi offer closes in days and the madman who owns 50 per cent of the business refuses to even consider it. You're the legal expert here. What can we do?'

'The short answer – and for the reason you've just stated – is nothing. One of you has to be dead before the other can legitimately sell, assuming the deceased has no family to inherit his share. Lewis is an only child.'

Damian's frustration got the better of him. 'Whichever way I turn he's fucking the business up. Because of him I stand to come out of this with bloody nothing. I wish he was dead. I really do.'

Shawcross heard the anguish in the other man's voice, remembered the slight, and wasn't unhappy. He rubbed salt into the wound. 'Accepting he's beaten you must be hard.'

63

My first sight of the loch took my breath away. I pulled into the side of the road, got out of the car, and walked to the water's edge. Seeing it roll flat-calm and glassy into the distance was a daunting, dispiriting experience, and I wanted to cry as the sheer enormity of what I was up against hit again. I hadn't been coerced or blackmailed. There was no one else to blame: I wasn't prepared and I should have been. Because it was what I'd wanted to hear, I'd eagerly allowed Rachel's information, deceptively vague and at the same time seductively specific, to fuel expectations in me that were already bloated and unrealistic. Loch Morar brought me down to earth with a crash they probably heard in Sauchiehall Street. When Interpol was after you, this was the place to come; it was huge.

Finding Lewis Stone's house hadn't seemed to me to be an impossible ask. Funny, if it hadn't been so important. Molly's death was the wound that wouldn't heal – it had hurt then and it hurt now. Every day since that awful time in the hospital with Mr Gupta I'd put myself through hell but on the drive north good sense had put in an appearance. Late, but, I hoped, not too late: I'd given myself three days to track Stone down and do what needed to be done. Then, win or lose, resolved or unresolved, I'd return to Glasgow and get on with the rest of my life. In the warmth of the car, I shivered. Three days or thirty-three, it wouldn't matter. On the banks of an ancient loch I came as close as I'd ever come to admitting defeat, turning round, and going home.

But I wouldn't because the difference between giving up and accepting was a chasm I'd never bridge. So, I went on.

It took eleven minutes – I counted them – to drive the road hugging the rocky north shore peppered with occasional inlets that would be beautiful on another day. When it veered left towards Tarbet and away from the water, I stopped and went back, disappointed and relieved in equal measure. Lewis Stone couldn't have chosen a better place to hide. Except, he wasn't hiding. That would've been admitting he'd done something wrong.

It was only the first bloody day and already I felt like pointing the car south. My life – existence would be a more apt description – was on hold in Glasgow. If there was nothing for me here there was little more in the city. Freddy and Molly, two people who'd been a part of me, were gone and I hadn't even replied to Sam's calls, knowing she'd ask where I was and give me a lecture I'd rather not listen to.

I needed to clear my head, sort myself out, and restore some balance, so when I saw the sign for Arisaig, I followed it.

The Silver Sands at Camusdarach weren't silver although they came pretty close – a glistening powder arc lapped by clear water I was powerless to resist and I walked a good half-mile in my bare feet. Molly would've said I was 'reconnecting'. I wasn't certain about that. She'd been misguided, wrongly imagining my relationship with Freddy had always been sweetness and light. That wasn't true; like everybody, we'd had our moments, but we'd sorted many a disagreement tramping together along a windswept Ayr beach on days just like this.

Looking out across the water, seeing Eigg and Rum

on the horizon, helped me regain my purpose and my courage. I could do this. I would do it. Because it was the right thing.

64

The Ubiquitous Chip in Ashton Lane had been the obvious choice for lunch. It was where they'd come nine years ago, the first time they'd met. He'd been about to begin renovation on two houses – one near Luss, the other in Helensburgh – she'd been a pretty young rep for a UPVC window manufacturer, building relationships and trawling for business. He'd had nothing for her – Victorian architecture and unplasticised polyvinyl chloride weren't intended to go together. Nevertheless, Colin remembered she'd paid the bill. Since then, he'd gone on to become a successful developer and she'd risen to Regional Sales Manager for Central Scotland.

Times might have changed; Fiona Kelly hadn't –

she'd been a good-looking younger woman and still was: slim, brunette and with a nice smile she used a lot. The market she was in was crowded but, even then, he'd known she'd do well.

She'd made an effort for today although he was aware the same couldn't be said for him – too many whiskies and not enough sleep had left him sluggish and haggard; his energy was low and there were bags under his eyes.

A waiter brought menus and asked if they wished to see the wine list. She glanced at Colin, willing to take her cue from him. He answered for both of them. 'No, I don't think so. Otherwise the whole afternoon will be a bust. We'll stick with water. Sparkling.'

She agreed. 'You're right, better not, although I've freed up the rest of the day for us.'

Colin understood what she was saying and let it pass. Fiona registered his reticence; if she was annoyed, she kept it hidden. 'So, what's new in your world?'

His initial reaction was to assume she'd heard about the break-up with Sam and was getting it out in the open before she made a move on him. Colin hoped he was wrong because he'd have to disappoint her.

He made a show of unfolding his napkin to buy himself time. 'What can I tell you that you don't already know? Costs have gone through the roof and there's a limit to how much we can expect our customers to shoulder before they decide to leave their money in the bank instead of giving it to us. As it is, supply chain issues and a shortage of core materials have increased prices by 24 per cent in the past year alone.'

Fiona nodded. 'Everybody's suffering. I suppose it's a question of holding on until things improve. Are you in a position to do that?'

'For the moment. Anyway – enough doom and gloom – what're we eating? And I've changed my mind. Let's have some wine. Something decent, eh? Anything you fancy.'

Colin's mobile rang. He lifted it, saw it was Sam, and didn't take the call. Fiona noticed and pretended she hadn't. She said, 'I was trying to remember how long it's been since I saw you.'

'It's been a while. You were about to get married. How long ago would that be?'

'Was I? Did I bore you blabbing on about bridesmaids and dresses and guest lists and all that bloody junk?'

'Not for a minute. You were sharing what you had

to share and were excited, and so you should've been. I was happy for you.'

Fiona put her cutlery down; she'd suddenly lost her appetite. 'Well – before you ask – it didn't work out. Actually, it was a disaster. On the plane coming back from our honeymoon, he didn't speak. Not a word. To give you an idea of the atmosphere, from the Seychelles to London is a thirteen-hour flight, so you get the picture.'

'I'm sorry.'

'Don't be. I'm not. It was a mistake. People talk about "not being right for each other" but it's true. Sometimes.'

'Has it put you off men?'

'Marriage, definitely. Men... well, that would depend on the man, wouldn't it? Let's just say I'm keeping my options open.'

Colin didn't share his own circumstances. The end of the affair had crushed him; he was a long way from being ready to try again – with this woman or anybody else. In fact, he might never be ready and replied defensively, 'Good for you. At the end of the day, we're strangers, all of us, and for most that's how it stays. Nobody knows anybody, not really. Marriage is a lottery. For a lot of folk and for a hatful of reasons, a miserable experience they're in no hurry to repeat.'

His mobile vibrated; he killed the call and brought his attention back to his companion. Fiona said, 'Wouldn't you be better just turning it off?'

'No, the office might need to get a hold of me. We're expecting the planning department to come back on the latest project with the usual list of objections.'

'I'd assumed you'd be well in there.'

Colin laughed. 'We were, at least, I thought we were. The guy we were dealing with left. The new people aren't as... amenable to our situation.'

'Then, good luck with that.'

'Thanks. Shall we order dessert afterwards or are you watching your figure?'

She feigned insult. 'Are you suggesting I should be?'

Before he could reply his phone rang again. This time he switched it off and put it in his pocket. Fiona leaned across, so close he could see a tiny fleck of yellow in her left iris.

'Is that your wife checking up on you?'

Colin lied without thinking about it. 'No,' he said, 'it's nobody.'

* * *

Colin lay on the bed, wondering what the hell was happening to him. He had a headache and not because of the wine he'd drunk at lunch. The meal had gone well enough, though Fiona Kelly might have a different take. From the beginning she'd made her interest in him obvious, hanging onto his every word as if it was the Sermon on the fucking Mount. At the end as they were leaving, she'd rested one hand on his arm and removed a speck that didn't exist from his lapel with the other, searching his face for the flicker of desire that would explode in a hotel bedroom. She'd wanted him. As straightforward as that. And why not? Fiona wasn't married and, in his heart, neither was he. Not any more. He'd done his best to disguise his reaction: the idea appalled him. But offending her wasn't right; she'd done nothing to deserve it. In Scotland, feeling horny wasn't a crime, at least, not yet.

They'd walked through Ashton Lane to Byres Road. On the pavement, she'd stepped away, studied him quizzically, and got ready to play her final card. 'Lovely to see you again, Colin. It really is. I'm glad it's all worked out for you. A guy with your talent... I never doubted it.'

'And you, Fiona. Next time we meet I fully expect you to be running the company. My people will speak to your people and all that nonsense. That's when we'll know we've "arrived".'

The compliment had pleased her and she'd smiled. It had faded from her lips and he'd guessed what was coming. 'This probably sounds odd but I'm not ready to go home, are you?'

'Well, actually—'

'How about finishing this at the Sky Bar? Have you been? The view is fantastic. Coffee's not bad, either. On me.'

He'd shuffled awkwardly. 'I'd love to, except...'

Fiona had moved quickly to cover her embarrassment. 'No problem. Just a thought. Thank you for lunch and don't do anything I wouldn't do. Believe me, that gives you plenty of scope.'

Colin had tried to repair the damage. 'I'm getting a taxi back to the office, where can I drop you?'

She'd rejected the offer without considering it. 'No need, I'm not in a hurry. I told you I'd left my diary clear this afternoon. Take care of yourself, Colin.'

He swung his legs off the bed onto the floor, sat up, and rubbed his eyes. Maybe he should ring Fiona and apologise for behaving like a prick. Tell her it wasn't her fault, but she was off the mark with her assessment: it hadn't 'all worked out' for him. Far from it. His whole life had turned to shit.

Not taking Sam's calls in the Ubiquitous Chip felt like another betrayal. Fiona sitting across the table had given him an excuse to ignore them. It had been easy. And the correct decision. But guilt wouldn't leave him alone and he couldn't shake the dreadful certainty something was wrong. His finger hovered over the call button, a second from making contact. He didn't because he understood only too well where it would go: Sam would hear his voice and read what wasn't there into it. Mistake concern for love. Worse, she'd realise she'd stumbled on the trigger that brought him running, press and press and press it until they ended up hating each other for who they weren't, loathing themselves for who they were. No, he couldn't do that, to either of them.

Colin didn't think of himself as a strong person, especially where Sam was concerned. Leaving her had required fortitude he hadn't credited himself with. Going back would only delay the agony, postpone the inevitable. When things calmed down – if they ever did – they'd discuss splitting what they had as rational human beings, fairly, without anger or resentment or malice. Before then, Colin hoped to God she wouldn't hire some Rottweiler of a lawyer to rip him apart.

He got into bed without bothering to undress, put out the light, and tried to sleep. An hour later, at twenty-five minutes to midnight and still awake, he realised Sam had stopped trying to reach him. Something was definitely off.

In the hotel that had become his home he called and heard it go straight to voicemail. Colin grabbed his car keys and ran for the door.

***

This wasn't the reaction of an indifferent husband. This was the frightened response of someone who cared more deeply than he'd known.

Colin leaned over the steering wheel, willing the car to go faster. Tonight – for a change – he was sober, otherwise not hearing from Sam wouldn't have registered. Too many evenings had ended with him clearing out the mini-bar before falling into bed. He'd told himself he didn't love his wife. That what they'd had, what they'd been – Colin and Sam; Mr and Mrs MacLean – had run its course. And he'd believed it. Of course, the truth wasn't conveniently black-and-white – he definitely wasn't 'in love' with her and doubted he'd ever know that with anyone again. But she meant a lot to him and always would. Instead of putting off the inevitable, waiting for the right moment to tell Sam, he should've ended the marriage, made a clean break with his conscience relatively clear.

He hadn't and this was the result.

He turned off the motorway at Junction 5 with tears in his eyes, remembering how he'd humiliated her. Had there really been no way to avoid damaging a woman who would never have given up on them?

Colin tried again to reach her – still no answer. More convinced than ever she was in trouble, he pressed the accelerator to the floor. The house they'd shared sat apart on a prime site, backing onto woodland at the far end of the estate; lights blazed in every room, upstairs and down. Colin slammed the brakes, the car screeched to a halt, and he raced to the front door.

It was unlocked and a new fear gripped him.

What the fuck was happening?

He stepped cautiously into the hall and checked the lounge and TV room without finding her. Fear morphed into an overwhelming terror Colin was barely able to control. He took the stairs, two at a time, and paused at the top, suddenly aware he might not be alone. Other houses on the estate had been burgled; maybe... he preferred not to dwell on it and let the thought go. Except, Sam hadn't tried to call him in hours. Was that why she'd kept phoning? Colin took a deep breath and forced himself to focus. He listened, hearing nothing except the tinnitus-hiss of adrenaline in his ears and the silence of the house. He tiptoed to the master bedroom, braced against Christ knew what.

Inside, there was no sign of her; clothes lay where she'd dropped them.

Colin was beginning to understand. Downstairs the kitchen confirmed the tale he'd suspected but hadn't wanted to admit. Sam adored this house, loved living here. That wasn't how it looked: the sink and draining board were full of dirty plates, the food on them almost untouched, knives and forks and un-washed cups and glasses; whisky, wine, and gin bottles overflowed from a black bin bag in the corner. From the smell, the window hadn't been opened in days and his terror instantly crystallised to anger; there was no fucking masked thief! She'd got drunk, forgotten to lock up and left the bloody lights on. Right now, she was probably in some fucking late-night drinking den getting even more wasted.

He went round the house switching off lights, banged the front door behind him and got into his car.

If it weren't so pathetic it would be funny.

Colin fired the ignition, about to pull away when he noticed he'd missed a light in the en suite. He cut the engine and went back into the house. The door to the bathroom was ajar; he pushed it open.

The first thing he noticed was the tumbler and the whisky bottle on the floor. Then he dropped to his knees; Sam was in the bath, her head resting on the porcelain; her eyes were closed, her skin deathly pale, and there was a blueish tinge to her lips. She was naked, her knees poking above the water that almost filled the tub. Her left arm was submerged, the right hung limply over the roll-top edge, fingers upturned, reaching for something only she had seen, directly above a pool of blood gathered on the tiles. Some of it had dripped from her wrist like pink tears down the outside. The old-fashioned razor blade she'd used lay smeared with red on the mat where it had fallen once it had served its purpose: Colin recognised it as Wilkinson Sword – the brand he used – saw the gashes where she'd cut herself and screamed, 'No! No! No, Sam! No!'

He slid his arms beneath her body, lifted her to the bed and laid her down, repeating her name over and over. He felt for a pulse and found none. Frantic with fear, he dialled 999.

'I need an ambulance! It's an emergency!'

The controller did his job, calmly asking for the information he needed. 'Where are you?'

'Newton Mearns.'

'And what is the emergency?'

Colin could hardly get the words out. 'It's my wife... my... wife... needs help. Please hurry.'

'I know this is difficult but take your time and tell me what's happened.'

'I can't. We don't have time. She isn't responding.'

'I understand that but—'

'You don't, you don't understand anything! I think she's killed herself!'

65

Lewis had no idea what time it was, except that it was late. The whisky tasted raw and harsh in his throat; tonight, the comfort he usually found in it wasn't there. He stared into the fire at the flames hungrily licking the logs chopped on his second day here with his father's rusty old axe and left neatly stacked at the side of the house. Damian turning up unannounced in Morar had been an unwelcome surprise and when Lewis had seen the figure waving from the shore he hadn't recognised him. How much better it would've been for both of them if he'd ignored him and kept on fishing.

He massaged his temple and closed his eyes, remembering the ugly scene that had kicked off the moment they'd met, and sighed. The argument didn't bother him – they'd had plenty of those over the years, resolved with a handshake and a drink in the Horseshoe – but what they'd become was more shocking even than the KILLER note Damian claimed to have had nothing to do with. His denial had sounded sincere yet Lewis didn't trust him and the lie, so easily and convincingly told, was just one more reason to sever his relationship with the man he'd once considered a friend.

He sipped his drink, set the glass down, and confronted a reality that couldn't be denied. Out on the water with fresh air and a brisk breeze colouring his cheeks, it had been easy to believe he was on the mend. Except, it wasn't true, because all he'd done was swap one hiding place for another; Sherbrooke Avenue in Glasgow for this remote place in the north. Unless he did something about it, his 'sanctuary' would become a prison without bars. He needed people, human contact, to be surrounded by voices and laughter, otherwise what was the point in carrying on? He had to stop running from the past and face his demons. That prospect scared him and, in spite of the fire, he shivered as a momentary quiver of fear seized him.

He waited for it to pass then went through to the

tiny kitchen where his mother had gutted and fried
the fish his father had caught, sensing her presence at
his shoulder, urging him to be strong. There was only
so much guilt, so much pain, anyone could handle and
Lewis had reached his limit. The whisky cascaded into
the sink and down the drain until the bottle was
empty. It was time to fight back and tomorrow he'd
begin.

* * *

When he woke up it was still dark but the resolve of
the previous night burned in him unchanged. Lewis
got out of bed, pulled on his jeans, and padded bare-
foot to the jetty as a crescent moon descended behind
the silhouettes of the tree tops on the far shore, scat-
tering the last rays of silver light before dawn arrived
on Loch Morar. He was witnessing the beginning of a
new day in all its majesty and felt hope stir inside him.
Back in the house, nervous but excited, he did some
stretches, drank two large glasses of water, and went to
look for his father's old running shoes. He found them
at the bottom of a wooden trunk in the spare bedroom. They'd been unused for so long the laces were
stiff, the canvas cracked and dry; when he turned one

of them upside down, grains of sand fell into his palm and Lewis smiled.

The drive through the forest was like an out-of-body experience, a dream he'd wandered into. His destination was Camusdarach with its sprawling arc of glistening sand and clear water, perfect for what he intended to do. He parked the Golf and walked to the water's edge. In the distance, the jagged crests of the Cuillin Hills on the Isle of Skye shimmered like a lost world in the early-morning mist. Lewis knew that this was where he was supposed to be – he'd been in a bad place but it was time to break the spell.

He started to run, replaying the awful night in his head, seeing the images, knowing how it ended, dreading it. Fear ate him from the inside and he almost gave up but he kept going, making himself picture her body, broken and bleeding in the road. Bile rose in his thoat; he thought he would be sick. Somehow he forced himself to go on, shouting at his tormentors, 'Fuck you! It was an accident! A horrible tragic twist of fate! I'm not to blame! There is no blame, do you hear me? There is no blame! Now, fuck off. I'm done with you!'

He stopped, exhausted, and rested his hands on his knees until the fire in his chest faded and his breathing returned to something resembling normal.

Lewis whispered to the voices in his head, 'It's over. I can't let you do this to me any more. I won't let you.'

It took more courage and strength than he'd imagined he had sitting on the cool sand talking to himself until there was nothing left to say. After a while, trembling, bathed in sweat and unsure if his legs would hold him, he made his way slowly to the car. At the house, he showered and changed his clothes, feeling tired but free. And while he was telling himself the truth, it was worth admitting Damian deserved an apology. He'd driven all the way up here to speak to him and been cut off before he could get a word out. On balance, he was right to want to sell Stone Free. The unpalatable reality was that Lassiter-Accardi was an immoral bottom feeder beholden to its shareholders and nobody else, but if they didn't buy the business somebody else would. Given the irreparable state of the partners' relationship and the money the Americans were willing to pay, it made sense. He'd call Damian later, ask him to accept the offer and take the buyout to the next stage. There were other opportunities out there and the next one wouldn't be starting in a lock-up down a side street in Glasgow with creditors hassling him, or drinking on the slate in the Horseshoe on a Friday night.

He thought about breakfast but couldn't face

eating and decided to settle for coffee, though not here – that was the old Lewis. If he wanted caffeine he'd get it surrounded by conversation, laughter and love, everything he'd missed, everything that made life worth living. And, damn it, he'd make himself speak to someone, anyone, it didn't matter who, and dare his demons to stop him.

66

I'd promised to give it three days and I'd kept my word. I hadn't quit, although more than once I'd felt like it because it had been fruitless, a total waste of time. I hadn't discovered Lewis Stone or his house and seventy-two hours after I'd checked into Mrs Gillies' B&B, I was depressed and defeated, weighed down by a sense of failure I could almost taste. Even in winter it was beautiful up here, but I wasn't a tourist – the spectacular scenery had no appeal. On the pier, with a chill southerly wind blowing around me, my positivity on the Silver Sands at Camusdarach might never have happened, and as I watched the arrival of the last CalMac ferry from the islands I knew I was ready to go home.

All that remained was one final miserable trawl of Mallaig before drawing a line under the whole misguided trip. I did the rounds in light rain that seeped through to my bones and added the finishing touch to my mood. As usual, Stone wasn't in any of the pubs or restaurants and I returned to my room, lay on the bed, and cried myself to sleep.

This morning, a calm I wasn't used to settled over me; I'd done my best. Unfortunately, it hadn't been good enough. Now my search was over I wanted back to Glasgow as soon as possible and didn't plan on stopping. When I paid my bill and checked out of Mrs Gillies's guest house, a coffee for the road seemed appropriate. The Bakehouse was as good as any; the pastries were first class. Several folk, locals by the look of them, had had the same idea and it took a few minutes to get served. I bought two almond croissants from the pleasant guy behind the counter, who put them in a brown paper bag, then I took it and my Americano to the seat outside and studied the harbour for the last time. Not much had changed. I guessed not much ever did in these parts. The orange dinghies and two of the three boats with bright-red hulls were still there; the fisherman in yellow overalls wasn't. I stared at the scene, wondering if I could be happy in a place like this, or was the grime of the city irrevocably ingrained?

From behind a voice said, 'Penny for them,' and I turned. He was taller than I remembered, the black windcheater making him look chunky across the shoulders. And he was older – under the rosy weather-beaten cheeks, his face was lined. The man I remembered being breathalysed in Byres Road and pacing the conservatory of his fancy house in Sherbrooke Avenue while I stood outside in the snow had seemed younger and fitter. He came towards me, smiling. 'Will a penny be enough?'

Staying calm, acting normal when every fibre in my body screamed, was the most difficult thing I'd ever done. Somehow, I fought down my shock and managed to reply.

'More than enough.'

'Good. I'm a bit like that myself. Do you mind if I join you?'

I'd come here to find this man. Instead, he'd found me. Spending time with him, pretending we were just two people having a casual conversation, was surreal and I wasn't certain I could handle it. Stone didn't notice. We sat side by side, looking out at the harbour and I quickly realised making small talk with a stranger was an art he hadn't mastered. For a long time we didn't speak, then, unexpectedly, he opened up.

'My parents used to bring me to Morar. They loved it.' He waved a hand across the scene. 'All this went over my head. I was too young to appreciate it. What brings you here?'

I was afraid the tremble in my voice would give me away. 'I wanted to get out of Glasgow for a few days. In fact, I'm on my way back there now.'

He hesitated, unsure of himself. 'Look – and please don't take this the wrong way – the fact is, I've been in my own company too long and I'm bored with me. This may sound strange so please feel free to say no. Would you like to have lunch? If it doesn't interfere with your plans, of course.' Unaware of my motive, he threw in a sweetener to get me to agree. 'Afterwards, we could walk on the Silver Sands before you swap paradise for Sauchiehall Street.'

I blurted out a reply that, to my ears, sounded stiff and forced. 'You've convinced me. To tell the truth, I could do with some company too. There's far too much time to think when you're by yourself.'

My reply pleased him. He tapped the side of his cup with his finger. 'Bloody good coffee, here. Hard to believe you can get such decent beans this far from the cities. Shall we have another, on me?'

I kept up the act. 'Thank you, that would be nice.'

So many nights had been spent imagining what I'd do if I came face to face with the bogeyman who'd stalked my dreams. In reality, Lewis Stone was nondescript, unmemorable: ordinary, the only word for it. The kind of guy you'd pass in the street and not notice.

He didn't look like a monster, but I knew he was.

67

Colin had gone in the ambulance with Sam, holding her hand, feeling how cold it was and knowing why. He pictured the face underneath the oxygen mask that had captured his heart in The Garage on Sauchiehall Street so long ago. What had he done to that girl?

Colin whispered, 'Sam, I'm so sorry,' and felt her fingers press his. 'Everything's going to be all right. Just don't go. Please, Sam, stay with me.'

Before leaving the house, the medics had worked to stabilise her condition. Colin had watched them bent over her body, totally focused on what they were doing. With nothing to contribute he'd stayed out of the way. Nobody spoke to him; he might as well not have been there. One of them had glanced in his direction. Colin couldn't meet his eyes.

At the hospital, they'd taken Sam away and left him alone to wait in a corridor. He'd fished coins from his pocket and bought a cup of coffee from a machine down the hall. On a good day it would be undrinkable. Tonight, it had gone beyond even that. Colin sipped at it until it was lukewarm and set it down on the floor. The clock on the wall ticked and his anxiety grew. Footsteps made him turn to find a young doctor identified by the name tag on his white coat as Dr Armstrong.

He said, 'Your wife will recover, Mr MacLean. Fortunately, she made a poor job of it. A little bit deeper and you and I wouldn't be having this conversation.'

'Thank God. Can I see her?'

'Of course, but we've sedated her. She's sleeping.'

'When can I take her home?'

Colin realised he sounded stupid but couldn't stop himself. The doctor understood. 'As soon as she's stronger, probably tomorrow, though that won't be the end of it. People need a compelling reason to attempt suicide – compelling to them, at least. I'll be recommending your wife see a psychiatrist. The scars will fade, eventually, but unless she gets the help she needs, she may try again. Take it one day at a time.

This isn't something you can fix. As her husband you might wonder why you didn't see this coming and blame yourself. If I'd only said this, if I'd only done that.' He shook his head. 'When someone close to us does this, guilt is natural – the most natural thing in the world. My advice, for what it's worth, is: if it knocks on your door, don't let it in.'

Colin's response wasn't what the doctor expected. He said, 'I appreciate that and thank you again for bringing her back to me. But what if I am guilty?'

68

Lewis Stone rowed with the assured strokes of a man completely at home on the water, quietly breaking the surface with the oars as we left the jetty and headed out into the loch. With the sun behind him framing his head in golden light, I couldn't see his face – a gift from God, because looking at him made me want to rip his eyeballs out with my fingernails and feed them to the fish.

I'd followed the red Golf that had killed Molly from Mallaig to here. Now, it was a red dot at the side of the house. Given the property's location – off the main road at the end of a narrow dirt track through dense woodland – my only chance of ever finding it was if Stone showed me the way himself. He had and I'd followed, scarcely able to credit I was actually here. Running into him just as I was leaving Mallaig after so many disappointments had been a huge slice of luck I couldn't have imagined in my wildest fantasies.

At The Bakehouse, he'd done most of the talking, easy, inconsequential conversation asking what had brought me here, had I enjoyed it, and did I agree it was a special part of the world. My impression was of a guy starved of company, in his own way as adrift as I was myself. These days, strange men coming on to me didn't happen but that hadn't always been true. Before Freddy, I'd had my fair share of them, creeps mostly, who only wanted 'one thing', as my mother used to say, and presumed it was fine to be open about it, as though directness made their sleazy behaviour acceptable.

Stone wasn't one of them. His interest in me wasn't sexual – I had no sense of that – he was being friendly, nothing more, enjoying being with another person and not wanting it to end. In The Bakehouse we'd finished our coffees and had started to go when I'd said, 'It's a bit early to be thinking about lunch, isn't it?'

He'd zipped his windcheater, grinning like a boy with a secret he was bursting to tell.

'Not really. We'll have to catch it before we can eat it.'

And I knew I had him.

* * *

There was no wind, no birds in the sky, nothing. The second after Stone stopped rowing an awesome silence swallowed us. The house was still visible but the Golf wasn't. He let go of the oars, breathing heavily. There were two rods in the bottom of the boat on top of a couple of smooth rocks that were probably ten thousand years old, and a bucket of maggots. Since we'd arrived at his place, Stone hadn't said much; his earlier talkativeness had gone. Having someone to share his isolation seemed enough for him and he'd busied himself with the boat.

He wiped the film of sweat on his brow with his sleeve and spoke without looking at me. 'Can you fish?'

'I've never tried.'

'So that's a no. All right, this is as good a time as any to learn. And sorry, how stupid of me, I haven't even asked you your name.'

'It's Alex.'

He held out his hand. 'Lewis. Pleased to meet you.'

Losing Molly felt like someone had taken a wrecking ball to everything I'd held dear. Breathing the same air as the man responsible should've made my skin crawl. During the nights when I couldn't sleep and lay awake thinking about him, Stone was pure evil. Normal didn't fit the picture in my mind. Discovering the devil liked to fish was, in its own way, shocking; horns and a forked tail would've made it easier to despise him. But he wasn't exactly a man on the edge either, someone haunted by his demons and his actions. From what I'd seen of him here and in Mallaig, rumours of a breakdown were wide of the mark. His grip was firm, confident, the handshake of a guy untroubled about his place in the scheme of things.

Untroubled by the sorrow he'd caused.

And the hate I'd felt for him returned stronger than ever.

He handed me a rod. I took it reluctantly and looked away. Stone misunderstood and quickly reassured me this wasn't a test I needed to pass.

'Watch what I do, then go for it. And don't worry, lunch doesn't depend on you. The loch's teaming with fish. I promise you won't go hungry.'

He dipped his hand into the bucket, threaded a maggot onto the end of the line, stood up and cast it across the water. It landed almost without making a ripple.

He smiled. 'Looks easy, doesn't it?'

I didn't answer. I couldn't. From the moment I'd decided to dedicate myself to righting the wrong he'd done I'd been worried – more than worried, terrified – not only about my ability to actually kill another person, but how. The answer was at my feet in the bottom of the boat and I knew it was now or never. From nowhere a surge of heat shot through my body as the plan I'd searched for materialised in front of me. I fingered Molly's scarf and took a deep breath before asking, 'What are the rocks for?'

Coming from him, the reply surprised me. 'The fish we catch will be our lunch. We're going to eat them so they need to be killed humanely.'

'And that's where the rocks come in?'

Stone nodded. 'And that's where the rocks come in. For years it was assumed fish couldn't feel pain. It isn't true. That's why it's important to stun them before bleeding them out. Don't be put off, I'll do that bit. All you have to concentrate on is reeling a couple of the buggers in. No need to be nervous, give it a try.'

'Let me see you do it again.'

'Okay. It can look complicated. Once you get the hang of it, it's simple. All you have to remember is...'

The words faded and once again I was in Byres Road.

Coming down the steps laughing, Molly and Sam winding each other up; slipping on the ice and Sam catching me; the beggar's empty red-rimmed eyes and his mongrel wagging its tail as my fingers ran through its coat; Molly falling into the road and Sam's outstretched hand trying to save her like she'd done with me; the screech of brakes...

Somewhere far away, Lewis Stone was speaking. '...don't snatch it, let the rod do the work...'

I closed my hand round the surface worn smooth by eons, feeling its weight in my palm, thankful for it. Stone sensed me behind him. He half turned and I caught him on his left temple; the dull thud of rock against bone echoed across the wilderness. His jaw fell open, the rod dropped from his hands as he stared, unable to believe what I'd done to him.

I tore off the wig that had become so much a part of me I'd forgotten I was wearing the damned thing. 'Recognise the family resemblance?'

Stone swayed but stayed on his feet. My lip curled and I snarled, 'You don't fucking know what I'm talking about, do you? Does the name Molly Kennedy mean anything? It should, you bastard! You killed her!'

In the small hours, I'd rehearsed this moment.

Maybe it was because he was concussed, but what I was saying didn't register with him – he had no idea why this was happening and I hated him even more for it.

Because he didn't remember. He didn't remember Molly.

I raised the hand holding the rock to strike him again; he kicked my leg and sent me reeling. Somehow, I managed to stay upright and threw myself at him, screaming, tearing at his clothes. A second blow broke his nose, spattering a crimson arc across the boat and into his eyes. Half blind, he fought for his life, grabbed the scarf and tightened it round my neck. Panic dredged strength from the well of resentment I'd carried in me since I'd lost Freddy. This bastard wouldn't beat me; I wouldn't let him. Our faces were inches apart and I could smell his fear as I hit him again as hard as I could. Stone's fingers wouldn't let go of the material. He staggered backwards, threatening to topple the boat, his jaw working as he tried to speak. I managed to make out the words escaping from his bloodied mouth.

'Accident... It was... an accident.'

Lewis Stone fell over the side and went under the water, one hand ironically still clutching the tartan scarf. When the ripples settled, I scanned the surface, dreading he'd reappear, but he didn't. The man who had killed my sister was dead and in the silence I cried and cried for Molly, for Freddy, and for me.

After a long time, I picked up the oars and rowed slowly towards the shore.

69

The machine Sam was hooked up to in the small featureless box of a room away from the comings and goings on the ward hummed quietly in the background, and not for the first time Colin realised they'd been lucky. It had been a long night, the longest of his life. All through it he'd watched his wife lying motionless under the sheets, appreciating just how lucky he was. He hadn't pressed anyone for details, though from what he'd witnessed, the end hadn't been far away.

If his instinct hadn't urged him to drive from the city to Newton Mearns...

It was wiser to avoid dwelling on what might have been; the reality was dark enough.

To give Sam the blood she'd needed had taken hours. Colin MacLean had never been a religious man – on his knees by the bed, hands clasped in prayer, wasn't who he was. Instead, he'd sat motionless in a plastic chair, anxiously waiting for Sam to wake up, determined that, when she did, the first face she'd see would be his.

The doctor who'd spoken to him had counselled against taking on guilt for someone else's actions. Good advice, well meant and easy to give, unless you knew better.

Colin had been too wired and upset to notice his own tiredness. Now, with light streaming through the room's solitary window, his joints ached, the day-old shirt chafed the back of his neck, and his eyes felt gritty. A nurse, dressed in an NHS Scotland navy-blue tunic and trousers, looked in to make sure all was as it should be and left satisfied. On her way out she smiled. Colin tried to return it and couldn't – his spirit was heavy, unable to shake the image of the ragged skin where the blade had cut and her blood dripping down the side of the bath.

He tried calling Alex again. When he didn't reach her he cursed under his breath and left a voice message that bordered on angry – where the hell was she?

The medical man's warning haunted him. 'The

scars will fade, eventually, but unless she gets the help she needs, she may try again.'

Sam stirred and moved in the bed. Immediately, Colin was out of the chair. Her eyes fluttered open, closed, and opened again. Then, as she slowly realised where she was, the tears came in anguished pitiful sobs. Colin awkwardly tried to comfort her, searching in vain for the words that would make it all better. 'It's all right. It's okay, Sam. I'm here.'

'Who found me? Was it you?'

There was accusation in her tone and Colin would've preferred to avoid questions.

'I knew something was wrong when you stopped calling so I went to the house. Thank God I did. Losing you like that would be more than I could stand.'

She buried her face in the pillow and wouldn't look at him. When she did it broke what little of his heart was left to be broken. 'You should've let me go. I wanted to die. I still want to.'

Colin gently caressed her brow. 'Not in a million years, Sam Kennedy.'

She clutched at the straw. 'I can't do this without you, Colin. It's too hard.'

He held her and whispered, 'You don't have to. I'm not going anywhere.'

70

I drove back to Glasgow on autopilot, barely aware of where I was, fear travelling every mile with me, crawling over my skin like the maggots on the boat, and I found myself irrationally checking the rear mirror for the flashing blue light that would mean I hadn't got away with it after all. That Lewis Stone hadn't died, that Molly's killer wasn't in the inky depths of Loch Morar, the fate he undoubtedly deserved. No. Somehow the bastard had survived. None of it happened. There was no light, blue or otherwise, just the voices in my head.

I crossed the Ballachulish Bridge and kept going. As I passed through the Great Glen, the sky began to darken, adding menace to an already intimidating landscape. In school, I'd learned about Glencoe's brutal history of bloody murder. Until that moment, it had been no more than a story from long ago. Now I understood what it meant and wished I didn't.

When I reached Tyndrum at the southern edge of Rannoch Moor, night had fallen and I reduced my speed until I was clear of the village, then picked it up again using full beam whenever I was the only vehicle on the road – which was most of the time. At a particularly sharp bend beyond the hamlet of Ardlui, from nowhere, Stone's disembodied face appeared in front of me. Not the chatty weather-beaten man I'd run into outside The Bakehouse in Mallaig, not that guy, but how he'd look after the sticklebacks and the eels had been at him: the head was bloated, inflated like a balloon, the nose missing where something had eaten it; on either side of what remained, the chubby lifeless cheeks glowed ghostly white below black bloodied holes where his eyes had been.

I screamed, took my hands off the wheel to beat the awful apparition away and almost ran into the water. A hundred yards further on I pulled over, sweating and shivering, and waited for my hands to stop shaking. Delayed reaction. With what I'd been through, not unexpected. My imagination was running riot. I was tired, scared, stressed, and easily spooked. Who wouldn't be? But, in the clear light of a new day, I'd recognise the truth and feel good because I'd succeeded: Lewis Stone was at the bottom of the loch, the police weren't coming – that was just me being silly – and I'd avenged Molly.

It had used up all of my energy, taken everything I had. And somewhere along the line I'd lost myself, forgotten I was one of the Kennedy sisters.

Sisters! Oh, my God! I'd been so laser-focused on Molly, Sam had gone out of my mind. Shit! She'd be going spare worrying about me when it should be the other way round.

I turned on my mobile for the first time in days to discover I was in demand – five missed calls from her and four from Colin. Why would he be phoning me? Please God, don't let anything bad have happened.

His last contact was a voice message, as terse as it was brief, and there was a catch in there I hadn't heard before, as though he'd been crying.

'Alex, where the fuck are you? Call me, it's urgent.'

* * *

Colin MacLean hadn't always been my brother-in-law although that wasn't how it felt because he'd been part of the family for so long it was hard to think of him any other way.

When Sam had first introduced me to her shiny new boyfriend, I'd liked what I'd seen and, even at that early stage, sensed something special between them. She'd stood nervously aside like an artist about to unveil a masterpiece, eyes wide, willing me to approve, afraid I'd find a flaw. She needn't have worried. There was no flaw. He'd seemed perfect for her; they'd seemed perfect for each other. And he'd obviously been in love with my sister.

Later, when she'd announced they were getting married, I couldn't have been more pleased: Sam was 'sorted'; Molly was in a relationship with Rufus, a long-haired dropout with a braided beard and a lazy smile who always had a joint going, played Leonard Cohen songs badly on a beat-up acoustic guitar, and wanted her to leave Glasgow to join a kibbutz in Israel – a very Molly thing to do. She was thinking about it. On Sam's big day the sun shone, Molly and I were her bridesmaids and the Kennedy girls, two of them, at least – by this time Rufus was history along with a parade of other totally unsuitable guys Molly had toyed with and dumped – looked all set for a happy ever after.

Only, that wasn't how it had worked out: Freddy

was in the grave; Molly died an unnecessary death under the wheels of a car; Sam's marriage hadn't lasted and her estranged husband had left an angry voicemail on my phone that paralysed me with fear.

Colin answered on the second ring and forcefully admonished me in clipped whispered sentences that left no doubt about his feelings. 'At long fucking last! Where've you been, Alex? I've tried your number umpteen times.'

The aggression surprised me and I stuttered a reply. 'What? I... I... had to take care of something.'

His fury erupted; he made no attempt to hold it back. 'Really? Well, I hope, for your sake, it was important.'

'It was. What's going on, Colin?'

'Nothing, everything's fine. *Now*.'

He emphasised the last word so I understood I was too late to be any bloody use.

'Is it Sam? Is she all right? Tell me.'

Colin spoke louder and I guessed he'd gone into another room. 'Yes, and thank you for finally remembering she exists. When she's strong enough I'll tell her. I'm sure she'll appreciate it.'

The sarcasm was starting to grate. I bit back an acid response and kept my tone even.

'I get that you're upset but taking it out on me

won't help. These last months I've been under a lot of pressure. I needed a break and went away for a few days to be on my own and get my head together. Because I didn't want to talk to anybody, I left my phone turned off, which maybe wasn't the smartest thing to do, I grant you. So, apologies for that. Now, stop fucking about and tell me what's wrong.'

He sighed and I held my breath. 'Sam tried to commit suicide.'

'What?'

'She cut her wrists.'

I couldn't believe it. Didn't want to believe it.

'Oh, God! Poor Sam! When was this?'

'Last night, she stopped phoning me. After a while I realised something wasn't right and came straight here.'

He was giving me the potted version, without the drama. Knowing that while I'd been righting a wrong in Mallaig my sister had tried to end her life made me want to be sick. I remembered the missed calls – five of them – and understood Colin's anger.

'Where was she?'

He mellowed and let me off the hook for now. 'It's a long story. We're at the house. I'll tell you when you get here.'

'But she's okay? Sam's okay?'

He considered his reply. 'As okay as anybody can be after that, yes. But it's early days, Alex, and, be warned, she's dreading having to face you.'

'That's silly.'

'Is it? You're her big sister and a pretty formidable woman – the one person in the world she looks up to and always has. She believes she's let you down.'

'And is that what you believe?'

Colin didn't rush to answer, weighing his response. When it came it was damning. He said, 'Remember the day Sam introduced us?'

'Yes, I do remember.'

'We were young. I was nervous; we both were. She was desperate to get your approval. If you hadn't taken to me she'd have ended it, there and then, and none of this would've happened.'

'You're blaming me for liking you?'

'No, I'm saying I misjudged you, Alex. I thought Sam could depend on you. I thought I could depend on you.'

Shame flushed my face. Not because he was right, he wasn't – it was worse than that. I hadn't forgotten, not really. I'd made a choice to put everything other than Lewis fucking Stone out of my mind and I'd succeeded.

Colin said, 'The hospital gave her a blood transfusion last night and let her out at one o'clock. They're overworked and under-staffed. Rightly or wrongly, alcoholics, drug addicts and failed suicides aren't their favourite people. She's sleeping. Where are you?'

I ignored the question – it was better for both of us he didn't know. Discovering his sister-in-law had murdered a man in cold blood wouldn't enrich his life.

'If Sam wakes up, tell her I'm on my way.'

I ended the call and pulled the car back onto the road.

* * *

He was standing at the front door framed by an orange light from the hall and didn't wait for me to get to him; he went inside and I followed. At the bottom of the stairs he turned and I caught the trauma of what they'd both been through on his face: the skin around his eyes was lined and puffy, the whites red-rimmed and bloodshot; exhaustion bent his shoulders like those of an older man, adding years. His angry tirade at me on the phone was a symptom.

Sam's husband was only just holding it together.

He spoke and the whisper was back, this time without the aggression. Colin hadn't forgiven me, yet I had the strong impression he was relieved I was there.

'Once you get used to the bandages, physically she doesn't look too bad. But that's the tip of the iceberg. If you'd seen what I saw...' He shuddered and shook the memory away. 'We can only imagine the mental and emotional distress under the surface. Seeing you might be the very best thing, or something you say might start her off. All I'm saying is don't tire her out; she needs to rest. Anything you want to ask, ask me, although I don't expect either of us will like the answers.' His fingers closed over the door handle but didn't open the door. 'Five minutes, okay? She'll want you to stay longer. Please work with me on this – it isn't negotiable – otherwise I'll throw you out. How I feel right now, I'd enjoy doing it, so don't tempt me, eh?'

Sam smiled a weak smile when she saw me. She was sitting up in bed, both wrists bound in thick white gauze wrapped round many times and held in place with bandage clips. The blood transfusions had given her complexion a glow, making her appear the healthiest person in the room, an illusion that shattered the moment she spoke. Her lip trembled and she dissolved into tears. 'I'm sorry. I'm so sorry.'

I held her tight and didn't let go until she'd finished weeping. 'Don't be daft, Sam, there's nothing to be sorry about.'

'Yes, there is. Look at the trouble I've caused. Poor Colin, finding me like that in the bath. I'm a selfish bitch who can't do any bloody thing right. You'd be better off without me.'

I scolded her gently, conscious of how fragile my sister was. 'That isn't true and you know it, Sam Kennedy. You've been in a bad place since Molly died, we both have. We didn't notice it creeping up on us until it was too late. Depression isn't called "the black dog" for nothing.'

Sam glowered at me, her mouth drawn tight with irritation. 'That's not why. Molly dying had fuck all to do with it.' She beat her hands on the bedclothes like a child having a tantrum, frustrated and teary. 'For once can it not be about her?'

'I'm sorry and of course you're right. That's not what I meant. This isn't about Molly, it's about you and your life.' I took her hands in mine, carefully avoiding the bandages. 'Sam, listen to me. I was where you are when Freddy passed. Somehow, I survived and so will you.'

I could've kicked myself. I'd been warned about not starting her off and that was exactly what I'd done. From somebody who should know better, it was a stupid mistake. I rushed to put it behind me and blustered on. 'But we can't have you rattling around on your own in this big house. Come and stay with me for a while until you feel better; we can keep each other company. Find a way through this together.'

A noise from the landing distracted me and I looked round. Colin was in the doorway, his expression as cold as the water of Loch Morar. He'd been outside listening and had overheard my error. But his displeasure ran deeper than a clumsy slip of the tongue; he hadn't forgiven me and maybe never would. He lowered his eyes, sending an unspoken message across the room that my time was up.

Sam saw him and smiled, instantly brighter. 'No,' she said, 'this is where I belong. And I won't be on my own. Colin will look after me, won't you, Colin?'

71

FOUR WEEKS LATER

Under the strip lighting suspended from the corrugated roof, sewing machines stood in lines, four abreast, like soldiers on parade all the way to the outsized Stone Free logo on the far wall. The noise in the factory was deafening. Damian Morton was out on the factory floor when his phone vibrated in his jacket pocket with a message from his secretary telling him two Police Scotland CID detectives were in his office. He kicked out at a stray fragment of material and cursed. Lewis had turned up, hadn't he? And here he was again, still managing to be a disruptive influence even when he wasn't in the building. Damian remembered his fist connecting with his jaw on the jetty and wished he'd hit the bastard harder.

The policemen weren't strangers; three weeks earlier they'd interviewed him after Lewis's housekeeper reported him missing, the senior man introducing himself as DI Flannigan and his red-haired colleague as DS O'Brien. Even without the titles it was obvious Flannigan was in charge.

Damian knew Lewis Stone better than any other person on earth and believed he'd become addicted to drama and taken it up north with him when he couldn't handle things in Glasgow.

Damian wasn't overly concerned with the policemen coming back. His conscience was clear; he'd done nothing wrong. On their previous visit the detectives had been friendly, the atmosphere informal, asking a range of general questions about his partner in an information-gathering exercise.

How long had he known him?

Was Lewis romantically involved with anybody?

To the best of his knowledge, did Lewis have financial worries?

What could he tell them about Lewis's recent movements?

Straightforward stuff, easily answered, until near the end when the DI had asked, 'When was the last time you spoke to him face to face?'

Damian had laughed. 'I might need a lawyer to respond to that.'

Their coppers' ears had pricked up at this. 'Really? Why?'

'Because he came at me with an oar and I decked him.'

A look passed between the officers. 'So, the meeting with your partner ended violently.'

Damian saw where it was going and reacted. '"Violently" isn't how I'd put it. Lewis tried to hit me and I defended myself. I'm telling you for two reasons – because I've nothing to hide and because that's what happened. As I drove away, he was on the jetty with his back to me, looking out over the loch. Ask his housekeeper, she saw me leave.'

'We will, Mr Morton.'

'Look, we'd been partners for a long time, friends even longer. Unfortunately – and it happens more often than you'd think – our relationships, business and personal, were over and we both recognised it. I've no idea where Lewis is and I don't want to know. But when I left him he was fine.'

Outwardly the policemen had seemed unmoved, yet Damian had sensed a change that had made him uneasy and remained after they'd gone.

And now they were back.

At his office door, Helen, his PA, whispered an apology. 'I told them you were busy; they insisted.'

He nodded. 'Don't worry about it. Let's see what they want this time.'

Damian didn't wait for the policemen to begin. He said, 'Let me guess. Lewis wants to charge me with assault, am I right?'

DI Flannigan didn't rise to it; his eyes bored into him. 'I'm afraid Lewis Stone won't be charging anyone with anything, Mr Morton. His body washed up two days ago. The housekeeper identified him this morning. Can't say I envied her that.'

Damian couldn't take it in and stared at them. The DI said, 'Do you understand what I'm telling you?'

'Of course I understand but I can't fucking believe it. How... how did it happen?'

'We don't know yet. After weeks in the water there was significant damage.'

'Okay, I get that. What I don't get is why you're here. Are you saying it wasn't an accident?'

'I'm not saying anything except, at this stage, foul play hasn't been ruled out.'

Damian gripped the desk to support himself. 'I... I can't believe it. We had our differences but... I didn't expect...'

Flannigan's next statement was like a hammer

blow. 'I'm afraid I'll have to ask you to come with us to the station.'

'The station? Why?'

'At the last interview you admitted you and your partner fought on the jetty, but you neglected to mention you wanted him dead.'

'Wanted him... What're you talking about?'

'We have a witness.'

'I don't care how many witnesses you've got, it isn't true.'

The detective stuck to his script. 'You'll have a chance to explain all that in Govan.'

'Am I being charged with murder?'

'For the moment, no. Otherwise DS O'Brien would be cautioning you. That he isn't means we aren't at that point, at least, not yet.'

Damian led the way, followed by the detectives. As they passed a horrified Helen, he leaned across and spoke with a calm that surprised even him. 'Call my lawyer. Tell him I've been taken to Govan and to get there pronto. It's serious. His card is in the top right-hand drawer of my desk.'

'Mr Shawcross?'

Damian's lips drew back in an ironic smile that morphed into a snarl. 'Not that bastard. Definitely not him.'

* * *

He used his keys to let himself in and heard his footsteps echo in the deserted factory. Going to his flat made more sense; he hadn't wanted to – the thought of taking the humiliation he'd experienced home had seemed wrong. In his office, Damian turned on the lights, took off his jacket, and slumped into the chair behind his desk, totally spent.

The ordeal – and it had been a fucking ordeal – was over.

For the moment.

The police had held him in a whitewashed room and before the interview even got going he realised a casual comment, spoken in anger, had taken him there.

Oliver Shawcross was a malicious bastard!

DI Flannigan had summarised their previous conversation, breezing through it as though it held nothing of interest. 'Lewis Stone was your friend and your business partner. At one time you'd been close. Two events caused that to change – Stone had some kind of a breakdown, and you got an offer to buy the business. You went to his home in Lochaber to persuade him to sell and ended up fighting with him. But when you left, Lewis Stone was alive. As far as it goes, fair enough.'

'And all easily verified. His housekeeper saw me leave. Ask her.'

The detective leaned across the table. 'Yes, you've already said, Mr Morton. Unfortunately, that doesn't help at this point.' Flannigan fired off a question. 'When did you arrive back in Glasgow?'

'I don't remember. Late.'

'Can anyone verify that?'

'I didn't fucking think I'd need an alibi so I didn't arrange one.'

The detective let the sarcasm fly over his head. 'Is that a no? Because the problem I have is making sense of your movements after that. Time of death hasn't been established. Given the condition of the body, it may well never be. And again, that doesn't work in your favour.'

The lawyer made a show of earning his fee. 'Is there a question in there, Detective Inspector?'

'Indeed, there is, and it's a big one. Where was your client in the hours and days immediately after his visit to Morar?'

'My client—'

Damian cut across him and spoke for himself. 'Was back in Glasgow doing his best to keep the company on track. You know – doing my job. And I don't expect anybody can vouch for my whereabouts 24/7. Seriously, could you get somebody to vouch for you?'

'Probably not, but then I'm not a suspect in a murder investigation.'

The lawyer came in again. 'Possible murder, detective.'

The detective shrugged, unimpressed. 'Semantics. We all understand what we're talking about. We have a witness who swears your client told them he wanted Lewis Stone dead. Well, he is. As for motive – look no further than Stone Free. One partner wants to sell the business, the other refuses. How did he intend to resolve that little conundrum? How did you, Mr Morton?'

'I didn't "resolve" anything.'

'Do you deny you said it?'

'No, I said it, but I didn't actually wish him harm. Haven't you ever blurted out something stupid? Of course you have, everybody has. Lewis was being unreasonable and I was angry and frustrated. Look, on his good days Lewis Stone was a strong character. Since he was involved in that accident, he hadn't had many of those. Dealing with him was impossible. He totally lost it and couldn't make a decision. Everybody was against him, or so he imagined, even your precious witness. Oliver Shawcross was on his way out. Lewis intended to fire his arse.'

He paused to let the DI take it in. 'Don't suppose he mentioned that little gem.'

Flannigan raised an eyebrow and he knew he was right. 'We will, of course, look into your assertion. Unfortunately, true or otherwise, you are still the main suspect in the case.'

The lawyer was on a roll. 'Can I ask if a crime has actually been committed or if, apart from a throwaway comment my client freely admits making, you have direct evidence tying him to Lewis Stone's death? Because, unless there is, we have no more to say.'

Damian watched the policemen's faces and snarled, 'You want proof of where I was, well, okay. CCTV will show that when I left Lewis I didn't double back. Check it.'

'Most of the roads don't have cameras on them.'

'So check the ones leading to it. Start with the factory. You'll see my car outside it every day until they fished him out of the water. If that doesn't do it, check my bloody phone log. Do your job.' He stood. 'Now, if you don't mind, I'm going home.'

* * *

The conversations he was about to have would be brief.

The deal Marsha Winter had offered was long gone and, from his previous experience of her, Damian believed there was little point in attempting to breathe new life into it. But she was a businesswoman. They might be able to come to a new arrangement. Then again, she was a tough lady and could blow what he was proposing out of the water – assuming she took his call in the first place.

A secretary put him through, a decent start. Marsha was the Marsha Winter he remembered – not unfriendly but to the point. 'Mr Morton. What can I do for you?'

'The situation here has changed dramatically. I think we might have something to talk about if you're still interested.'

Her reply was the first crumb of good news he'd had in a while. She said, 'I'm always interested in talking business. Let's set up a meeting.'

He saved the lawyer till last. Oliver Shawcross was expecting to hear from him and was thankful he hadn't come in person; it wouldn't end well.

Damian chose every word carefully, certain that this was the last time he'd speak to this man. 'It's me. Having a nice day? Let me spoil it. Towards the end,

Lewis and I didn't agree on much. But there was one thing we were totally united on. That you're a snake. A fucking reptile. Since he isn't here to do it in person, I'll do it for both of us. You're fired, Shawcross! Stone Free's new owners won't be using your services. Neither will anyone else when it gets out you can't be trusted. And expect a visit from the police. No need to thank me. Only too happy to return the favour.'

EPILOGUE
BUCHANAN STREET, GLASGOW

Six weeks later

Twenty-three days after I'd seen blood spill from Lewis Stone's wounds into his disbelieving eyes, and watched him fall from the boat into the cold depths of Loch Morar, the body of a man was recovered from the water. It wasn't a total surprise; I'd been expecting it. In some ways it was a relief, but I was glad I wasn't there.

In Glasgow, the news had become my latest obsession. I avidly followed it on TV, in the national papers, even the Lochaber section of *The Oban Times* online, scanning for the story that would surely begin the final chapter of Molly's saga. Searching had unearthed an interesting statistic: fifty people, give or take, drowned every year in this country – one more shouldn't attract suspicion. That was the lie I'd told myself every morning when I wakened, sweating and rigid with fear, with fragments of yet another nightmare lingering in my fevered brain.

I'll never forget the evening the story broke: I'd rushed home from work so as not to miss *Reporting Scotland* on BBC and was eating a microwave dinner off a tray on my knee. Towards the end of the show, the female presenter's voice took on a note of sadness. Somehow, I guessed what was coming and nervously edged the volume up. The screen filled with a landscape I recognised and the fork dropped from my quivering fingers.

It was too early for details. Beyond the fact the deceased wasn't local, his identity was unknown.

The whisper in my head that had started on the drive home from the Highlands had never stopped urging me to go to the nearest police station and get it over with, confess and face the consequences of what I'd done. But it was small, easily shouted down by the strident voices of self-preservation. And there were many of those. Getting caught had been a big concern, a close second to the fear of failing Molly. Now they'd found him there was nothing to do but wait for the knock on my door that would mean they'd come for me.

Except, there was no knock, they didn't come, and Mrs Gillies, the Silver Sands at Camusdarach, and the red speck on the shore at the side of the house, faded until it might all have been a dream.

I'd gone back to work, picked up my life in a way I hadn't since Freddy died, and felt I was benefitting from being around people again. One morning, Rachel was in the queue at the dispensary. She saw me and came over. We chatted for a minute or so before she awkwardly brought up the subject I'd been dreading.

'You've heard about Lewis?'

I said I had.

'Tragic, wasn't it? Just when you were thinking about reconnecting with him. I'm sorry.'

I faked grief that was actually relief. 'I left it too late.'

She leaned in conspiratorially. 'Actually, the police were questioning his partner. Seems they thought he had something to do with it.'

I felt the colour drain from my face and a tingling in my fingertips. It hadn't occurred to me some innocent bystander might be dragged into this. 'They didn't say that on the news.'

'Well, they let him go, probably because they couldn't prove it. And the talk is now that he committed suicide.'

Rachel studied me to see if her words had hit home. And, right away, I got why she was here. It wasn't a coincidence. I might've been in contact with Stone; she'd seen a chance to impress her workmates. When I didn't give her the reaction she was after, she prattled away to hide her disappointment – the usual platitudes. 'He'd so much to live for. Everybody at the factory is gutted. Nobody was expecting it. We have no idea how anybody really feels, do we? We see what they have and assume they're happy.' She'd hesitated, uncertain of her ground. 'Look, if you're ever at a loose end and fancy a coffee, give me a bell. I owe you one.'

'Thanks, I will.'

Rachel was devious and duplicitous, but she wasn't sharp – she'd known my interest in Lewis Stone and got the information on his whereabouts for me, put two and two together and come up with an opportunity to be in the limelight. All she'd leave with was an empty promise of coffee and a girly chinwag.

I was off the hook.

Sam was a different story. At first, I'd visited her

every day, chatting about nothing very much, never staying long. Colin hovered in the background, protective to a fault in case I undid his wife's progress with another ill-chosen comment, willing to be unpopular to keep her safe. She clearly relished being the centre of attention, yet it was obvious her husband didn't want me there and the visits soon became phone calls.

Today I was in town. I'd already treated myself to coffee and cake in a little place in Gordon Street and was mooching around window-shopping when I spotted them, arm in arm, coming down the steps at the Royal Concert Hall at the top of Buchanan Street, Sam holding tightly to Colin. She said, 'Well, hello, stranger. Fancy meeting you.'

She seemed well, the Sam of old, revitalised, the fragility that had surrounded her gone. We hugged, the sleeves of her coat rode up and I caught the scars, pink against her pale skin. I said, 'So, how are things?'

Sam looked at Colin with a light in her eye I remembered from the best times with Freddy, when we'd thought we'd be together forever. 'Wonderful. I mean, really wonderful, aren't they, darling?'

Before he could reply she threw her arms round me again. 'Oh, Alex, this is so good, we don't see you nearly enough. Come for dinner on Sunday. Colin's turned out to be a fantastic cook. My very own Gordon Ramsay.'

Colin looked less than delighted and I said, 'I'll call you.'

'Do that, sister. We desperately need a catch-up.'

A shop window drew her attention and she was off, yelling over her shoulder, 'Talk among yourselves! I'll only be a couple of minutes!'

Making small talk with Colin wasn't what I wanted. From the look on his face, he felt the same. The guy thought I'd let Sam down; he didn't like me. But we had common ground – we both loved Sam – so I offered an olive branch and hoped he'd take it.

'Congratulations, Colin. Whatever you're doing's working. I've never seen her so happy.'

He stared at me and I thought he was going to cry. 'I can't go on, Alex. I can't take it.'

I replied like an idiot, completely missing what was in front of me. 'If you need a break, Sam can stay with me.'

He grabbed my shoulder, his fingers digging into me through the coat. 'You're not listening. I went to the house because I realised something wasn't right. I went to help. To check she was okay. As a friend. As a friend, Alex.'

'Thank God you did or Sam would have died.'

Colin slowly shook his head. 'No, no, you don't understand. Nobody understands.'

'Understands... what? What are you saying, Colin?'

Despair broke over him and his eyes filled up. He said, 'I'm trapped. I'm trapped, Alex. I'll never be able to leave. If I do she'll try again and succeed next time. I couldn't live with that on my conscience.'

Colin wiped tears from his cheeks, the words tumbled out, and I got why he'd been so anxious for nothing – including me – to come between Sam and her recovery: the sooner she was well, the sooner he could escape.

'You heard her a minute ago – telling herself a lie, pretending it's all wonderful, pretending I love her when she knows I don't. How can I when I'm still in love with somebody else and always will be?'

It was shocking, heartbreakingly sad, yet it explained so much.

Sam was my sister; I loved her. But even I could see what she was doing to this man wasn't right. I put a hand on his shoulder. 'Oh, Colin, how awful for you. That's emotional blackmail. You have to find a way to tell her, you have to.'

With an effort, he pulled himself together. 'No, it's gone beyond that. The whole sorry mess is down to me. It's my punishment, my penance for being a bastard.'

I tried to find something meaningful to say and came out with the same old tired clichés. 'Relationships end, marriages break up...'

Colin's eyes wandered across Buchanan Street to Sam talking to the shop assistant in the doorway, unaware of our conversation. He gritted his teeth and I saw for myself that whatever they'd had wasn't there any more.

'Not hers. Not your sister's.'

'I'll tell you what I would say if it was the other way round. Contact this woman, let her know how you feel and, if it's still possible, be with her. Three unhappy people isn't the answer to anything. I'll help Sam find a way forward without you.'

His eyes narrowed and he stared at me. 'You don't know? You really don't know?'

He'd lost me. Colin sighed, a sound that came from the bottom of his soul. 'I said this bloody disaster was my fault and it is. I made a terrible mistake.'

'What mistake?'

'I married the wrong sister. It was Molly I loved.' He ran his fingers through his hair and I caught something in his eyes I hadn't seen before: defeat. 'The irony is that, of all the times to discover it, I waited until my wedding night. An innocent kiss from my new sister-in-law lit a fire in me I couldn't put out no matter how hard I tried and, believe me, Alex, I did. But Molly...' His voice cracked and he turned away. 'She felt the same. We were going to pick the right time to tell Sam and move in together. It never came.'

Seconds earlier I'd been angry at Sam for holding this man hostage. Now, my heart broke for her. 'Dear God, Colin, promise me you'll never tell her. Promise me. I need to hear you say it.'

His eyes welled up again; his voice cracked. 'Can't you see that's what this... this charade... is all about? She knows.'

'She... what?'

'She found our messages on my phone just before your night out before Christmas.'

Sam joined us, clutching a carrier bag. She looked at us in turn and smiled. 'Did somebody's cat die?' She laughed, hooked herself onto Colin and started to walk away. 'Call me about Sunday. If you don't, I'll assume you're coming.'

I didn't go home – I couldn't. I sat on a bench in George Square and tried to make sense of what Colin had said until the late afternoon sky began to darken, kicking myself for being a blind fool. I'd assumed that the 'problems' Sam had talked about over the years were other women. I'd had no idea it was Molly. Yet there must have been signs at family gatherings – loving glances; gentle touches that lingered too long. How could I have missed them?

* * *

I woke in the dark with a ringing in my ears, too afraid to open my eyes, and the clock on the bedside cabinet ticking the seconds away towards dawn, daring me to deny what had been in front of me all along. Colin's voice haunted me, his words echoing in my brain.

'She found our messages on my phone just before your night out.'

Against my will I replayed that night in Byres Road...

...*coming down the steps laughing, Molly and Sam winding each other up; slipping on the ice and Sam catching me; the beggar's empty red-rimmed eyes and his mongrel wagging its tail as my fingers ran through its coat; Molly falling into the road and Sam's outstretched hand trying to save her like she'd done with me; the screech of brakes...*

Suddenly I realised I'd seen what I'd wanted to see that night in Byres Road, but Lewis Stone had it wrong, too – it wasn't an accident.

Six days before Christmas Sam had murdered Molly.

Molly had stolen her husband, stolen Colin, and Sam hadn't been trying to catch her – she'd deliberately pushed her in front of the car.

It was more than I could take in, more even than the awful truth Colin had shockingly revealed to me in Buchanan Street. And as the full implication dawned, the horror of what I'd done in Morar swallowed me like the cold waters of the loch and I couldn't breathe. I felt the rock in my hand, smooth and heavy as it smashed against his skull, and saw his blood spill into the disbelieving eyes of an innocent man.

Imagine you had a secret so terrible you couldn't tell anybody. Ever. Because if you actually said the words out loud the world would see who you really were.

ACKNOWLEDGMENTS

With every book I write, the list of people who contribute seems to grow. In the interests of brevity, I'll keep this short. Although the story is set in Glasgow, much of the action takes place on the rugged West Coast of Scotland and I want to thank the lovely folk who took time to walk with me over the Silver Sands of Morar as the sun set behind the islands and talked about the loch they'd grown up with and known all their lives. What a stunning place to call home. I envy you.

The team at Boldwood Books who seem to win awards with an alarming regularity (at least for the rest of the industry). But, above and apart, my gratitude goes especially to Sarah Ritherdon, Sue Smith and Candida Bradford, who all strived, once again, to make me look so much better than I really am and succeeded.

Why she should always be mentioned last is an injustice that needs to be rectified. My wife, Christine, who has never met a plotline she couldn't resolve and selflessly shares her insight into the human condition and her rich imagination with me during the process. Thanks, baby.

MORE FROM O. J. MULLEN

We hope you enjoyed reading *Three Sisters*. If you did, please leave a review.

If you'd like to gift a copy, this book is also available as an ebook, paperback, hardback, digital audio download and audiobook CD.

Sign up to O. J. Mullen's mailing list for news, competitions, updates and receive an exclusive free short story from Owen Mullen.

https://bit.ly/OwenMullenNewsletter

ABOUT THE AUTHOR

O. J. Mullen is a highly regarded crime author who splits his time between Scotland and the island of Crete. In his earlier life he lived in London and worked as a musician and session singer.

Follow O. J. Mullen on social media:

- twitter.com/OwenMullen6
- facebook.com/OwenMullenBooks
- instagram.com/owenmullen6
- bookbub.com/authors/owen-mullen

THE

Murder

LIST

**THE MURDER LIST IS A NEWSLETTER
DEDICATED TO SPINE-CHILLING FICTION
AND GRIPPING PAGE-TURNERS!**

**SIGN UP TO MAKE SURE YOU'RE ON OUR
HIT LIST FOR EXCLUSIVE DEALS, AUTHOR
CONTENT, AND COMPETITIONS.**

SIGN UP TO OUR
NEWSLETTER

BIT.LY/THEMURDERLISTNEWS

Boldwood

Boldwood Books is an award-winning fiction publishing company seeking out the best stories from around the world.

Find out more at www.boldwoodbooks.com

Join our reader community for brilliant books, competitions and offers!

Follow us
@BoldwoodBooks
@BookandTonic

Sign up to our weekly deals newsletter

https://bit.ly/BoldwoodBNewsletter

www.ingramcontent.com/pod-product-compliance
Lightning Source LLC
Chambersburg PA
CBHW010657100726
47900CB00010B/2696

* 9 7 8 1 8 3 7 5 1 5 0 0 4 *